THE LOST GIRL

MARK GILLESPIE

INKUBATOR
BOOKS

Published by Inkubator Books
www.inkubatorbooks.com

ISBN (eBook): 978-1-83756-326-5
ISBN (Paperback): 978-1-83756-327-2
ISBN (Hardback): 978-1-83756-328-9

PROLOGUE

At around thirty-seven degrees Celsius and rising, it was on course to become one of the hottest days ever recorded in the UK. The sun was a seething, shimmering orb in the sky. This was the sort of heat that made headlines.

The soft, pale sand on Bournemouth Beach was crammed with bodies and beach umbrellas. The umbrellas came in so many different colours that from above, the beach looked like a work of pop art. A bass drum, fat and punchy, thumped from distant speakers. Seagulls squawked. Thousands of human voices intermingled with the occasional dog bark.

The man and woman had come with their family.

They were sitting close to the water. Their three young children were beside them, sitting under the second beach umbrella. The family had been on a road trip for the past week and a half, travelling down the east coast of the UK. They were having such a good time, in fact, that they extended the holiday. Now they were travelling along the south coast, stopping at Folkestone and Brighton before reaching the coastal town of Bournemouth, well-known for its seven-mile stretch of golden sand beach.

The woman's parents were also on the trip, but travelling in a separate vehicle.

They went into the water several times for a paddle and to cool off. At the woman's insistence, they never stayed under the sun for too long before returning to the shade under the two beach umbrellas, one for the adults, one for the kids. The woman fussed, as was her way. Making sure the kids were drinking their fruit juice. Eating their snacks.

There was no indication that anything was wrong.

The twins played with their bucket and spade. A gift from their grandparents, purchased back in Folkestone. Their sister was beside them, drinking her blackcurrant juice, her teddy bear sitting on her lap. She put the straw to the teddy bear's lips. Urged him to drink because it was so hot.

The woman sat beside her husband. She tried to read from a cosy mystery novel but, although it was a good book, it was hard to concentrate. She put the book down and glanced up and down the beach.

So many people, she thought.

It was hard to breathe, not only because of the stifling heat but the lack of space was doing her head in. She could only imagine how much litter was going to be left over when everyone went away. It would be like a bomb had gone off. This wasn't her idea of a good time but she'd been outnumbered. Her husband and the kids wanted to visit the beach. They'd gone through a hard time recently back in Edinburgh and she didn't want to be a spoilsport. All she could do was make the best of it and ensure the kids didn't get burned.

Her mum and dad were somewhere nearby. Wandering around town. Not interested in the beach.

She picked up the book. Tried again to read but a sudden cry from the water made her look up. Not a cry. More like a scream.

No one else around them reacted at first. There was so much going on, so many people, and this was just another noise. And yet it stood out. Not only that, the screaming got louder and became more desperate.

Her husband jumped to his feet. He'd heard it all right. Now he pointed to a cluster of swimmers in the water, not that far from the beach. Movement. It came from behind them, a little further out to sea. Arms flapping. A head bobbing in and out of the clear blue water. The desperate swimmer trying to signal for help.

"That guy's in trouble," the man said.

Others had noticed the swimmer's distress by now. They rushed close to the water's edge, some of them going in until the water was up to their knees. They pointed. They waved their arms, yelling for help. The cluster of swimmers in the shallows had seen it too but no one was making a move to help him. It was as if they didn't believe it was happening. Maybe they didn't understand the seriousness of the situation.

Fortunately, the RNLI lifeguards were all over it. Two men in red and yellow wetsuits were already paddling out on surfboards. They moved fast, reaching the distressed swimmer and helping him onto one of the boards. They were coming back in to the sound of applause, and as soon as it was over, it didn't feel like a big deal anymore.

The woman breathed a sigh of relief. For a moment, it was like she'd had an out-of-body experience. She'd be glad when they finally got off this beach. Back to the hotel room, the air-conditioning fanning them at full blast. This sort of heat wasn't good for anyone. Certainly not for that swimmer who'd overestimated his abilities.

"Darcy!"

Her husband's voice.

"DARCY!"

She looked at him. The drama was over, wasn't it? Why was he shouting their daughter's name like that?

"What is it?"

"Where is she?"

What happened next would remain foggy over the years. A nightmare, half-lost. It was as if the trauma had ravaged the woman's memory, and maybe it did so to protect her from reliving the horror day and night for the rest of her life.

The man said the same thing over and over again. "She's gone."

She's gone. His arm shook as he pointed to the second beach umbrella. Eyes bulging. *She's gone.* The boys were exactly where they were supposed to be, underneath the umbrella, sitting in the shade. So close that their arms were touching. Shovelling up golden-brown sand with plastic shovels and dropping it into the bucket.

She *was* gone. There was no sign of their daughter. Nothing to say she'd ever existed except a faint impression on the sand where she'd been sitting.

It's all right, the woman told herself. *It's all right.*

The little girl had just wandered behind the beach umbrella. That's it. She was no more than a few metres away in one direction or the other. Perhaps she'd been startled by the excitement of the near-drowning. Who hadn't?

"Don't panic," the woman said.

A quick check around the back. She wasn't there. Look to the left, to the right. Not there.

She's gone.

Panic rising. Sweat seeping from her pores. Heart thumping. So many faces and none of them the face they were looking for.

Her worst fears began to solidify.

The man started yelling. Hands cupped over his mouth, screaming their daughter's name. He ran a few metres one way kicking up sand, then stopped. Ran the other way, then stopped. Yelling, yelling, yelling. Everyone in the vicinity had settled down after the swimmer's rescue but now they stirred again. Heads turned in their direction. Annoyed expressions. A look of concern. Of curiosity. The woman's body shuddered with fear. Terror pricked her skin like sharp needles. This was a waking nightmare, or rather the start of one.

She screamed.

Their little girl was gone.

Thirteen years later

PART I

THE RETURN

1

SOPHIE

Darcy's coming home.

She's waiting for us in the police station in Glasgow. It's her, I *know* it's her. Common sense and logic tell me it's just another imposter claiming to be my long-lost daughter. That I'm in for more disappointment. There have been plenty of imposters before. Plenty of disappointment.

Not this time.

She *is* coming home. I feel it in my bones. There's a connection between a mother and her child and it's never broken, not by distance, not by time, not by anything.

It's 8.02pm, Sunday night. My husband Mike and I are driving west along the M8 from Edinburgh to Glasgow. The journey from our house to the police station, according to Google Maps, will take fifty minutes. Feels like we've been driving for hours already. My palms are soaked with sweat. Twice we've stopped on the hard shoulder because I felt dizzy and sick with excitement.

Mike sucks in a deep lungful of air and grips the steering

wheel. His eyes are locked on the endless motorway. He glances at me, his face wrinkled with tension.

"Are you alright?"

"What?"

"Are you *alright*?"

It's a hollow question. Neither one of us is all right and truthfully, we haven't been for years. We've continued. Persevered. Thirteen years of heartache, pain and not knowing what happened to her since that day on Bournemouth Beach. Only memories left. The fear of losing those memories. Or even the slightest fading, which ends with her angelic face blurring into the blind spots of my mind. That would be like losing her all over again. She might as well have never existed. No, I couldn't bear it.

The not knowing. Not knowing why someone took her, my precious little girl, who belonged at home with her mum and dad. With her brothers.

"I'm fine," I say.

I can't sit still. I'm even biting my nails and I never bite my nails. It feels like I've got no control over anything. A sudden downpour crashes off the roof and windows of our SUV.

It's a bad sign, I tell myself.

What if it's not Darcy?

The SUV's headlights plough through the darkness pressing in all around us. Autumn has settled in early across the UK. The cold pinch of winter is here in advance. What little summer we had in Scotland is over.

The motorway is quiet. There are other cars but it feels like we've got the M8 to ourselves tonight.

I brave a smile. Turn in my seat so that I'm facing my husband.

"Are *you* okay?"

He keeps his eyes on the road.

"Mike?"

"Fine. It's just–"

Another long sigh.

"Just what?"

"Soph, I'm terrified. Terrified it's not her. Terrified it *is* her."

"I understand."

Finally, he glances at me. Then, it's back to the windscreen. "I don't know how I'm supposed to feel right now."

Even now, I can't stop looking at him. Mike's still so handsome after all these years, and that's even more impressive considering the weight of those years. He's still the cool kid with the cigarette dangling in between his lips at the school gate, two years older than me, an awkward gangly girl whose nickname was 'Giraffe'. He's still *that* Mike. That's what I see when I look at him. Not the dark circles under his eyes.

"It's okay," he says. "Whatever happens, we'll be okay."

"I know."

We're saying all the right things to one another. But words aren't enough. Neither one of us will be satisfied until this excruciating drive is over and we're looking at the girl who walked into Cathcart Police Station tonight. Who told the people inside that her name was Darcy Drummond.

We got the call just over an hour ago. We've had calls before. *Lots* of calls. I've lost count of the number of times that a girl or a young woman has turned up, claiming to be Darcy. And that's just the ones we've heard of. Most claims don't reach us before they fall apart. The imposters always tend to surface on social media. They don't go to the police.

They don't come to us. They're on social media, telling the world before they're revealed as frauds, scammers and attention-seekers. One girl from Ireland made it pretty far. She looked the part and landed a few TV spots and high-profile magazine interviews before the DNA test ruled her out. Still, she made good money.

The police have never called us and asked us to come to the station. Not until tonight.

As soon as possible if you please, Mrs Drummond. We really need you both here.

The officer I spoke to hinted of evidence, something of vital importance that we had to see for ourselves. *Come to the station*, he said. *Make no fuss. Keep it quiet.*

My heart hasn't slowed down since.

The windscreen wipers go back and forth in a hypnotic dance. They make a bird-like squawking noise on the laminated glass when the rain eases off. I ask Mike to turn them off. He comes back from whatever daydream he was trapped in. Turns the wipers off and clears his throat before speaking.

"There's a part of me that doesn't want to believe it."

His eyes are wary, like he's expecting me to hate him for saying that. But it makes perfect sense. It's been a long time since hope was a friend. Not only did it stop being a friend, it became a dangerous enemy.

"Me too."

He lets out a sigh of exhaustion and falls back, deflated, into the seat. His arms are outstretched and he seems far away from the wheel. For a second, it looks like he's about to turn on the radio. He doesn't. It's another few minutes before he talks again.

"I can't stand it. All these new books, documentaries and

podcasts that come out around the anniversary. It's like clockwork. All the theories about what happened to her. They're just a reminder of how we failed her."

I nod.

"I know."

The anniversary of Darcy's disappearance is coming in fast. It comes in faster every year, and here we are again. Thirteen years. The media will be all over it. The content creators will twist and distort reality for clicks, conjuring up sick narratives about how we, Mike and I, killed Darcy, hid her body and then covered it up with a kidnapping story. Journalists at the front door, badgering us for interviews. Many of them the same journalists who tried to crucify us for Darcy's disappearance back in the day. They would've gladly seen us burned at the stake despite the fact there wasn't a shred of evidence against us. Didn't stop them knocking on the front door, calling or emailing, asking us for interviews. Playing nice when it suited them.

Serious journalists and spotty teenagers on the internet. They all wanted content.

Bastards.

"I think it's her," I say to Mike. Outside, the rain starts up again. A trickle. "Why else would they call us out like this? They must have *something*."

My chest feels like someone's sitting on it. The air inside the car is too warm.

Mike looks through the windscreen with blank eyes. He's reluctant to engage with my optimism. Afraid. Behind those eyes, I wonder if he's reliving the nightmare of Bournemouth Beach all over again. It's a look I've seen before.

"If we'd just kept our eyes on her," he says, confirming my instinct.

Whoever's sitting on my chest just got a whole lot heavier. This is the beginning of a conversation we've had a thousand times before. What we did. What we didn't do. What we should've done. We've blamed ourselves and forgiven ourselves too many times, and I can't do it again.

"Mike, don't."

He blinks hard, as if waking from a deep sleep. There's a slight nod of the head.

"You didn't tell anyone, did you?"

"Of course not."

"What about the kids?"

"The kids? No, I don't want them getting their hopes up."

"They didn't say anything before we left?"

"Maria asked why we were going out so late. I improvised. Said it was something to do with work. That I'd drunk some wine and needed you to drive me. Said the same thing to Mum when she came over. I think she knew I was lying. I couldn't care less right now. They can ask all the questions they want later."

"What if it's not Darcy?"

My body goes cold. "Then it was a work thing."

And if it is Darcy? What then? We've got four other children to consider. The twins, Tom and Nick. They're fifteen now, barely two when Darcy went missing. They have no memory of her. It's like she never existed for either one of them. They don't remember that day on the beach. I wonder if they've somehow blocked out the intense panic and madness that followed her disappearance. There are two other girls. Maria, our eleven-year-old, looks a lot like Darcy. The brains of the family, she's a shoo-in for Oxford and Cambridge. Lola is the baby of the family. Five years old and just the sweetest little thing. I see Darcy in all of them.

Mike groans. He sounds like a bear waking up. "Your dad's not going to be at the house when we get back, is he?"

"Nope. Just Mum."

"Thank God for that," he says, scratching his five o'clock shadow. He looks at me. Raises an eyebrow. "What about Margo? You didn't say anything to her, did you?"

"Margo?"

"Isn't she your best friend?"

"I don't have enough friends to single one out as the 'best'."

"She's a reporter though."

"Mike," I say, trying to sound calm. "We're the only two people who know what's going on tonight. You and me. And the police, of course."

"Sorry."

"Even if I did want to talk about it," I say, "what would I say? They'd think it's just another hoax. Poor Sophie, they'll say. She's back on the pills."

"I'm sorry," Mike repeats.

A quick glance at my smart watch tells me my heart rate is through the roof.

Mike's eyes go blank again. "Not long now."

I close my eyes. Listen to the hum of the engine and try to control my breathing. I can feel the prickly heat of Bournemouth Beach on my skin. The way I fretted about not having enough sun protection on the kids. Scottish skin burns easily. I know mine does. Darcy was right behind us, sitting cross-legged on the sand under the umbrella. *Right there*. Drinking her juice, playing with her teddy bear, and as far as I could see, no one was paying any particular attention to us. It was *so* busy. I still hear her singing to herself. The twins beside her with their bucket and spades, sitting closer to me and Mike. But they were close. I've told people that and seen the doubt in their eyes. The suspicion. The wariness. *I know you killed her.* I remember the sudden disturbance in the water. A man's voice crying for help and the surge of panic that spread rapidly across the beach because we thought we were about to witness someone dying. He sounded so scared, but it didn't last long. Two lifeguards charged in and got the swimmer out of the water. There was a hearty round of applause. Cheering and laughter. A good story over drinks and dinner for those who weren't there. But yes, we were distracted. And when we turned around, Darcy was gone. The twins were there, acting like she'd never existed. There was no distress on their faces.

That moment will never leave me.

Hard to describe. It felt like I'd been turned inside out. Upside down. I've never felt such horror in all my life, but horror doesn't even begin to capture that moment of realisation. I'll be surprised if anything ever comes close. It was chaos. Like a nightmare. Mike and I were jumping around like possessed people. We grabbed the twins. Running. Screaming. Calling her name. Our eyes skimming the enormous beach and seeing nothing but strangers on all sides. Some looking at us like we were mad. Others doing their best to ignore us. We asked if anyone had seen her. I hadn't given up. Couldn't give up. I was convinced she'd appear at any second, carrying her little bucket and spade. That cute smile on her face. Not understanding the deranged look of terror on Mummy and Daddy's faces.

So, what do I know about this girl in the police station? This young woman claiming to be Darcy.

She's approximately seventeen and, according to what she told the police, she's been living with a man and a woman all these years in Cathcart, Glasgow. That's less than an hour's drive from where we live in Edinburgh. I won't digest that. Not until I see the girl with my own eyes and know for sure that she's my blood.

Something terrible happened in that house. The two kidnappers are dead, I know that much. And although no-one's said anything outright, I get the feeling that Darcy was responsible for the deaths. That's all I know.

"Not long," Mike says. Feels like he's been saying that forever.

This time, he's right.

The lights of the motorway are gone. The SUV is silent as it glides onto a slip road, and there's little traffic as we follow the satnav towards the south side of the city. My heart's racing. I feel sick again by the time we pull into the car park at Cathcart Police Station.

Mike turns off the engine. The silence burns and we grab each other by the hand. I glance over at the station entrance.

"We can do this."

He nods.

We summon up the courage to step out of the car. Mike locks the car and we walk hand in hand towards the door. I feel a rush of vertigo and when I close my eyes, I'm back on the beach. Screaming her name.

I open the door quickly. Scared stiff that I'm about to lose her all over again.

2

DARCY

The blood on my fingernails is so red under the bright lights. Caked at the edges. Crusty and dry, like flaking red nail polish.

I ball my hands into fists. Put them under the table.

This police interrogation room is like the ones I've seen on TV. The sharp light above my head. The long table in the middle, resting on chunky metal legs that are a bit wobbly. Two chairs on either side and, of course, the mirror. I see my reflection there, but I know there are people on the other side of that mirror. Police officers. Watching me.

I feel lightheaded, like there's not enough blood in my brain. I wish I could lie down on the floor, elevate my legs and feel okay again. I want to close my eyes but when I do that, I see Trevor and Hattie lying dead on the floor.

I don't want to linger on their final expressions.

It's all about moving forward.

It's been all go since I walked into the police station and talked to the woman behind the front desk. I could tell she didn't believe me. There was a look of irritation on her face, like I was out to ruin her evening. It went away when I showed her what I had in my bag. Things moved fast after that. She called someone. A man and a woman came along and, eventually, I was brought into this room. People have been asking the same questions. Same questions, different faces. Uniformed officers standing in the corner of the room. The whirr of a fan on the ceiling. And of course, the big mirror to my right.

Am I supposed to feel like a criminal?

I'm waiting for the next person to come along and ask the same questions. In the meantime, one of the uniformed officers brings me another can of Coke. My third. Some hot chips would be nice. Lots of salt.

"There you go, love," the woman says, putting the can on the table. "Sure I can't get you anything else?"

I shake my head. Maybe I'll ask for those chips later.

I pull the tab back, making the can hiss. The policewoman is trying hard not to stare at me as she backs off into the corner of the room. Can't blame her. She's not looking at me; she's looking at the legend. That's something I'll have to start getting used to. That look.

"Are they here yet?" I ask.

"Who's that, love?"

"My parents. My *real* parents."

The smile fades. Maybe she doesn't know how to respond. Maybe she's not allowed to say anything about them. "They're not here yet, love. They're on their way over from Edinburgh. Won't be long."

"Okay."

I sip my Coke. So much sugar. I tap my fingers on the table and it's like the caffeine is waking me up again. Ugh!

The blood on my nails is so *red*. I'm like something out of a horror film.

I hide my hands and wait.

The officer leaves the interrogation room and closes the door behind her. I'm alone again.

Except for the people behind the glass.

3

SOPHIE

It's all a blur after we walk into the station.

Mike and I do our best to keep it together as we introduce ourselves to the woman at the desk. The look on her face tells me we could've skipped the introduction. Feels like we're movie stars checking into her motel.

"Wait here," she says.

Then it's all go. People come and it's like everything is moving in fast-forward. We're given names and ranks but I hear none of them. A man with a bald head in a grey suit seems to be in charge. He leads us down a long corridor. I smell coffee. I hear muted voices trickling out from other rooms. People walk past. They stare and I guess most of them have seen us on TV over the years. *Mike and Sophie Drummond. Those poor people. Those killers.* It's okay, I'm used to it and so is Mike. I can decipher a look in two seconds and know that the person standing in front of me with a smile thinks that I murdered my daughter. Not an easy thing to get used to, the suspicion that flares up in their eyes.

Being in a police station isn't easy either. There was a

time when it felt like certain, influential members of the police force were against us. I'm talking about the highest level. And they were determined to prove we did it.

At worst, we killed our daughter and got rid of the body. At best, we're negligent parents. On that last charge, we have no defence.

My head spins as the bald man leads us into a dimly lit office space. The smell of coffee continues to follow me like it's my own perfume. Warm air trickles through a small, portable heater. The unnerving silence in the station lingers.

We're briefed by the man and another woman in plain clothes. I catch the guy's name this time – it's Ian. The woman is Hannah. She's lean, fifty-something and speaks with a refined English accent that makes me wonder how she ended up in Cathcart. Their ranks still escape me but it doesn't matter. Seems like we're okay to use their first names. Special treatment, I guess.

Ian repeats what he said on the phone.

"Earlier this evening," he says in a gruff, Glaswegian accent, "a young woman walked into the police station and identified herself as Darcy Drummond."

I feel Mike squeezing my hand.

"Apparently, she's been living under the name Poppy Burton for as long as she can remember. She only found out recently who she was. According to the story, she escaped from a house here in Cathcart. There was–"

Ian hesitates. He looks at Hannah, like it's her cue to take over. She nods and takes the lead.

"There was an incident in the house. The people who lived there are now deceased."

I nod but it's hard to take in what they're saying. It's too much and, right now, all I want is to see her. I'll know with a single look if it's my Darcy they're talking about or another imposter. I don't want to speak to these people or anyone else and, quite frankly, I don't care if two child kidnappers are dead. Good riddance. Hallelujah. Light the fireworks. Nothing else matters until we see her. My daughter's been waiting thirteen years for her parents to find her and take her home. Well, here we are, sitting in an office while she's somewhere else in this very building.

That hits hard. She's here.

It's Mike's voice I hear in my head.

It's another imposter. You have to prepare for the pain of disappointment.

Fortunately, they don't keep us long. After the briefing, we're led down another corridor. It's a short walk that feels like a marathon. More faces, peering at us from the surrounding offices. The police station is neverending and it feels like we're wandering through an endless mansion of law enforcement. Some of them smile at us. I want to believe there's sympathy for two people who lost a child. Even if we failed her.

"This way," Ian says.

We're led into a small room. Feels like the inside of a giant freezer with dimmed lights overhead. It's so quiet. Like we've just walked into a holy place. I walk ahead of Mike, my shoes clicking on the floor. There's no one else in the room.

I stare at the two-way mirror looking into an interrogation room. My heart stops. My feet feel like they've left the ground.

"Mike."

I grab hold of his arm. Maybe he's the one who grabs me. Either way, we're holding each other up as we stare through the glass.

"Mike. Do you–"

His voice is choked. "I see her."

She's beautiful. She's perfect. She's Darcy and she's seventeen years old, just like she ought to be. It's like looking at a younger version of myself. She's tall, slim and dressed in a checked shirt and blue jeans. The colours on her clothes have long since faded. Blonde hair falls over her shoulders. She's sipping a can of Coke. There's also an empty plate with crumbs on the table in front of her. A female officer in uniform stands in the corner of the room with her arms folded, eyes down to the floor. The girl – Darcy – stares straight ahead. She's a beautiful and tragic exhibit in a museum. A doll trapped behind the glass.

"It's her," I say, letting go of Mike's hand. My legs are strong. I step back, unable to take my eyes off her for a second. "Mike, it's her."

"I think so too."

"I *know* so. Look at her."

I'm laughing and Mike's crying. I've forgotten that there are two other people in the room with us. We grab each other again and I feel Mike shaking like a frightened child in my arms. I tighten my grip around his waist. I want to let him know that it's okay. That the nightmare is over.

We stay like that for a long time. Locked in each other's arms, staring through the glass at our daughter.

All those people who think we killed her. All the hate mail we received in the aftermath of her disappearance. The death threats. God, it almost destroyed our marriage. Our lives.

If only they could see us now.

See her.

Ian talks in a quiet voice. "She can't see you. You can see her, but she can't see into this room. Not even a little."

Mike and I let go of one another. He's smiling now and I wipe the tears from my eyes. Then, I walk towards the glass like I'm walking on a frozen lake in springtime. She's so pretty. So tall. The height comes from my side of the family. That's why they called me 'Giraffe' in school. The pale skin. So pretty. Her posture is a little stooped and there's a look of exhaustion in her eyes. But I see the strength there.

My heart skips a beat when Darcy turns towards the glass. It's like she heard me walking over. I gasp and feel our eyes meet.

"She can't see you," Ian repeats.

"Maybe she can."

I look at Mike.

"She looks like Maria, doesn't she?" A sudden wave of euphoria sweeps over me. It's like I've taken a heroic dose of the world's happiest drug. She *does* look both like me and my second daughter, Maria, with her sandy-blonde hair, almond-shaped eyes and mouth.

That girl is my blood.

"I see it," Mike says.

A young officer in uniform walks in, carrying two glasses of water. He hands one to Mike, the other to me, before offering us tea or coffee. We refuse the offer of a hot drink, but somehow manage to thank him for the water. My hands shake as I bring the glass to my lips.

"What was the other thing?" Mike says to the two police officers. He puts his glass on the window ledge. Still looking at Darcy. "You said there was something important. Something that made you call us."

Ian nods. "A few things, actually."

"What?" I ask. I'm finding it hard to concentrate. All I want to do is run into that interrogation room and grab her. But I know we're not quite there yet.

Hannah walks over to the door. Pulls it back, revealing a small desk at the back of the room. There's a see-through plastic bag sitting on the desk. She brings it over, holding it aloft so it's closer to the ceiling light. In the meantime, Ian puts on a pair of disposable gloves.

He pulls out the item from inside the bag.

"We found this in the kidnappers' house."

I gasp.

"Do you recognise this?" he asks.

I don't have to answer. My face is all the answer they need. Ian's holding up the pink t-shirt with *Daddy's Princess* printed in glittery letters on the front. Darcy wears it in the famous photo that was taken on Bournemouth Beach, the one where she's playing with her bucket and spade. The last photo we ever took of her, about an hour before she went missing.

"Oh my God," I say.

Hannah brings out two other bags. Ian then pulls out the tattered remains of a crumpled teddy bear she called Marvin. She was clinging to Marvin at the moment of her disappearance.

The third item we're shown is the white bucket hat she wore that day to keep the sun off her head.

"These were found in the attic of the house," Ian says. "There were some other children's toys in there too, nothing that belonged to Darcy. Which means there may have been others. We're not sure."

"That's why we wanted you over here as soon as possible," Hannah says. "This isn't a regular Darcy Drummond imposter. This isn't someone crying out for attention. We've got evidence. And we've also got–"

She stops herself.

Two dead bodies.

I wait, but no one says it.

"You're sure about these items?" Hannah asks.

Mike nods. "The teddy bear's still only got one eye. He was tattered like that. And the t-shirt was specially made."

"We're sure," I say. "Those are Darcy's things."

Ian and Hannah exchange looks. To my surprise, Ian looks a little overwhelmed and, sure enough, he eases himself down into a seat. He utters one word that comes out like a sigh of relief. "Okay."

I stare into the interrogation room.

"I want to see her."

"And you will," Hannah says. "Very soon. But we're still talking to Darcy about what happened. About her life with the kidnappers. It's important that we establish what happened while it's still fresh. We also have to find out if there were other children in the house."

I lean my head against the glass.

Not an imposter.

"We have to be *sure*," Ian says. "Nothing's one hundred percent certain until we perform the DNA test."

Hannah walks over and I feel her hand on my shoulder. "But it's looking good. It's looking very good."

4

DARCY

Are they standing behind the glass?

I look over while I'm waiting for the next person to show up and ask questions. I stare at the mirror, see only myself in the glass. My hair and nails are filthy and I smell like someone who's been in a house with two dead bodies for a week. Which is how it was. I can still smell them decomposing. Two giant lumps of rotten fruit sprawled out on the kitchen floor.

Are you watching me, Mum and Dad?

Why aren't you in here? It's been thirteen years and you should be here, pulling me off this chair and getting me out of this police station. *Where are you?* People in uniforms have been coming and going for hours. Questions, then more questions. Have a drink. Have a sandwich. Want some chocolate? Answer some more questions while we record and rustle some papers. Rinse and repeat.

I'm tired. I just want to go home. And yet, the Drummonds are strangers to me. What if they don't like me? I'm not the little girl they lost on the beach. What if I don't measure up to the memory of that little girl? She's a woman now and look at me – the blood is stuck to my fingernails. What if it never washes off?

"Can I go now?" I ask the nice woman standing in the corner.

She speaks in a soft voice, almost childlike. "A few more questions and then you can go meet your parents."

Her smile flounders a little.

"They're here?" I ask.

"I think so, yes."

I lean back in the seat. My legs are stiff and my back's sore. The light on the ceiling feels like a hot laser burning a hole in my brain.

"Home," I whisper.

The door opens and someone new comes in. Another woman. She's a lot younger than the other ones who've questioned me so far. Her black hair is severely tied back and she's dressed in a grey, business-style suit that clings to her slim figure. Must be hard to breathe in it. Even though she's nice and says hello, there's a hardness in her eyes.

She puts her phone on the table. Preps the recording app, says her name, the date and what she's doing. I know the drill by now.

She pauses the app.

"I'm Tracey," she says. "It's nice to meet you, Darcy."

I nod.

"Are you comfortable?" Tracey asks. "Is there anything you want before we start the interview? Food? Another drink?"

I glance at the mirror.

"I've answered all the questions."

She nods. "I know. I'm sorry it's taking so long. We're just gathering information about what happened to you. Filling in the gaps. You're a big deal, you know? But this is the last time, I promise. After this, we'll take you to your mum and dad."

Tracey doesn't take her eyes off me. She's studying my every little reaction to what she says. Like she's looking for something. A chink in the armour, perhaps? She called me Darcy but does she really believe that's who's sitting across the table?

I feel my heart pounding. There is one part of the story that we haven't really gone into enough detail about. I'm going to have to talk more about Trevor and Hattie, aren't I? They want details about the kidnappers.

"Are my mum and dad here?"

She smiles. "Yes."

"What did they say? Do they believe it's me?"

Tracey leans back in her chair. "Things are looking good, Darcy. That's all I can say for the moment, but certain items were found in the Burton house. Items that go a long way to confirming your identity."

"What items?"

"We'll talk about that later. Now, shall we crack on with the interview?"

"Okay."

"So," Tracey says, restarting the app. "For the past thirteen years, since the age of four, you've been living with Trevor and Hattie Burton. You thought of them as your mum and dad? As your biological mum and dad, correct?"

"Yes."

Tracey nods as if to say, *you're doing great*. "It's clear from previous interviews that you have little memory of that day on the beach, and who can blame you?"

"I was only four."

"That's right. So, let's talk about your life with Trevor and Hattie, shall we? Specifically, I want to focus on this past week."

I shrug.

Tracey leans forward, her elbows pinned to the table. Hands clasped together. "What changed, Darcy?"

"What do you mean?"

"Well, you've been living a reclusive life with the Burtons for thirteen years, and as far as you were concerned at the time, you're their biological daughter. Flesh and blood. But something happened, right? Something changed. Set you on the path to discovering your true identity."

I nod.

"What happened, Darcy?"

"I overheard a conversation."

Tracey lifts her elbows off the table. Her eyes shimmer with intensity as she looks at me. "You overheard them talking about...*you*?"

"Yes."

"When was this?"

"A week ago."

"Uh-huh."

"They thought I was out," I tell her. "I was supposed to be on an errand. But I forgot something and came back. They didn't hear me open the door, I guess. Didn't hear me close it. And they kept talking, not knowing that I could hear them because my bedroom is right above the living room. All I have to do is put my ear against the floor and I can hear everything."

Tracey nods. She pushes the phone across the table so it's closer to me. "What were they saying?"

I look her straight in the eyes. Then, I lean back in the chair and clench my fists under the table. The dry blood pinches my skin.

"They were planning to kill me."

5

DARCY

THE INTERVIEW

W*hat happened that day, Darcy?*
The day I overheard their conversation?
Yes, that's right.

My parents, I mean Trevor and Hattie – guess I should start calling them by their names, right? They were never my parents.

Call them whatever you want just now.

I'll call them Trevor and Hattie. As much as I can.

Anyway, they thought I was at the local shop buying bread. Hattie sent me there sometimes. The shop is a five-minute walk from the house. But I didn't get out much. Those little outings were like walking to the end of the world and back again. But it's getting cold and that day I was about to leave the house without a jacket. I stood on the doorstep for a while, deciding if the chill was enough to make me go back inside and grab a coat. Yep. I hadn't closed the door and I pushed it open, not making any effort to be quiet.

I guess they were so caught up in...in what they were talking about.

I walked upstairs to my bedroom. Opened the door and pulled my winter jacket off the hook and started threading my arm through the sleeve. I could hear them talking in the living room, directly under my bedroom, but I didn't think much of it at first. Their voices were muffled. But then Trevor said my name. Who wouldn't listen? So I put my head against the floor.

Are you okay, Darcy?

I might have to pee soon.

Do you want to go now? We can pause the interview for a few minutes if it's urgent.

I'll be okay.

You were saying? You put your head against the floor and...?

We've got no choice. Dad, I mean Trevor, kept repeating that over and over again. Mum was crying and he kept raising his voice to talk over her. He said they'd be in big trouble if they didn't do it.

You mean...?

Uh-huh. I didn't know it then, not at the start. I didn't have a clue what they were talking about at that point. I remember thinking that I didn't want them to know that I'd heard them fighting. But that was the beginning. Look at me. I've still got their blood on my hands. Look, it's stuck to my nails.

Why don't we take a break and get your hands washed? Does that sound good?

What would you do if you found out that your parents wanted to kill you? You'd do what I did, wouldn't you?

Tracey?

You'd kill them first.
Wouldn't you?

6

T *ell me about living in that house, Darcy. What was it like?*

Depressing. Sad. Lonely.

In what way?

It's all part of the same story. For as long as I can remember, I've gone by the name Poppy Burton. Darcy Drummond is someone else. It's hard to think of myself as that missing girl, the one in the photos, the one who everyone's been talking about for all these years. They've written books about her. Made documentaries. But she's not me. Not Poppy. And yet, that's who I am.

Can you tell me about your life before overhearing that conversation? What was normal for you?

Normal?

Yes.

Normal was never going anywhere nice with them. Never going to the city. Never going anywhere. Never meeting anyone. We were a drab, unspectacular family as far as the outside world was concerned. We were the colour grey, but less interesting. No one ever noticed us. We kept ourselves to ourselves. That's what it was like for years.

How old are you, Darcy?

I'm seventeen.

And your birthday?

August 11th. But that's not right, is it? Darcy was born in March.

What else can you tell me about living with Trevor and Hattie?

They kept me indoors for most of my life. That's why I'm so pale. I'm kind of sick-looking, don't you think?

You look fine to me.

I've seen pictures of my real mum on the internet. She's beautiful, not like Hattie. She's got the same colouring as me. I did get out of the house sometimes but they wouldn't let me go past the row of shops where I got the bread. Newsagent. Baker. Hairdresser. End of the world. That's been a rule since forever.

I speak well, though, don't I?

I'm sorry?

I speak well for someone who never went to a proper school.

Very well. You've never mixed with other children?

Nope. No friends ever.

They home-schooled me. That's the reason I don't talk much. This is the most I've ever talked in my life, I think. Lessons were structured. English. Maths. Science. All the stuff I hate.

What sort of lessons do you like?

Drawing, but that's something I taught myself to do. It had nothing to do with them. I like to draw my favourite cartoon characters, nice landscapes and whatever, just to escape how boring my life is, I guess.

It's not boring anymore, is it?

No.

Drawing is easier than talking to people. Hattie liked to draw pictures. She even had a book, a sort of journal where she drew some of her happiest memories. Kind of like a photo album but with drawings instead of photos. You've seen the book, haven't you?

Yes, we found that book.

Do you want to know why she made that picture book?

Why?

She was worried about ending up like Trevor. Slowly losing her mind. All her memories fizzling out.

Trevor had dementia?

I don't know. But he was starting to forget things. It was happening more and more. A thought would come to him and then before he could grasp it, it would slip away. You could see the frustration in his eyes when it happened. Mum had her moments too, but she wasn't that bad. Nowhere near it.

What sort of woman was Hattie? Besides being worried about memory loss.

Simple.

Simple?

Simpleton – isn't that the word? Not very clever. I thought she had a good heart though. I guess I was wrong.

Was Trevor clever?

He was in charge. Looking back, I think he was the one who came up with all their little ways to control me.

Like what?

When I was young, *really* young, they used to make me

watch the news with them. It was a thing. We'd all sit down together at about ten o'clock in the morning. And although I couldn't understand much of what was being said, I was bombarded with the worst images. People getting stabbed in bus stops. Pandemics. School shootings. Rape. Wars. Always the bad things.

No good-news stories?

No, I didn't see any of that.

And that was a deliberate move on their part?

Yes. I found out much later it wasn't the real news I was watching. They'd been showing me carefully edited video tapes. I was too young to realise at the time that I was watching the same five or six reports over and over. All I saw were the pictures. And I remember the way they made me feel.

You were afraid to go out?

They told me I was safe as long as I stayed inside the house. And later on, when I did go outside, it was never for long. Those things I saw never left me. *The world's a bad place*, they'd say. *A bad place, Poppy. A dangerous place.*

Still, I longed to go outside sometimes. When I was younger, I wanted to play with other children. That's when Trevor and Hattie would put on the cartoons. Sit me down in front of the TV and distract me. *Stay inside*, they said. *That's a good girl.* I did too much sitting down and now I'm no good at exercise. My back hurts sometimes. They gave me vitamin D because I never got enough sun.

Not socialising with other children. That must have been hard.

Can I see my real mum and dad now?

Soon, Darcy. Let's just get this interview done and dusted, shall we? So, apart from watching cartoons, how did you spend your time in the house?

Home schooling, like I said. Maths, English and Science. I read books sometimes without being told to. Apart from that, I watched TV, mostly cartoons. I could just sit on the floor and watch them all day. I did that lots of times. Laughter is the best medicine, don't you think? Cartoons made me forget the bad stuff. They also made me feel good about myself. There's a can-do attitude in cartoons and I think that's what helped me after I found out what Trevor and Hattie were planning to do to me.

How did it help?

It helped me spring into action. Good always triumphs over evil in the classics. *Snow White and the Seven Dwarfs –* that's my favourite.

So, it's fair to say that your day-to-day relationship with Trevor and Hattie was somewhat...strained?

Suppose so. I don't know what happened to make them kidnap a child. There's something seriously wrong with them. There *was* something wrong with them. And yet there were a few photos around the house, taken in their younger days. They look happy. They're smiling. There's nothing sinister about them.

Are there any photos of you?

None that were ever framed. They didn't want my face on show. I understand why now. Electricians, plumbers, joiners and others – they came to the house sometimes. I was always told to stay in my room.

Would you describe them as happy people?

No. I've seen Hattie sitting on the end of the bed with her pills and a glass of water in hand. A glazed look in her eyes. This was more than once. She never swallowed the pills though. But she was restless, especially at night. Sundowning, Trevor called it. She got anxious after dark. He was anxious all the time. Maybe it all goes back to stealing me. It was that anxiety that, I suppose, made them decide to get rid of me.

Let's go back to that. What do you remember about that conversation you heard through the walls?

I remember all of it.

7

I remember Hattie's shriek. Feeling it move the foundations of the house, like the beginning of a powerful earthquake. I felt her breathless struggle in my own lungs, a struggle to get the words out of her mouth.

"No...we can't. No...we're not doing this."

"Hattie. Please listen to–"

"We can't seriously be talking about this, Trevor. Stop. Listen to yourself."

"We _have_ to do it."

"Why? She's our baby girl. We brought her up and it doesn't matter what anyone says – we're her parents."

"Hattie!"

"No!"

Trevor sounded sharp that day. Strong. In control. All the lights were back on in his mind, the bulbs operating at full power. Usually, there was a weird tremor in his voice. Usually, he stuttered. But he sounded like a young man. The house, walls and floors trembled as he bellowed at Hattie.

"She's not our child, for God's sake. Is she?"

I pressed my ear to the floor. Not sure I'd heard that last part right. The words were surely distorted.

"She is," Hattie yelled back.

"They're looking for her."

"Please," Hattie said in a pleading voice. Again, I could feel the raw emotion in her voice. As if the pain swirling around inside her was my own. "We can't seriously be considering this. Not *this*. She's our daughter and I don't care whose blood flows through her veins. She's Poppy Burton."

"Hattie, you must see reason. You must."

"I'm begging you, Trevor. Let's just forget this. Forget we ever spoke about it. We'll get through this, one day at a time. Nothing bad is going to happen, you'll see. No one will ever find out."

"Hattie," he barked. "Pull yourself together. This weakness of yours will be the end of us."

A slapping noise came through the floor. I knew that Mum – Hattie – was hitting her head with her hands. Literally beating herself up. She did that sometimes when she was upset. Really upset, like she was now. I still had no idea what they were talking about.

I felt lightheaded. Like there wasn't enough blood reaching my brain. It was like I'd left the house and walked back into an alternate universe.

"We can't drag this out for much longer," Trevor said. "She'll be back soon."

Thank God, the slapping had stopped. But the desperation in her voice was still there.

"Please, Trevor. No."

"We have no choice anymore." But he sounded less sure this time. At least, that's what I thought listening through the floor. The tremor was back in his voice and he sounded like a musical instrument going out of tune.

His feet thumped on the floor as he paced the living room. Sounded like a baby elephant trying to find a way out of the house.

"We *have* to."

I pressed my ear tight against the floor. Took short, shallow breaths as I listened.

"You know what happens if we *don't* do it," Trevor said, his pacing coming to a sudden stop. "Don't you, my love? They'll come for us. A dawn raid, that's what'll happen. Do you want to hear that hammering knock on the door at six o'clock in the morning? The sound of dogs barking. Loud voices. The feeling of hands dragging you out of bed?"

"Stop it!"

"We knew the risks when we took her," Trevor said. "We even talked about it afterwards when it was all over the news. No, my love, I can't take another anniversary. All the media. All the attention. Latest theory. Have you heard? She's still in Scotland. They even mentioned Glasgow! Don't you feel it? They're closing in on us."

Panic lifted his thin, reedy voice up several octaves.

"Her name is Darcy Drummond. That's who she is. That's who she's always been."

I took my head off the floor.

Darcy Drummond?

There was a long, drawn-out silence in the living room. What was happening in there? Why weren't they talking? Had I made a noise? What now? Those clumsy footsteps would explode up the stairs, stopping on the other side of my door. A knock. *Poppy? Are you in there?* The door handle would rattle. Then it opens. His beetroot face staring at me across the room. Eyes frantic. Trying to figure out what to do with me.

Thank God, they started talking again.

"Is it settled?" Trevor asked.

Hattie's voice was a brittle croak. "Is there no other way?"

"No, my love. We have to let her go. We...umm...we have to..."

The mind he'd cultivated for years was full of holes and there was nothing he could do to stop more holes coming. The eyes would go blank. Then, he'd jump back into the flow. Restart. Like someone had fixed the faulty wiring.

He'd exhausted his voice pleading with Hattie. Now he sounded old and weak. "We're too old to get caught. You understand, don't you, my love?"

Silence.

"Hattie, I need you to say it. We can't go on like this. Worrying about every little thing. It's making us sick. We're too old to get caught. Can you imagine what they'd do to people like us in prison? They'd rip us to shreds, you know that, don't you?"

A whimper came back. Then, a single word. "Yes."

Trevor spoke in a gentle voice. "It's settled then?"

I stared at the floor, waiting for the answer. I didn't have to wait long.

"Yes."

8

That must have been very traumatic for you, Darcy. I can't imagine how you must have felt.

Just imagine the two people you trust the most betraying you in the worst possible way. You'll have an idea.

Easier said than done.

The difference between living and dying was forgetting to put my coat on. If I'd wrapped up, I never would've gone back and overheard their conversation. I wouldn't be sitting here. They'd have wrapped me up and got rid of the evidence.

Tell me about those first few moments after you heard them talking. What was going on in your mind?

Confusion. Panic. Horror. My brain was trying to find ways to cope. I remember standing up off the floor, heart pounding, telling myself that it was just a game. We did play games long ago when I was little, before they lost interest. Hide and seek was my favourite. We played tag. Board games like Operation and Buckaroo.

This was a game too. It had to be.

But I knew it wasn't.

I thought about the news clips they force-fed me as a child. Was something bigger than us happening out there in the wider world? An apocalyptic event? All those images flooded back to the surface and, sure, maybe that was it. Civilisation had collapsed. Just like it was on TV, with people turning against one another, stabbing and shooting. Climate change. Immigrants. Gun crime. Knife crime. The world had lost its mind.

But...

But what?

There were no blaring sirens outside. No scared voices. No bloodcurdling screams. Everything was so quiet.

They *were* going to kill me.

What happened next?

I stood there in my bedroom for what felt like a long time. It was probably only a minute or two. I was numb. That girl's name was doing laps in my head.

Darcy Drummond?

Right.

You were supposed to be out on an errand. How did you get out of the house?

That wasn't what I was thinking about. Not right away.

What were you thinking about?

About Darcy Drummond. I had to get more information.

More information?

The Google thing. I can't just ask a question there and get what I want. Trevor and Hattie told me there were a lot of bad people on the internet. It's poison, they said. Kills off your brain cells. Makes you as mad as the people outside. Watch your cartoons and be a good girl.

They've got the router controlled at home pretty good,

using apps that limit user time, restrict websites. They can pause the Wi-Fi whenever they want.

You're standing in the bedroom thinking about Darcy Drummond. About getting more information. What are Trevor and Hattie doing?

They were quiet for a while. Then they started talking again.

"We need a proper goodbye," Hattie said to Trevor. "We're not getting rid of her like an old chair."

"Hattie–"

"I mean it."

"Why prolong this?" Trevor asked. "Why make it harder for ourselves? The risk increases every second she's alive. We could sit her down for dinner tonight and–"

Hattie let out a shriek of protest. Sounded like someone who'd burned their hand on a hot stove.

"No!"

"Hattie!"

"We took her off that beach, Trevor. We brought her into our home, didn't we? We called her Poppy. *Daughter.*"

In the end, Hattie negotiated a few more days for me. And Dad came up with the idea of how they'd do it.

"We'll make dinner," he said. "How does that sound, my love?"

"Dinner?"

I remember he sounded giddy. Almost like he was looking forward to it. "Yes! Remember those lavish family meals we used to enjoy on Sunday evenings? All of us gathered around the big dining table with the classics playing in the background. Bach. Rachmaninoff. You remember, don't you?"

"That's a memory from *your* childhood, Trevor."

"Oh...right."

Another long silence. This time, I was certain the conversation was over. I started thinking about how to get out the house when Mum, I mean Hattie, spoke.

"Sunday dinner," she said. "I'll make all her favourites."

Trevor's voice was little more than a whisper. "She won't feel a thing."

"She won't," Hattie said. "I'll make sure of it."

"We'll do our research."

Wow, Darcy. I can't imagine. That must have been very frightening for you.

It was. They kept talking. Persuading themselves it had to be done. Even though I knew I had to get out, I kept listening.

"Look at us, for God's sake," Trevor said, his voice a choked bellow of exhaustion. "We're sick with worry. Look at *you*."

"What about me?"

"Hattie! You've lost so much weight since this anniversary came back under the media spotlight. It's not healthy. We've endured twelve anniversaries already. You don't think I hear you throwing up at all hours of the day?"

"She's our little girl," Mum said. "What if we're overreacting? What if it all blows over in a week or two?"

Once again, Trevor's voice shot up an octave.

"Overreacting? Over-bloody-reacting, are we? They're saying she's still in Scotland. Some of them are narrowing it down to Glasgow."

"Well, it's to be expected. It *is* the biggest city in the country."

"We're at the mercy of fate, my love. We don't know what's going on. What if someone remembered something from that day on the beach? Perhaps an old home video clip has surfaced and we're in it."

"You're scaring me, Trevor."

"I'm scared too. We *should* be scared. Scared of the police kicking down our door in the middle of the night."

Hattie yelled. "Stop it!"

"I've always been scared of the police," Trevor said. "You know that. Scared of authority. Imagine what it would do to us. We'd be humiliated in a public trial. They'd call us monsters, not understanding how much we loved her. How much we *needed* her. They won't see past the tabloid head-lines. We'll be vilified. Sentenced to life in prison. We'll be high-profile targets for all the other inmates. We aren't strong enough to survive. That's why she has to go. We'll be safe then, my love. And...and it'll be like we never knew her."

9

---

o, the conversation ended. Then what?

S I had to get out of the house. From my room, there was a clear path down the hallway, down the stairs, to the front door. It was that easy, but I had to do something first.

What?

Well, I had to get on the internet, remember?

To research Darcy?

Right, but I didn't have a phone, which meant getting one of theirs and taking it with me. Mum carried her phone in her pocket. That was no use. Dad – Trevor – didn't. His phone was always upstairs in their bedroom, plugged into the charger at his side of the bed. He hardly ever used it. Didn't like them. Was always saying how they were making people stupid. He was a newspaper, slippers and pipe man.

Probably didn't have a password. That's what I was hoping for.

One step at a time. I had to get out of the house because I was supposed to be at the shops and I didn't know what they'd do if they realised I'd been in the house all along. I didn't know these people anymore.

But I knew what they were capable of.

Fighting back the urge to be sick, I crept towards the bedroom door. The floor taunted me by groaning under my weight. Lucky for me, the TV was now on in the living room. A man's voice, muffled and distorted, filled the house as he read the news headlines. I could picture Trevor sitting there in his favourite seat. I wondered if, somehow, with his mind the way it was, he'd forgotten about killing me.

You never know.

Hattie was in the kitchen. That much I knew for sure. Distancing herself from Trevor and getting things ready for dinner. Making everything look normal.

Bread. I was supposed to be getting bread. That was their little way of shutting me up when I asked about getting out more. A five-minute walk to the shops. I was supposed to be happy with that.

I had to fight the urge to make a run for it. But I had to be sneaky. I had to be quiet and clever. I needed Dad's phone.

My sweaty fingers gripped the door handle. Pulled down, down, slowly. I winced at the squeaking noise, wondering why all of a sudden the handle turning sounded like the shriek of a frightened bird.

I closed my eyes. My heart was like a drum. While I tried to breathe, I envisioned both of them standing outside my door. Their eyes huge and doll-like. Grimace-like smiles on their faces. *Poppy. Are you in there, darling?*

I had to go for it. After pulling the door open a few inches, I peered through the gap. Looked right, then left. Now or never. I tiptoed out of the bedroom, the muffled news broadcast still cloaking any sounds that might trickle downstairs. I could do this. Trevor wouldn't get up during the news. He didn't move much in general. With any luck, he'd already fallen asleep in front of the TV.

I snuck into their bedroom on my tiptoes.

The house continued to groan like a sinking ship underneath me. On my way to the bedside table, I crept past the full-length wardrobe mirror. Saw the girl there and wondered who I was looking at.

It looked like...*me*. Like someone pulled out of a burning building who didn't fully understand what was happening. My skin was a sickly marble colour. Beads of sweat pooled on my forehead.

We must kill her. We must kill Poppy.

And yet, despite everything, there was a strange fluttering excitement inside me. A tingling that made my arms and legs feel weightless. Was it the possibility that I was someone else? The excitement of the butterfly as she emerges from the cocoon?

Who is Darcy Drummond?

My God, their bedroom is so neat. The bed perfectly made, not a crease in sight. Curtains pulled, carpet freshly hoovered and nothing lying on the floor. I hurried over to Dad's side of the bed. The phone was on the bedside table, plugged into the wall and charging. I pulled the lead out at the wall. Hid it under the pillow just in case one of the would-be killers came upstairs when I was gone and noticed it lying around.

I shoved the phone into my pocket.

Done.

I straightened up. *Keep going*, I told myself. *Breathe*. I talked to myself. Found an encouraging voice in my head that told me this was my chance to be a hero like in the cartoons. No such thing as bravery without fear.

And I've never been so scared as I stood there, knowing that it was time to make for the front door.

I walked downstairs. Crept past the living room door which, lucky for me, was still closed. Everything in my body tightened up, got heavy. It felt like I was dragging a piano behind me. It got harder to breathe, like someone had a hand over my nose and mouth. The news presenter behind the door was talking about a school blowing up in Syria. I covered the downstairs hallway in less than half that report. *Creep, creep, creep. Door, door, door.* A loud thump from the living room stopped my heart. Might have been Dad dropping something. I didn't hang around to find out.

I ran on my toes. Scurried forward, pushed the handle down and pulled the door open. A cool breeze spilled inside. It was a gentle reminder to keep moving forward.

Nearly there.

I closed the door behind me. Stumbled down the concrete steps, willing my legs to make it down the garden path. Didn't matter if I'd forgotten anything else. I wasn't going back there for anything.

My fingers wrestled with the latch. The gate swung open and closed. Then, I found myself on the road, backing away from that house.

I thought I heard someone calling.

Then, I ran like the devil was on my tail.

I KNOW what you're thinking. That I should have stopped the first person I saw. Grabbed them by the arm, clung on to them like I was a crazy person. Told them what I'd heard. *That one down there. The house at the bottom of the street. Two people, Trevor and Hattie Burton. They're going to kill me!*

But I didn't. I just kept going, and even if I did tell someone, who'd believe me? It sounded crazy just thinking about it in my head.

Besides, I had to find out about this Darcy Drummond. I had to know who she was.

And quite possibly, who I was.

I ran flat out for about five minutes. Willing my legs to impossible speeds. I zoomed past the hairdresser, the newsagent, a tanning salon and a second-hand bookshop. There was *so* much going on. People walking on both sides of the street. Suddenly, I was hot. Then, I was cold. *We have to kill her. We have to kill Poppy.*

I found the café at the end of the shops. My heels skidded to a complete stop and I peered through the window, seeing it was busy inside. Groups of people gathered around the modest space, eating and drinking. A few scattered loners on their phones or reading books. On the front door there were posters for music and comedy gigs and at the centre, a small sticker that said 'Free Wi-Fi'.

I sucked in the air. Heart slowed. Sensation returned to my legs after the mad sprint.

I pushed the door open and it was instantaneous sensory overload. All those voices snapped at my ears. The shriek of cutlery scraping off plates. Someone dropped a glass and it smashed. And behind everything, the constant whirr and hum of machinery.

But you didn't leave?

No. But I wanted to.

The woman at the counter smiled at me. She had

coloured beads in her hair and a Beatles t-shirt that said, *Happy Road*. No, I mean *Abbey Road*. Her smile relaxed me a little. I approached the counter, pulling Trevor's phone out of my pocket. With a beetroot-red face, I asked her how to connect to the Wi-Fi. I made up a story about looking for a clothes shop in the area because that's what girls my age do, isn't it? I had to blend in. Just being there, I felt I stuck out like a sore thumb.

The woman gave me a small card. It had the Wi-Fi password on it. Asked me to bring it back when I was finished. I asked how it worked and, after giving me a funny smile, she took the phone off me, went to 'Settings' and hooked it up. She told me all I had to do was go into the browser and look up what I wanted. I gave her a look and she showed me how to get into Google.

"Do you want to order anything?" she asked.

"Can I have a glass of water?"

"Of course."

"Is it expensive?"

She smiled. "Oh, we don't charge for a glass of water. Take a seat, sweetheart, and I'll bring it over."

"Thanks."

I had to be quick. I found an empty two-seater table in the corner and, shutting out the noise all around me, typed the girl's name into Google.

That brought up a flood of pictures and articles.

I pressed my thumb on the first picture. That took me to an American-based news page and, after shutting down an onslaught of ad bubbles, I was free to look at the article. One of three freebies before I had to start paying, according to them. There she was, front and centre – Darcy Drummond, a blonde-haired girl of about four. Sitting on a crowded beach, dressed in a pink t-shirt and wearing a white hat. It was like a jolt of electricity surging around my body.

There *I* was. That girl was me.

So many pictures, but none that I could remember. But still, look at her. Look at me. I read the articles as much as I could, as fast as I could. The blogs. The book pages. I skimmed the blurbs. It was like reading about someone else and I only looked up to thank the woman who brought me the water. Doing my best to look normal.

According to the articles, thirteen years had passed since four-year-old Darcy Drummond was kidnapped on Bournemouth Beach. *Kidnapped*. The kidnappers were never caught. No one knows what happened to her. Now, interest in the case was heating up again because of the anniversary closing in. Happened every year by the sound of it. New documentaries, podcasts, articles and claims of fresh evidence. New witnesses coming forward. Weird theories and wild speculation about what happened to Darcy.

Most of the world, it seemed, believed the missing girl was alive.

I put the phone down on the table. Dizzy. The words floating on the screen and me trying to blink it out. No words could explain how I felt. I just stared into space, shutting off all the noise inside the café. That was it. The butterfly was out of her cocoon. Poppy Burton never existed.

I looked at her face. Looked at the parents. The twin boys she would have called brothers. *My* brothers.

The heat was rising in my chest.

Anger.

They kidnapped me when I was a little girl. They stole me and took me away from my real family – my mum, dad and two brothers. They locked me in that house, feeding me scary news stories and making sure that I grew up scared instead of curious.

And now they wanted to get rid of me?

Darcy, I have to ask. Why didn't you ask someone to call the police? Why did you end up going back to the house?

Because I hated them. I *hated* them. They stole me and now, just like that, they had no more use for me? They wanted to throw me away like a piece of rubbish.

I hated them. And I had to go back because whatever the law was going to do to them, it wasn't enough.

---

hat happened next?

W I hurried out of the café, knowing I was late. Very late. I still had to pick up the bread. Go back to the house, act normal, just like they'd be acting normal despite what they'd just agreed to do. Our worlds turned upside down, both of us hiding it. I got a sourdough in the end. The woman who worked in the shop, Mrs Holland, tried to be chatty with me. She called me Poppy and for a second, it was on the tip of my tongue. The truth. *My name isn't Poppy.*

You wanted to tell her?

Maybe. But I didn't say a word. I took the bread, tucked it under my arm, then went outside and started running again. Running helped. My thoughts couldn't touch me if I ran fast and hard enough.

I got home, shot up the path and stopped at the door. *Here we go*, I thought. I don't have a key and once I close the door over, that's it, I'm locked out. We have this weird ritual where I have to prove my identity before being allowed into the house. I thought it was a game. I thought lots of people did these things for security reasons, given how the world was teetering on the edge of collapse. How stupid. Four knocks followed by three questions from Trevor about our daily routine. Little things that only the three of us know. Breakfast. Lessons. Whatever. Sometimes he's holding a knife when he opens the door. Always, this fearful look on his face. I thought it was his forgetfulness.

I did the secret knock, answered the questions, and he didn't have a knife this time. But I could tell he was agitated.

Once inside, I did my best to act normal.

"What took you so long?" Trevor asked.

"The shop was busy," I lied. "And I walked slow because I was enjoying the fresh air. Sorry – didn't mean to take so long."

"You walked *slowly*."

Even then, still trying to control me.

"Oh."

"Never mind," he said, turning back towards the living room. I watched him go, realising how frail and stooped he was. Now I knew about the fear inside him. The fear of police. Of authority and someone breaking the door in for a dawn raid.

These people were planning to kill me. Today was Wednesday. On Sunday, at around five o'clock, I'd be dead.

What was it like after you came back?

I tried to act normal. Dropped the bread off in the kitchen. Spent some time talking to Mum and she could barely look me in the eye. If I hadn't known, I would've asked her what was wrong. It was that obvious. But I didn't say anything. Knowledge was my superpower, not theirs.

Mum – Hattie – was the hardest to take. She'd agreed to

his plan. Trevor – we've never been that close. Looking back, I'm like a toy he got bored with quickly. It was different with her though. With Hattie. At least, I thought it was. But she was under his spell. Always was.

I know this can't be easy. Tell me if you need a break.

I want to go home.

Soon, Darcy. Very soon. I just want to get a picture of the last few days leading up to...Sunday.

Me against them. Good versus Evil. The hero versus the two villains. They lied to me for years and taught me to be scared of the world through videotapes. But even a brief trip to the café showed me things weren't that bad outside the house. Beyond the street. I grew up thinking that the house was an island surrounded by sharks. I thought that's why they locked the doors and checked them over and over again. I thought that's why the doorbell made Mum jump. Why we had the secret knock.

Lies. All of it.

But I had the upper hand. They didn't know I knew about their plan. About my last supper on Sunday. Good vanquishes evil. All those cartoons, all the lessons I've learned, they were all building up to that moment. To Sunday. The last supper. I *would* escape, but not before punishing them for stealing me from my family. They wanted the Sleeping Death for me but I'd give it to them first.

Darcy?

I can still see them lying on the kitchen floor. Limbs twisted and bent out of shape.

You're not in trouble. You know that, don't you?

Why did they steal me?

I don't know. I suppose they wanted a child. We've still got so much to learn about Trevor and Hattie, and why they did what they did.

I had to do it. There was no shortage of pills in the bathroom cabinet upstairs. Labels that made no sense to me, except for the warning about side effects, abuse, addiction and overdose. Like I said, I've watched Mum crush up a big box of pills and put them in a glass of water. She didn't know I was lurking at the door. Didn't know I was listening to her crying. But she never drank the poison. The contents of the glass always went back down the sink.

Life would go on.

Something kept her in this world. I wonder if it was me.

11

I didn't sleep a wink that first night, and neither did Hattie.

The sundowning made her restless. She couldn't sit still at night and sometimes she liked to sit in the bedroom, drawing in her picture journal. When that didn't calm her down, she might go into the bathroom and crush pills again. Bring the powder back with a glass of water. Sit on the edge of the bed and stare into space.

Having said that, she was most likely restless that night because of what she'd agreed to do.

You must have been terrified.

I lay awake most of the night. Flinching every time the floorboards creaked upstairs or downstairs. Especially upstairs. Thing is, my bedroom doesn't have a lock on it. What if they'd changed their mind about doing it on Sunday? The sooner I was gone, the less anxious Trevor would feel about the police finding him. Maybe they were planning to move house. To disappear. They just needed me out of the way. I could see it happening. Quiet footsteps creeping down the hall. Hushed voices. My door flying open, an explosion of speed that should've been beyond them and by the time I sat up in bed it would be too late. The needle would've sunk into my skin.

But nothing happened.

I did manage to sleep for a few hours. And something happened when I woke up. Because I woke up angry. It was like the feeling was sitting on the edge of the bed all night, waiting for me to open my eyes so it could jump inside me. I wasn't scared anymore. There was just this fire burning up inside me.

I could hear them downstairs in the kitchen. They were fighting too, and it was a bad one. The sort of fight between a husband and wife that might get physical. That's not like them. Trevor's the least physically scary man you'd ever meet. Small, a little bit hunched over. Looks like the stereotypical bookworm.

I didn't have to listen in. I knew what they were talking about.

Finally, it went quiet. Like they'd remembered I was still in the house.

Tick-tock. Not long until Sunday.

What about the regular household routine? Did your lessons continue?

No more lessons. Mum said we were having a break from all that. I mean, *Hattie* said. I didn't ask why. She was still pacing around the house a lot, even during the day. She was so restless.

Must have been tense.

Yes.

What did you do to pass the time?

I watched TV in the living room. Cartoons. Lots of

cartoons. That's what I was doing when I heard footsteps approach from behind. The floor made a loud cracking noise and I felt cold all over. The hairs stood up on the back of my neck.

"Poppy?"

It was Hattie.

"Poppy, darling?"

I had to act like nothing unusual was happening. I wasn't supposed to know. But I did know and I was sure that knowing was all over my face.

"Hi," I said.

She sat down beside me on the floor. That was a painful process for her and she groaned while her joints clicked like a percussive instrument. She was trying to smile but the expression on her face resembled a wince.

She looked at the TV. Then, at me.

"Are you okay, my little precious one?"

My little precious one? Is that what she called you?

Horrible, isn't it? And yet, I sort of liked it. That day, though, after everything I'd overheard, it was flipped upside down. It scared me more than anything.

Anyway, I nodded.

She leaned into me a little. I felt the warmth of her arms through her jumper. "Dad told you about the–?"

"About the family dinner this weekend?"

I could hear her insides clench up.

"Yes."

"He did."

"That's good."

She rocked back and forth gently. Her eyes locked on the TV, lips moving like she was speaking quietly to herself. Her picture book sat closed on her lap. Beside her on the floor, the old tin box of coloured pencils. She must have been drawing before she came to find me.

"We haven't had a proper family dinner in ages," she said. "You'd like that, wouldn't you?"

I pretended to watch TV.

"Hmm."

"*Snow White and the Seven Dwarfs* again?" she said. A nervous chuckle trickled out of her. "How many times have you seen that one?"

I felt the arteries in my neck tighten.

"I like it."

"It's your favourite, isn't it?"

"Maybe."

"Well," she said, rubbing my leg like it was an eager-to-please spaniel seeking affection. "I'm going to make all your favourites for dinner on Sunday night. And dessert. You'd like that, wouldn't you?"

You'd like that, wouldn't you?
You'd like that wouldn't you?
You'd like that, wouldn't you?

Before I could answer, there was a shuffling-of-feet noise behind us. I knew it was him. He didn't ever walk – he scraped his feet on the floor. We turned around and Trevor was standing in the doorway. Watching us. He looked back and forth between us, his expression blank. Then he mumbled an apology for interrupting before scraping off down the hallway.

Did you and Hattie talk about anything else?

Not much. I watched TV and she did a little drawing. I think she just wanted to spend time with me.

"Can't wait for Sunday," I said at one point.

Zap. Like she'd had an electric shock.

That nervous chuckling. Then she looked down at the book, browsing through her older sketches. I glanced too, but none of them made any sense to me. She wasn't good. She drew like a child but not in a good way. Still, for her it wasn't about how good they were. Just the act of drawing seemed to comfort her. Drawing memories.

"I'll help with the food on Sunday."

"Oh no," she said quickly. "You don't have to do that. I'll do everything."

"I want to help."

"Poppy–"

"Just the starter. I was planning to make minestrone soup."

"You've never made it before."

"First time for everything, isn't there? I'll have to start doing more cooking around here. I want to look after you both as you get older."

Hattie's eyes filled as she clung to the picture book like it was a blanket on a cold night. She swallowed hard.

"Okay, sweetheart. You make the soup."

"Is everything okay, Mum?"

The way she looked at me. It was hard to hate her in that moment, even though she'd agreed to Trevor's last supper. But I saw the conflict in her eyes. No, conflict isn't the right word. The agony. It wasn't easy to look at. This woman used to read stories to me at bedtime. She read to me when I was ill. My love of stories began with her in my earliest memories. She bought the DVDs of my favourite cartoons. She was always bringing me food and stuff to drink. Showering me with kindness.

She was no killer.

"I'll make the soup," I said. "It'll be my project."

The smile on her face was strained. She managed a weak nod.

"Whatever you want."

I remember how much I wanted her to confess. Right there. *Just say it*, I thought. *Say it and I'll forgive you.* Maybe we could've fixed it somehow, just the two of us. But she said nothing. So she was still willing to go through with it. Still and always under his spell. Willing to poison me to death.

Good versus Evil.

"I was talking to Dad earlier," I said, an innocent smile on my face. "He suggested that we should go on a picnic this week. Just me and him."

A crease appeared on Hattie's forehead.

"What?"

I nodded. "Daddy-daughter time. He said we should take a special trip together. This week – it has to be this week."

Hattie's face turned chalk-white. "A special trip? *This* week?"

I nodded. "We've never done anything like that before. I wonder what made him want to take me away somewhere all of a sudden."

"Take...you...away."

"Yes."

"When?"

"Friday. Maybe Saturday."

"And it'd definitely be just the two of you?"

"Oops. Don't say anything, okay?"

Her shrill laugh hurt my head. "Of course not."

I turned back to the TV, watching my favourites while Hattie pretended to look at her book. But I could feel her shaking beside me.

12

What about Trevor? Did you play mind games with him too?

These people kidnapped me. Now, they wanted to kill me. Yes, more mind games.

Sorry, I'm not judging you, Darcy. Far from it. I'm just trying to find out what happened in the build-up to Sunday.

A distraction technique. To heighten the tension between them, fuel the distrust and use it to my advantage. That way they'd be focusing more on each other and less on me. Because I was preparing my own last supper.

So, what did you say to Trevor?

I approached him later that day. Walked into the living room while he sat on his favourite chair watching TV. Hattie was at the shops so there was no better opportunity to mess with his head.

There was a cup of tea in his hand. Biscuit crumbs on the armrest. He didn't look at me even though I'm sure he knew I was there.

"Hi, Dad."

I stood beside the armchair. Closer than I would've liked to. He was such a strange and awkward little man. I was never comfortable around him – and vice-versa, I think. He made my skin crawl in a way I couldn't explain. His eyes twitched. He'd fart sometimes like he was the only person in the room and never think to apologise. Disgusting. Finally, he noticed me standing beside him. His beady eyes were all over me like I was a cockroach making for the kitchen.

"Poppy. What can I do for you?"

So stiff. So formal.

I sat down on the armrest. The TV was blaring away. Some guy in glasses talking with a woman about a local election that was coming up. I sold a big smile on my face, or at least I tried to sell it. Hoped it didn't look as fake as it felt. *This man*, I reminded myself, *is not my father. He stole me. He wants to kill me because my existence is inconvenient.*

"When are we going for that picnic?" I asked.

He made a loud snorting noise. Shifted in his chair, not looking at me.

"Hmm?"

"When are we going for that picnic?"

"What's this about a picnic?"

When he finally looked at me, it was as if I'd spoken in a foreign language.

I smiled. "You were talking about a picnic yesterday. Don't you remember? You said it was time we livened things up around here. A picnic. Just the two of us. Daddy-daughter time – that's what you called it."

His face wrinkled up. I saw the little twitch flaring up in his eyes. "Daddy-daughter time? I said that?"

I frowned.

"You didn't forget, did you?"

I could almost hear the clanking of machinery inside his head. His mind was like a sieve. I could have said anything and there was no way he'd be sure that I was telling the truth. That would be cruel. We don't do that sort of thing to nice people, do we? Well, he wasn't a nice man. He was a kidnapper. And a murderer-to-be.

Still, it was a long shot that he'd believe me. We didn't have these sorts of conversations. Not ever. We existed under the same roof together but apart in our own little bubbles. I don't know why he took me. Why he thought a child would make a difference. That's why he looked so puzzled as I pretended that we'd made plans.

"You did forget," I said, slapping the back of the chair. I was probably overdoing it at that point. "Didn't you?"

He must have thought I had a screw loose.

"Well–"

"Not to worry. We hadn't committed to a date or anything like that. I just thought I'd remind you that we'd talked about it."

"The picnic?"

"The picnic."

Very clever. If Hattie brought the subject of a picnic up later on, there was every chance that it would show on Trevor's face that he knew. Now that you'd planted the seed. That would make him look guilty in her eyes of conspiring to kill you before Sunday. Without Hattie.

Yes.

But I wasn't finished there.

No?

No. I still had to plant something in his mind. About what Hattie was doing behind *his* back.

Of course.

I stared at him. He was watching a mouthwash advert on TV and acting like it was the most engrossing thing ever. I could tell he was desperate for me to go away. He didn't want to be reminded of my existence. An existence he would snuff out in a few days if I let him.

I didn't go away. I sat there on the armrest, waiting for the advert to end before speaking again.

"Dad?"

"Hmmm."

"Speaking of family time."

A loud sigh. Those beady eyes on me again.

"Yes? What is it now?"

"Mum said she was thinking about taking me on a trip."

It was like he froze for a second. Then, he sat up in the chair. Peered at me through those narrow slits carved into his head. He tried to smile but his face was out of practice and didn't know what to do. It was like there was a gargoyle looking at me.

"A trip? What sort of trip?"

He spoke with a tremor in his voice.

"Don't know exactly," I said. "She sat down with me earlier while I was watching TV. You saw us earlier, remember?"

"Oh yes."

He was blinking furiously. Like someone had just shone a bright light in his eyes.

"She's thinking about something exciting too. Something for me and her. Said we could go away for a couple of days. Girl time, as she called it."

"Girl time?"

"This weekend."

"This weekend? *This* weekend?"

"Yes. Before the big dinner on Sunday."

"*Before* it?"

"Yes."

"Oh right."

After that, he was back to staring at the TV. But the crazy blinking and constant finger twitching was a dead giveaway.

You rattled him?

They wanted to keep me in the dark. Keep me in the dark until Sunday and then wipe me out. But now I was the one pulling the strings. And it felt good.

13

I know what it must have looked like to the police,
seeing them lying on the kitchen floor like that. All
bloody and disgusting. The soup. Bits of flesh. All that
mess. But it was them or me. And none of it went as planned
anyway.

*We'll get to that part soon, okay? For now, let's talk about the
build-up to Sunday. What else were you doing leading up to
that day?*

Darcy?

I'm tired. I don't usually talk this much.

*You're doing great. Take a sip if you need to. That's right.
Better?*

Hmmm.

So, what were you doing leading up to Sunday?

I crushed pills on the Friday and Saturday.

There was a lot of sneaking around, waiting for the right
opportunities to get moving. I worked in frantic spurts. I was
upstairs when they were downstairs, raiding their medicine
cabinet in the bathroom. Ever since I was young, I'd been

told to stay away from the medicine cabinet. Dangerous, they'd say. Pills. Well, it only makes you want to get closer, doesn't it? I knew there was a pill crusher in there somewhere. After rummaging around, I found it in Mum's toiletry bag under the bathroom sink. The crusher looked like a tiny jar. You open the lid, pop the pill inside and then screw the lid back on. Then you squeeze hard. I worked away at it. All their medications, taking as much as I could from each little bottle without making it too obvious. I didn't know how much I was supposed to crush. How much powder does it take to stop a heart?

Me or them.

Good versus Evil.

I couldn't even pronounce the names of the chemicals I was crushing. Didn't matter. As long as they worked. Mum sent me to the shops on Friday, which gave me a chance to go back to the café with the Wi-Fi. Which I did. This time, I watched videos on Dad's phone, his headphones in my ears. Read some posts on forums. Most of the pages I visited online popped up with a suicide warning. The internet thought I was about to kill myself.

What about the mind games? How were Trevor and Hattie coping with that?

They were quiet. The shouting had stopped and I knew what I'd said about Daddy-daughter time and girl time had to be eating away at them. I kept chipping at it. A little word in one ear, a little word in another. I was sure that Hattie thought Trevor was planning to kill me ahead of schedule. On the other hand, Trevor thought that Hattie's fictional girlie day out was her way of getting me away. Saving me from the last supper.

I was proud of myself. I'd caused a distraction. They were

focusing more on each other than me. The possibility of betrayal. Meanwhile, I persevered with the pill crushing. I'd built up a nice collection of white powder that I kept inside a big plastic bag. Looked like it was enough. I'd find out soon.

I also had to figure out how to make the soup. And another question arose – was it okay to put the powder in the soup or was that too hot? If it was too hot, could I put it in their water? Would they see it? Taste it?

The more I thought, the more I tried to convince myself to back out. I could still run. Go to the police.

But I couldn't. It had to be me that served justice because otherwise, I wouldn't be the hero. I'd be a...what do you call it...bystander.

One thing was for sure. They'd never steal another child again.

Well, you were certainly brave.

Friday and Saturday were slow days. There's this old sun clock on the wall in the living room and the big and little hands seemed to be going backwards. *Tock-tick. Tock-tick.* Slow, slow days. I stayed away from Trevor and Hattie as much as I could. Wasn't easy. Mum kept trying to get close to me. Putting her big fat arm around me. Sometimes she'd sit down beside me at the TV and start drawing in her picture book. Therapy, I suppose. We all needed our therapy for the madness to come.

She asked me about the picnic with Trevor. My answers were always vague. Nothing planned, not yet. But it's definitely happening.

Trevor asked about girl time with Hattie. I did the same thing with my answers.

The big advantage I had going for me was that my fake mum and dad didn't know I'd overheard their conversation that day. I was innocent. I had no reason to make up stories about picnics and girl time. I was doomed. The last person they'd suspect.

I did other things to chip away at their fragile minds. Little things. We had this small brown suitcase tucked away in the spare bedroom upstairs. Covered in dust. Never got used because nobody ever went anywhere. I pulled it out of the cupboard one afternoon, dusted it down and left it sitting on the upstairs landing.

So that Trevor would see it?

Yep. So he'd think it was Hattie. And then I'd take it away and put it back in the cupboard. Let him think he was seeing things.

He deserved it. They both deserved it. You don't just kill people, you don't get rid of someone when they're inconvenient, do you?

No.

I took two more trips to the café for the internet. I got quite good at using it and I was comfortable around the people because I didn't have to talk to anyone. There I was, researching how to use prescription pills to kill my parents while eating a brownie. I didn't get many sugary treats at home.

With any luck, Trevor wouldn't notice the trail I was leaving on his phone. I didn't know how to get rid of search history and obviously I wasn't going to ask a stranger to do it for me because they'd take one look and think I was suicidal.

I did my work, researching poison. Researching how to make minestrone soup. I learned that I couldn't put the crushed powder into the soup as the heat would affect it. I'd put it in their water or something else at room temperature.

Sunday was getting closer. I was the hero and that meant being brave, even though I was scared out of my wits.

But it was time.

Time for the last supper.

14

Sunday night. They'd dimmed the lights in the house. Candles were lit and there was soft, classical music playing on the downstairs stereo, something that didn't get used much. Mournful strings called out to me. The house felt like the inside of a cathedral.

I can still see it. Hear it. The smell of the food wafting upstairs from the kitchen. And the white dress they gave me to wear.

They bought you a new dress?

They did. That gesture alone would've rung the alarm bells even if I'd never overheard that conversation through the wall. They never gave me clothes. Well, the basics. Jumpers and trousers. Warm socks. Plain shoes. Nothing bright or summery. Nothing eye-catching. But this dress was like something out of a Disney fairy-tale. It had a stunning floral lace pattern and a wide skirt that billowed from the hips. It was magical. A perfect fit and I felt like a princess. That was Mum. She got it for me.

You mean Hattie.

Yes.

Are you okay?

I remember the way she looked. Lying on the kitchen floor. Arms and legs all twisted, covered in blood and soup.

I know this is hard for you, Darcy. Would you like that break now?

No. I just want to finish.

Okay.

I'd watched cartoons all day. That helped me to relax because when I wasn't watching cartoons, I was working on the soup in the kitchen. Working alongside Hattie. Strange when you consider that we were both plotting to kill one another.

And what about the tension between Trevor and Hattie?

The mind games?

Yes.

Spilling over. Even on Sunday night when it was obvious that none of it was happening like I said it was. Mum wasn't running away with me. Dad wasn't taking me on a poison picnic. Didn't matter to them. The seeds were planted and growing. They still suspected the other of plotting against them.

They'd been drinking all afternoon. Hattie was on the red wine and Trevor hoovered up all the Scotch from a big bottle that was barely ever touched. The smell was awful. They barely said a word to one another. Their faces were bloated and red. Eyes puffy. Twenty years of ageing in a single week.

Where did it all go wrong for them? There were photos in the house – not many, but there were some hidden in drawers of them in their twenties, young, fresh-faced and smiling. Hard to believe it was the stale old couple that I lived with. Where had those people gone? What made them kidnap a child?

Maybe they couldn't have children of their own. We don't know much for sure yet.

I lived with them for years. And I barely know anything about them.

What about you? How were you feeling at this point?

Weird.

That creepy classical music was playing downstairs. I hated it. But the dress was on and I knew I couldn't stay upstairs any longer. I'd been putting it off for long enough. It was time to go down and face the last supper.

I opened my bedside drawer. Pulled out the bag of powder. Then, I rolled it up and tucked it into the dress as best I could. Feeling like I was in a dream, I walked out of my bedroom. Down the hallway, putting my foot on the top step. It creaked under my weight. *The next time I take these stairs*, I thought, *they'll be dead.*

My body went tight, like someone was suffocating me.

I turned back, ran straight into the toilet and threw up everything that was inside me. I tried to keep the sick off my dress. Didn't want to leave any traces. Everything had to look normal when I went downstairs. I'm oblivious to their plans, remember?

I could smell the whisky floating up from the living room. It made me gag, but there was nothing left inside me to bring up. I was hollow. Telling myself I couldn't do this. Telling myself it was a bad dream and that I'd wake up as someone else who'd only been dreaming they were me.

The soft strings of death wafted upstairs with the whisky reek.

Why didn't I run away? Why didn't I just go to the police?

"Good versus Evil," I said, spitting into the water until my mouth was dry. I flushed the toilet. The tank filled with water and that's when I heard it. The noise coming from downstairs. It wasn't the music. It wasn't the sounds of dinner being prepared.

What did you hear?

Raised voices. Shouting. That was the beginning.

Let me guess. The mutual suspicion, fuelled by alcohol, had spilled over at last?

I've never heard them shout at each other like that before. And along with the shouting, the sound of breaking plates. Scary banging noises. Thump-thump-thumping. Sounded like they were fighting. *Really* fighting.

Physically?

Yes. I wiped my mouth dry. Then, I crept out of the bathroom on tiptoes. I stood at the top of the stairs, a hand clamped tight over my mouth. Listening. They were still screaming at one another. I heard words like betrayal. Others that you never heard in our house. Liar. Bitch. Whore. *Fucking* whore. Trevor was swearing like he was out of his mind, and he hardly ever swore. Not like that. More banging. Thumping. They'd both gone crazy and the house shook with anger.

"You think I don't know what you were planning to do with her?" Trevor yelled. "Hmm? Do you think I'm a fucking idiot?"

Another barrage of 'F' and 'C' words.

"You were going to run away with her, weren't you?" he said, his voice cracking under the strain. "I *know*."

There was a horrible choking noise. Sounded like someone gasping for air and I had this image of him with his hands around her throat.

I was relieved to hear Mum's voice.

"Don't you dare call me a schemer, you pathetic coward. I don't know what you're talking about. You're the schemer! You and your picnic. What happened? Too scared to go through with it in the end?"

"What?"

"Don't deny it. LIAR!"

"Keep your voice down, for God's sake," Trevor said. "She's upstairs. She'll hear you."

Bit late for worrying about that, I thought.

"Were you or were you not taking her away from me?"

"You're crazy," Trevor said. "We made a plan. We agreed we'd do it tonight, didn't we? Why would I take her away?"

And yet, I could hear confusion in his voice. The doubt. He didn't trust himself. So much fell through the holes in his mind and into the oblivion of forgetfulness that he couldn't be sure. And maybe he was trying to get back to that conversation I'd had with him in the living room during the week. When I'd talked about the picnic. Maybe it *was* real. He'd always been so neat and orderly throughout his life. In control. Now he was falling.

"Well?" Hattie said. "Were you going to...*do it*...without me?"

"Shhh, haven't we got enough on our plates?"

"Answer me."

"No," he said. "I don't think so. There *was* something about a picnic, but there's no way I'd–"

"Bastard."

"Hattie! Don't talk to me like that."

Their voices grew louder.

"Admit it!"

"No."

"How dare you stand there calling me all sorts of names when you were the one plotting to take her away. You lying piece of–"

A thump. Then, I heard a shriek. Sounded like a screaming fox inside the house. I stood at the top of the stairs, my fingers gripping the slippery banister. Blood whooshed in my ears. I didn't know what to do.

The chaos downstairs turned to silence. Except, that is, for the classical music that continued to play. Everything happened so fast. Raised voices. The thumping, screaming and now this. Dead silence.

What did you do?

I waited for something to happen at first. When it didn't, I walked downstairs. What else could I do? The music was like a siren, luring me towards the kitchen. There was another noise, something I couldn't make sense of, just underneath the sad strings.

I walked closer. Then, I understood.

Dad's wheezy breathing. Now it was loud enough to drown out the orchestra.

I approached the kitchen in a daze. Numb. Not feeling my body as it went through the motions of movement. Then, I stopped in the doorway.

What did you see, Darcy?

The aftermath. Mum was lying on the floor, twitching and then perfectly still. Flat on her back, arms out like a human cross. Legs bent, all twisted up. Blood spilled from a wound on her head. The soup pot was overturned and her nice dress was covered in it. Her final exhale had a word trapped in it. But I couldn't make out what it was.

Her eyes were open. Looking up at the ceiling. Already, they looked like glass.

Not real.

Trevor was standing with his back to me. The wheezy breathing was frantic now, like he was surging towards a panic attack. He was reaching for her. Mumbling to himself. To her. I don't know what happened but if I had to guess, I'd say Hattie ran at him and he pushed her backwards with too much force. She must have hit her head on something. The worktop, maybe. Knocked the soup over. Cracked her head open.

Trevor turned around slowly, his eyes wild with horror. His skin was yellow and glistening with sweat.

"Poppy."

Those hands reached for me now. His fingertips twitched like he was air-typing. Tears streaming down his face.

"It was an accident. I didn't mean–"

Accident? The kitchen looked like a bomb had gone off in it. Looked like they'd been throwing things at one another. There were bits of food everywhere, on the floor, stuck to the walls. Pots lying overturned. Scattered cutlery. The table itself was a mess of plates and a jug of water tipped on its side. The fruit bowl had tipped over the edge, spilling apples, oranges and ripe bananas.

Trevor looked at Hattie. Then, back at me.

"Didn't mean it."

He staggered over to the kitchen table like a doomed man wading through quicksand. Picked up the bread knife. Turned back to me. There was nothing in his eyes anymore.

"Better this way."

"What?"

"We'll all go together."

"Dad–"

He shuffled towards me. "You'd like that, wouldn't you, Poppy? To go and see Mum. She's waiting for us, you know."

"Stop," I yelled, backing into the doorway. My hands were outstretched like two little shields, for all the good they'd do me against that knife.

He was smiling now. A dead-eyed smile.

"It's okay, it's okay. It's better this way."

I yelled at him. I even told him that I knew I was Darcy Drummond but that bombshell went straight through him. Maybe he didn't hear it. Most likely, he didn't care. He kept nodding. Kept scraping his feet on the floor as he sped up his approach, the blade angled high above his shoulder, the tip pointing at me.

"We'll go together. Go as a family. Coming, my love, we're coming right behind you."

And then he sprang at me. He was inches from catching me with the knife when his slippers skated off the lake of soup. There was a look of shock as his balance betrayed him. He did a silly dance, arms flailing, then his back tipped over at an impossible angle. There was a loud crack as he landed on the floor. A horrible cry of pain.

Hattie's dead arm was touching his face.

"No!"

Trevor looked like a giant insect turned over, kicking air, trying to get back up. Somehow, he managed. He limped towards the doorway. A crazed smile emerging through a red mask of soup.

The knife was over his shoulder again.

"My love—"

I couldn't run. I didn't dare turn my back on him. So, I circled the outskirts of the kitchen. Slipped past the table, edged along the worktop and, once there, I picked up a smaller knife from the rack. About half the size of the one Trevor was wielding. But it was lighter too.

He saw me grab the knife. Made a panicked whimpering noise.

Then, he ran at me.

It came down to speed in the end. We were both armed. Both terrified. I was just faster than he was and I felt like I had some superhuman strength that came to the rescue. I don't know how I was able to put the knife in him. But I did it. I'll never forget the way it felt, the blade cutting deep inside him. That wet, slicing noise. The look of horror on his face as he realised that I'd won.

Darcy?

I don't know how to feel about it. I did what I had to do, Tracey. I know it looks like I stabbed him too many times, but I had to be sure. Me or him. Good versus Evil.

Okay, I think we've got enough now. What do you think? Think it's time we got out of here and met your real family?

Darcy? Would you like to–?

When it was over, I walked into the living room and turned off the classical music. I had no idea what to do after that. I was a complete blank. Nothing would ever be the same again. So, I turned on the TV. Grabbed a copy of my favourite DVD and put on *Snow White and the Seven Dwarfs*. That felt nice. Familiar. I stayed like that for days, watching TV and trying to forget what was back there in the kitchen.

PART II

The Man in the Gold Watch

15

MARGO

I still don't understand it. That girl – let's assume for one second that she really is Darcy – could have run away. She *should've* run away. And yet she didn't. Instead, she went back to the Burton house, and for what?

To punish them.

What sort of person does that?

The question spins around my head when the phone rings. I answer and it's Sophie Drummond. Did she have some inkling that I was just thinking about her family? About the girl claiming to be Darcy. Then again, who isn't thinking about the Drummond family right now? It's the biggest news story in the world.

"Hey, Sophie."

"Margo, how are you?"

Her voice is a long, elegant exhale. That's how rich people talk, at least the ones I've encountered. Even when they're stressed to the eyeballs, life sounds like it's a breeze.

"It's been a while," I say. "I was wondering if you'd call."

"Been a bit busy," Sophie says.

"I noticed."

We both chuckle. It eases the tension somewhat.

It's been two weeks since Sophie's eldest daughter, Darcy, walked into a police station in Glasgow and told the officers who she was. That must have come as a shock. Darcy Drummond has been missing for thirteen years and it's no exaggeration to call her the world's most famous missing person. Darcy's disappearance was big news. BIG news. Blonde-haired, blue-eyed angel, daughter of rich white doctor and architect stolen from a beach. The world was outraged. And yet despite the ferocious media attention, no one ever came close to finding Darcy. The police, under pressure from all sides, arrested multiple suspects and went after known child trafficking rings. They did everything they could but it wasn't enough. Failure. That meant more outrage. The family was blamed, first for taking their eyes off Darcy and then they were accused of being involved in her disappearance. Everyone else on the beach was blamed. *How could a little girl just disappear like that?* The police were blamed because all their suspects were released without charge. In the end, it was a media circus that overshadowed the tragedy of a little girl's disappearance.

"Margo, how are *you*?" Sophie says. "Let's talk about anything besides you know what. Is that okay?"

"That's okay. I'm good, thanks. I've missed the sound of your voice."

"Likewise."

"Haven't missed you on the mat beside me in yoga though. Making everything look easy while I have a stroke doing the basic poses."

Sophie laughs. "I've been doing yoga on YouTube. Well, I've done it once. It's hard to find time for myself right now."

"Understandable. I guess it's hard for you to leave the house."

"Something like that."

I'm sitting on the couch in Mum's living room, the phone pressed against my ear. My bare feet are propped up on the coffee table. Tracksuit bottoms. A hoodie with all sorts of wear and tear and stains on it. Staring at the TV with the sound down. It's one of those horrible daytime TV shows – some kind of *Judge Judy* rip-off set in a courtroom. Since coming back to live with Mum, this is what a lot of my after-noons look like. Same clothes. Same shit on the TV. God help me.

"Okay," I say, doing my best to sound chipper for Sophie. "I know you don't want to talk about it. Let's talk around it. How are you holding up?"

"Hanging in there."

"Mike? The kids?"

"Same."

Short. Clipped answers. Sophie sounds tired and hoarse. Like she's been up for days, and it makes me wonder why she called in the first place. Maybe she wants to hear a voice that isn't Mike's or her parents' or even one of the kids'. Must be pretty claustrophobic in that house, even if it is massive.

Of course, I want to ask about Darcy. How's she doing? She's got two twin brothers she hasn't seen since she was four. Two younger sisters who weren't born thirteen years ago. That's just for starters.

Man, how do you even begin to put the pieces back together again?

That's if it *is* her. They brought her home. I'm sure the tests have been done and she's still with the Drummonds. I don't know. It's just such a massive thing to accept – that

Darcy Drummond has been found. Most people, myself included, believed that girl was dead a long time ago. Not that I would've said as much to Sophie.

I can't stop thinking about what happened. About what brought Darcy out of the shadows after all these years. Little snippets of information have come my way, from the news and the occasional text from Sophie. It's clear that Darcy overheard the Burtons talking about something important. That conversation, it's said, gave her true identity away. Now comes the part I have trouble with. She got out the house that same day. She did chores or something like that and went outside to go to the shops. She could've told someone. But she went back to the Burton house. I can't get my head around going back there. What sort of girl finds out that she's been kidnapped, given this false identity for thirteen years, and goes back to punish the kidnappers?

Then again, what do I know?

I have no idea what she felt. How she feels now. I might have done the same thing in her situation. The Burtons are dead and, although I don't know the details, I get the feeling that Darcy was directly involved in their deaths. Hands-on. Maybe I'm wrong. I'm not about to ask Sophie for all the gruesome details. At least, not yet.

"Darcy's home," Sophie says. "That's all that matters."

She speaks in a hushed voice. Maybe she doesn't want Mike or her parents to know that she's talking to anyone outside the family. Especially a wannabe journalist.

I won't bombard her with questions. She called as a friend so I'll have to zip it, even though I want to know about the DNA test. The girl is still there. After so many imposters, it's hard for me (and everyone else for that matter) to believe that it's the real Darcy. The evidence must have been strong. What was it? What else did they have before the DNA test that made them bring her to the Drummond house?

"I'm frightened to go to sleep at night," Sophie says.

"Why?"

"In case I wake up and she's gone."

"Is that why you sound so exhausted?" I ask.

"I'm fine. How's work?"

"Like it always is," I say. "Like swimming upstream with no arms. Having said that, I've never been so popular. Thanks to you."

"Oh?"

"A couple of weeks ago," I say, "I'm no one. I'm the anonymous freelance journalist begging all the bigwigs for a payday. Pitching article ideas, getting polite rejections that are essentially telling me to piss off. Now though, I'm waking up to dozens of texts and missed calls. Emails flood my inbox. Editors. Contacts. Journalists. All inching their way in. *Oh, you know the Drummond family, don't you?*"

Sophie laughs but it sounds weak. We're talking about it. She doesn't want to go there and yet here we are.

"The world's waiting for you guys to speak," I tell her. "Not to mention waiting for their first glimpse of Darcy. Let me guess, there's still an army of press vans parked outside your house, right?"

"Good guess."

"How's that working out?"

"Well, our neighbours aren't too happy about it. But we've never been the most popular residents."

"I'll bet."

I hear a beat of silence.

"Anyway," Sophie says, brightening her tone a little.

"While we're on the subject of the world waiting for us to speak–"

"Uh-oh."

It's uncomfortable being a journalist and a family friend. They're the Drummonds, for God's sake, and like it or not, they're world-famous for all the wrong reasons. The gorgeous, successful and wealthy couple who turned their backs on a child for a couple of seconds on Bournemouth Beach, only to pay the ultimate price. Every parent's worst nightmare, and instead of sympathy, they were met with a hostile undercurrent of suspicion. Particularly from the press.

That's why I don't talk about work with Sophie.

I'm small fry. Smaller than that. But I am the press.

And for what it's worth, I like the Drummonds. They're good people and yep, maybe they did mess up that day but there are millions of people all over the world who do the same thing and don't get punished for it. They take their eyes off the kids, even if it's just for a few seconds. Enough time for disaster to strike – but nothing happens. Sophie and Mike weren't so lucky. Fate gave them so much and took even more. They aren't saints. They're ordinary people but it grates on others because they live in a big house in Morning-side, one of the more upmarket neighbourhoods in Edin-burgh. Mike's an architect. Sophie's a doctor. But the real money in the family comes from Sophie's side. It comes from the Wallace side. Her dad, Edward, is a big deal in the world of finance. Old money. Goes back generations.

"Margo? Are you listening?"

"Sophie," I say, picking up the remote control off the couch and switching off the TV. The courtroom thing is major cringe. "I have no ambition to interview you. And I'm not recording this phone call even though it'd make me rich and I could finally move out of my mum's house."

Sophie laughs. "You wouldn't take the job if offered?"

"We're friends."

"You must be curious."

"No more than anyone else. It doesn't take a journalist to be curious."

"You're right."

"Anyway," I say, "I wouldn't know where to start. What question to ask first."

"Yes you do," Sophie says without skipping a beat. "You'd ask if it's really her. Or if it's another imposter."

Man, she's good.

"It's been two weeks," I say. "And unless you tell me otherwise, she's still there. I'm sure all the tests have been done."

"They have."

"And?"

"They came to the house last week. Usually, you have a long wait for the results. But, all things considered, we got upgraded to high-priority. Rapid testing. It's gaining traction in the forensic community, so they said. Reserved for law enforcement or wherever information is needed fast."

I can only imagine the expense of 'rapid' DNA testing. And yet, I doubt the Drummonds had to pay a thing. Not in a case as high-profile as this one.

By now, I'm on the edge of my seat, wanting Sophie to confirm it once and for all. But I have to show restraint. I take my feet off the table. Outside, the sound of kids playing swingball in a nearby garden is deafening.

"Did she cope with the test okay?"

"Not really," Sophie says. "I'm glad we did it at home."

"What happened?"

"She was a nervous wreck when they came to the house," Sophie says. "There were two of them. Darcy took one look and thought they were going to lock her up for what happened in the Burton house. She's overwhelmed, literally. All the police, psychologists and care workers and so on. It's neverending. Anyway, we let her go upstairs. Lola went with her. Darcy and Lola have become the best of pals, thank God. She freaked out a bit upstairs. She doesn't trust anyone, I don't think. The tester was patient. He gave her space. Gave her time. The sample came back later that night."

"That night?"

"Two hours. Crazy, right?"

"And–"

She laughs. "Go on, Margo."

"It's her?"

"Yes. It's Darcy. She's home."

I exhale loudly. At the same time, I'm thinking about all the pictures of four-year-old Darcy that have become so familiar over the years. On TV, the internet, in books and newspapers. The gallery whirrs through my mind. That face. She was just so damn cute. And over the years we kept getting fresh images speculating about what she'd look like now – as a ten-year-old, a twelve-year-old, fifteen-year-old, and so on. Did any of them get it right?

"My God, Sophie."

"I don't blame you for doubting," Sophie says as I struggle to find the right words. "Don't feel bad. I don't blame anyone for doubting after all the imposters."

"Yeah but...HOLY SHIT."

She laughs. "I know."

My heart's pounding as I clear my throat. My backside is

still perched on the edge of the couch. "Mind if I ask another question?"

"Of course."

"You took her home before the DNA test, right?"

"Right."

"Which means there had to be something else. Something that convinced you she was the real Darcy. And the police must have been convinced too."

There's a pause. I sense that Sophie's hesitant to tell me too much.

"They found her things in that house. The Daddy's Princess t-shirt. The white bucket hat. Her teddy bear, Marvin. All hidden away."

"Wow," I say.

"I know."

"After all the shit you guys had to put up with over the years. All those bloodsucking journalists who tried to blame you."

"Which is why I'm talking to you."

Oh boy.

I'm staring up at the ceiling. It's flawless, like everything else in my mother's house. No cracks, blemishes or mystery stains to ruin the aesthetic.

God, I miss having my own place.

I know what's coming next. Sophie knows that I'm desperate for a break. It's been nearly a year and a half since I walked out of a steady job in advertising to chase the dream full time. I'd been freelancing on the side for several years but it was never enough to satisfy the hunger inside. So, after saving a little money, I went for it. Quit the day job. It was a leap of faith that backfired. Rent became a problem. Several months later, I had to give up my beloved flat and move back in with Mum, who's been wearing a told-you-so face ever since. Now, I'm hustling for paid articles, both online and in print. Getting paid crumbs for the lowest of the low. Pitching story ideas that come back faster than a boomerang. So far at least, I'm hardly setting the world alight.

"There's an exclusive here, Margo," Sophie says. Her voice is formal. All business. "And I want to give it to you."

"Sophie–"

"Those vultures sitting outside the house won't leave us alone until there's a story. An official family story."

"I don't know. We're friends. It doesn't seem ethical."

"We need someone we can trust. And forgive me if I'm out of line here, Margo, but I think you need this too."

"My bank account sure thinks so."

"Someone has to write it. Why not you? You're a damn good journalist and you need a break."

"What about Mike? What does he say?"

"We've both made up our minds. We want you to do the story. Come over to the house and interview us. I can't give you or anyone else a photo of her though. Her privacy is too valuable and I'm going to fight tooth and nail to keep it."

"That's a tough ask," I say. "In a world drowning in cameras."

"She deserves a life. Not a circus."

"I get it."

"So, that's a yes?" Sophie asks. "You'll do the interview?"

My heart's in my throat. I don't know why there's this weight pressing against my chest.

"Listen, Sophie. I'm just a freelance nobody. Even if I do it, I can't control what happens after I pass it on to the bigwigs. Other people will be involved. The headline. The editing. They can do whatever they want."

"I understand. Will you do it?"

I'm not sitting down anymore. I don't even remember standing up but I'm pacing the living room like it's an Olympic sport. Wishing that I still smoked. Wishing that I had a stiff drink in hand. Eventually, I stop.

"Okay. I'll do it."

16

MARGO

Usually, I'm the one standing on the sidelines. I'm the onlooker, standing somewhere in between the credentialed reporters and the crowds. Looking on enviously. And why not? I'm a nobody in this business. Small-fry or smaller than that. I'm not affiliated with any giant media conglomerate and I have zero reputation to speak of.

Today, I walk past them all.

The big guns are gathered outside the Drummond house. Journalists, renowned in both print and TV. Famous faces. Household names. People I've looked up to for years. People who've repeatedly ignored me, my pitches and my requests for assistance.

I step out of the taxi (sent and paid for by the Drummonds) and a private security guard approaches the car.

"Good morning, Miss Martin," he says, opening the door. "I'm Frank and I'll take you up to the house."

Frank's a giant of a man. Black suit. Shaved head, grizzled features. Ticks all the boxes when it comes to what you want your security personnel to look like.

I nod and say thanks as Frank holds the door.

Wow. This feels like the big time. Like I'm deep down in the rabbit hole. A voice inside reminds me to play it cool, to act like I belong.

I don't look at the crowds. Straight ahead. One step at a time, the morning breeze blowing on the back of my neck.

Frank escorts me towards the big house with the late Victorian architecture. The Drummond house is located in Morningside, the leafy Edinburgh district a few miles south of the city centre. Here's the sort of fancy house that anyone even remotely aspirational wants for themselves. It's a different world. I can't imagine what the uptight neighbours think about all these vans and journalists and crowds clogging up their street. I suspect most of them have disappeared to their holiday homes on Loch Lomond.

"This way," Frank says, leading me towards the house.

There are other big and burly men in dark suits in front of the house. A couple of women with hard faces. We walk past them and Frank announces my arrival into a walkietalkie. It's over the top but then again, Darcy is a big deal. I wonder how much the Drummonds paid for all this security. I suppose it's worth it to stop people trespassing, sneaking around the house, trying to get the first photo of seventeen-year-old Darcy. There hasn't been a single picture yet and it's driving the world mad. Money-crazed photographers wait like vampires. They don't care that the poor girl should have a normal life when the heat dies down. That anonymity is best. Kindest. Everyone wants the prize.

I do it. I glance over my shoulder and it feels like everyone on the street is looking at me. I'm getting more than a few strange looks from the established media personnel huddled outside the house. Print, TV, podcasters.

I don't want to look smug. Yet, I'm desperate to wave.

Large, mature trees hide the front of the property. There are only glimpses, which adds to the intrigue. Those trees, along with the small army of hired security, make it a tough ask for any photographer in search of something substantial. Getting inside the Drummond house right now is the Holy Grail of journalism. It's also like trying to break into Fort Knox.

Thank you, Sophie, I think.

One last look over my shoulder. The rabid dogs taking photos. Giving me the hard stare. Like *I'm* the story.

What the hell?

I wave.

Frank leads me past a second, smaller line of security at the front of the house. Holy shit. There's a thrill at being here, I admit it. But I can't help thinking about the other eight million children who're reported missing around the world every year. I wonder how many of them vanish without a trace. Without all *this*.

"This way, please," Frank says in a gruff voice.

He knocks on the front door. The door opens and a tall, pale-skinned woman I've never seen before gives me the once over before ushering me inside. I don't like the way Miss Snooty Pants looks at me. Like I'm dirt on the carpet. I have no idea who she is. I know the Drummonds have someone who cleans for them every week but it's not exactly *Downton Abbey*. I'm nervous as I walk inside. This doesn't feel like visiting a friend.

"This way, Miss Martin," says Miss Snooty-Pants.

We leave Frank outside. She leads me down the hallway,

her feet eerily silent on the floor. Like she's gliding. A woman made of air. In contrast, I've always been a heavy walker. I get it from Mum. Wee woman syndrome, someone once said.

I do love the Drummond house. Gigantic, lavishly furnished rooms on the first floor. Bay windows at the front and back, letting in the perfect amount of light. The kitchen has a massive dining area, an Aga, a utility room and everything else a kitchen in this sort of house is supposed to have. I've been here before several times. Thank God. I'd be bricking it even more if this were my first visit.

I hear hushed voices up ahead. Snooty and I slow a beat, then turn into the living room. Before going in, I pat down my blazer, wondering if smart casual was too casual for this gig. I want to look professional but not overdressed. In we go. The curtains are drawn in the living room. Blinds pulled down. Gloomy ambience prevails in Castle Drummond, with floor and table lamps turned on everywhere. Oh my God, it feels like I'm making a big entrance.

There they are.

The Drummonds.

I see *her*. The one that everyone wants to see. Darcy is sitting cross-legged on the floor in front of the TV, watching some Disney cartoon with little Lola beside her. She doesn't look my way. They must have told her I wasn't here to prod and poke her or to extract a DNA sample. Otherwise she'd be climbing the walls.

"Margo!" Sophie says, standing up off the couch. She looks fabulous in a cream sweater and jeans combo that shows off her Amazonian figure. God, I hate her. She'd look perfect in a binbag. "Oh, it's great to see you."

We embrace. Her grip is strong.

"You too," I say, giving her a squeeze. And then I whisper

in her ear. "Thanks for this. You should have seen their faces out there."

We break off the embrace and she winks at me. Her eyes are clear, thank God. Sometimes, Sophie can be a little foggy. Not today.

"Margo," Mike says, walking over. "Nice to see you again."

I'm about to offer my hand but Mike gives me a hug. We break it off and there's a stiff but polite greeting exchanged with Sophie's parents, Edward and Liz, standing in the background. The kids are scattered around the living room. *My God, that's Darcy Drummond.* Tom and Nick give me an awkward wave. They're shooting up in height like it's a race. *Darcy Drummond – right over there.* Maria offers a polite hello. Lola's usually friendly but she's busy at the TV with Darcy.

Shit, I think.

Darcy Drummond. How am I supposed to act? Like it's no big deal she's sitting right over there?

It's frightening how ordinary she looks. Tall, skinny and blonde. Prominent bones. Angular. A younger version of Sophie if ever there was one. And it's not hard to see that Maria and Darcy are related either.

Maybe I still didn't believe it. Even with the DNA results.

It's her. It's Darcy.

She might be seventeen but there are dark circles under her eyes. I can't even begin to imagine what she's been through. I want to talk to her. They have to let me talk to her for this article to become something special. That's the gift. Not another conversation with Sophie and Mike, although that'll be part of it. She has to be involved.

I think about the girl in the famous photograph. About

the DNA test. The pink t-shirt, the clothes and teddy bear. About the Burtons and what must have happened inside that house a few weeks ago.

I was wrong. I'll bet most of the world was wrong too. It's not a hoax and she's not an imposter.

She came back.

17

SOPHIE

I'm ecstatic when Margo arrives.

A friendly face, that's what I needed. Someone outside of the family circle. Someone who isn't a police officer. A psychologist. A whatever.

I throw my arms around her and squeeze so tight I risk breaking her. Margo's so petite and bird-like. And she's warm too, which is nice. She hugs me back and it feels genuine. Like she's pleased to see me.

I feel bad for using her like this.

But she'll get paid well for the interview. Very well. The money will be like nothing she's ever seen before and it'll get her name out there in a competitive field. She needs the break. She deserves it.

There's an awkward silence after she says hi to everyone. I see the way she keeps looking over at Darcy. It's okay; it's to be expected. Everyone who's been in the house, whether it's a personal or professional visit, does the same thing. Darcy's always at the TV. Lola, her best friend in the house, is beside her. I hope Margo isn't expecting too much. Darcy's been sitting there for about three hours straight. I worry about her eyes but right now the TV is her safe place and we're not ready to interfere with that yet. When she's not watching TV, she's in her room. That's the pattern. Distant. At least Lola's getting in. Lola's such a quiet, good-natured girl. She doesn't talk much either. Maybe that's what Darcy needs right now.

It's okay. We just need time.

What we really need is to get rid of these journalists camped outside the house twenty-four seven. To get on with our lives. We need an interview done and dusted. Put it out there as soon as possible. And Margo's the one to write it.

"You look amazing," I tell her.

I've always admired Margo's sense of style. She's small with a curvy frame, reddish-brown hair and large eyes. She says what she thinks. Not much filter in the woman. I love how she gave up the corporate world to chase her dream.

And I'm more than happy to help her along.

I *am* helping her. Everyone wins with this article.

Margo's polite smile tapers off. She's no dummy and she can read the room. I wonder if she knows why I picked her for the job. Like I say, she's no dummy. She'll know soon enough and she'll be pissed off. Hopefully the money and attention will make up for it.

Right now, she's absorbing the atmosphere in the living room. The world might be celebrating Darcy's return but inside the house, it's awful. It's like a funeral. Darcy isn't talking to anyone except Lola. Mike and Dad are at each other's throat as usual. Tom, Nick and Maria don't know how they're supposed to act around their long-lost sister. Her presence is a disruption.

And I feel like I'm the one who's supposed to hold it all together. Somehow, I feel responsible for the inadequacy of it all. But for now, I have to smile. We have to get through this interview and hope it'll get the media frenzy off our doorstep.

"Well," Mike says. "We're here to do an interview. Margo, are you ready to–?"

"Let the poor woman catch her breath," Dad says. He steps forward as if to claim the centre of the room. His cold glare never leaves Mike. "Offer her a drink, for God's sake."

Mike's back stiffens. He gives Dad a filthy look and, thank God, leaves it at that. But I saw it. I'm sure Margo saw it too. The simmering tension between the two men in my life never ends. Never. Dad never forgave Mike for taking his eyes off the kids on Bournemouth Beach. Yet, he was able to forgive me for the same crime. But, according to the gospel of Edward Wallace, it was Mike's fault. The man's job is to protect his family. Mike didn't do that. Truthfully, we both screwed up that day and we've never shied away from the fact. But, no matter how much self-loathing Mike's carried inside all these years, he won't back down in front of the great Edward Wallace. He's not a submissive man. The coolest kid in school, Mike Drummond, is still there, some-where inside the broken, middle-aged man I live with. I still see that boy sometimes when he plays with Lola. When he forgets his troubles. I was a year and a half younger than Mike when I fell head over heels in love with him at school. He had all the popularity and street smarts. I was an excep-tional student. The giraffe in a skirt, dreaming of medical school and making my parents proud. Somehow, fate brought us together. At some point, our worlds clashed and we started going out. The odd couple. Then. Now.

I'm sure Dad wishes he'd sent me to boarding school.

His contempt for Mike was there from the start. It oozed

out of Dad, like sweat from pores. Mike comes from a working-class background in Niddrie. He didn't bring anything tangible to the Wallace family, like money or status. Handsome, sure, but what good was a pretty face? Money didn't get wrinkles. Real wealth didn't sag, not ever. Didn't matter to Dad how hard Mike was working towards bettering himself. Proving himself. That he was striving to ditch the teenage rebel and pursue the goal of studying architecture.

Mike wasn't good enough. Never was. Never will be.

It doesn't help that Mum's so passive. She never helps when the tension arises. And she doesn't do anything now, even though I'm embarrassed in front of Margo. Mum just sits there on the couch, stony-faced, neck veins like fraying rope. It's me who has to break up the fights. To keep the smile on her face for the sake of everyone else. And I'm sick of it.

I haven't opened the bedside drawer in almost a week. No pills. Haven't even been tempted.

That last part is a lie.

I'm doing my best. Darcy's felt the tension too since coming back. We've suggested outings, albeit that's a little hard with the press camped on our doorstep. I hate those people. So many of them believed (or wanted to believe) that we murdered our daughter and, without a shred of evidence to back up their claim, spread the story far and wide. And they did so with glee. Doing whatever they could to get us convicted. I won't let them anywhere near her. She's not ready for the cameras and, with any luck, Margo's interview will send them all packing.

Margo talks in a quiet voice. "Are you sure this is a good time?"

I thrust my hands into my pockets to hide the shaking.

"It's fine. You'll have to forgive us, Margo. We're a little on edge."

She nods. "Understandable."

Margo glances at Darcy again. I look too this time. She's still there, sitting cross-legged on the floor, too close to the TV. Staring up at the screen like she's a disciple at her guru's feet. Why does it feel like she's still gone? I think she's worn out. Maybe I'm just projecting. For now, we have to let her be.

Give it time, I tell myself. She'll come around. She'll open up and let me in.

18

MARGO

"Where will we begin?" Sophie asks.

She's sitting on the couch beside Mike. They're holding hands but I get the feeling that Sophie's restraining him because he's still riled up about Edward. There's a distant look in his eyes. I don't know where Mike's head is at right now but it's not here.

Sophie's parents sit on the opposite couch. They wear facial expressions that could only be described as grim.

Let's just get started, I tell myself. *See what happens.*

I smile at Sophie. Glance at my handwritten notes, trying to shake the feeling that I've walked into a fresh crime scene. I'm rattled, not so much by the mood, but by the way Darcy's just sitting over there at the TV with Lola. Is she coming over or what? I understood about the photograph but is there any harm in getting a quote or two?

The Drummonds are acting like this is it. And if that's true, if Darcy's not involved, what does that leave me with here? The ten-thousandth interview with Sophie and Mike? That's not exactly going to shake up the world, is it?

I wonder if the strain is showing on my face.

"Why don't we take it from *that* Sunday night," I say, setting my phone down on the coffee table. I make room amongst a pile of family photo albums lying around. One of the books lies open and I see a gallery of Darcy's childhood photos on display. Looks like she's at a water park with Mike and Sophie. She couldn't be much more than two years old here. I imagine Sophie brought the albums out, hoping it'd spark something. Make her smile. Get her away from the TV for five minutes.

I open the voice recorder app. Mumble an introduction with the time, date and participants. Then, I hit play.

"The police called you here," I say, "asking you both to go to the station in Glasgow. What happened next?"

Sophie and Mike talk freely. They take it in turns, leading me through the series of events that happened on the Sunday after the bombshell phone call. Arranging a babysitter. Trying not to say anything to the kids. The 'tense' drive from Edinburgh to Glasgow. Walking into the police station and talking to various officers before getting their first glimpse of Darcy in an interrogation room. I'm under-whelmed. It's a pedestrian retelling of events and even their first glimpse of Darcy sounds boring.

They're not giving me enough. Not by a long way.

Is that deliberate?

I glance over at Darcy again. Our eyes meet for a split second, then she's back to the TV. I can't prove it but I get the feeling she's listening to every word. She puts an arm around Lola's shoulder. Loses herself in the bright Disney anima-tion. Or at least appears to.

My eyes return to Mike and Sophie. Sophie's talking now. In a way, I'm still looking at Darcy.

I want to talk to her. I want to ask her why she went back there to punish the Burtons. God, that's the real story. *Why didn't you run? What did they make you become?* I want to ask Darcy about living in the Burton house for the past thirteen years. Does she have any memory of what happened that day on the beach?

That's the story. We wouldn't even need a picture with a story like that.

Fuck. I see what's happening and it's a disaster. This interview is bland and generic. We go through the motions and halfway through, other people visit the house, so we take a five-minute break. I'm introduced to a couple of detectives. An elderly couple are shown in by Miss Snooty-Pants. Jimmy Gold and his wife Sarah worked for the Drummonds years ago on another property in Edinburgh. Jimmy was their nightwatchman. Sarah, the chef.

I'm polite to these guests but my disappointment has to be showing.

We resume the interview and Edward chips in from the other side of the room. The old man has zero tact, telling me in a loud voice that Darcy's had several panic attacks since the DNA testers showed up. Sometimes, Edward says, it feels like everyone's walking on eggshells around her.

"Dad," Sophie says, glancing over at Darcy, who shows no sign of overhearing. "That's not relevant."

Edward shrugs. He turns his back on us and goes back to talking to the former nightwatchman and his wife.

The interview sinks like the Titanic. I feel so deflated. The Drummonds talk and say very little of substance. This is not my interview and it never was. I get the feeling they want this done and dusted. The generic story of a family reunited with their long-lost daughter, sister and granddaughter. Zero insight into what happened to her. Zero contribution from Darcy. It's bland, unspecific drivel. The avoidance of an interview. I know I should push harder but, if I'm honest, the Drummonds and Wallaces are intimidating. They're gathered here in numbers, not least of all Edward, who isn't the sort of man you want to cross in a hurry. Besides, they've thrown me a professional lifeline and I'm not about to bite the hand that feeds me.

I'm a coward. I'm also the worst journalist in the world.

Fuck. Fuck. Fuck.

The Drummonds are pretty much asking their own questions. Sophie does most of the talking. Mike chips in here and there but he's fizzling out like a faulty bulb. I see the dark circles under his eyes. The laboured smile. Still, he's always got the bling to stay shiny on the outside. Expensive shirts. Designer jeans. The massive gold watch. He likes his chunky rings too. All the stereotypical symbols of affluence, just to feel like he belongs with the rich family he married into.

There's no interaction between Darcy and the other Drummond children besides Lola. Mike says at one point she can't remember the twins, Tom and Nick. The boys are growing so fast. Their blond hair has dulled to a mousy shade of brown. Tom's a little heavier and I know he's more into video games while Nick's into running. Eleven-year-old Maria is smart and beautiful, just like Sophie. There are good genes in this family. Having said that, a lot of rich people are headcases.

The interview is close to hitting a wall. I wonder if they can see the disappointment on my face and if so, do they even care? The story, when it's published, will be watered down. It'll sell and it'll be forgotten. And so will I.

"Any more questions?" Sophie asks, after they finally shut up.

I feel like my tongue is twice the size of my mouth. All I can do is shake my head even though I have a hundred questions for Darcy.

Edward leans forward on the couch. A tight-lipped smile on his face. "Well, that's enough, eh, Margo?"

It's not a question.

Mike reacts. I think he's been waiting for an opportunity to hit back.

"Edward," he says through clenched teeth. I see Sophie squeeze his forearm. "We're still talking. Margo calls time on the interview...when she's ready."

Thanks, Mike, I think. The illusion of control.

Edward's eyebrows stand up. Apart from that, he maintains a good poker face.

"Careful, Mike. You almost sounded like a man there."

Mike stands up like he sat on a drawing pin. Fists clenched at his sides. Glaring at the old man across the room. I freeze. Time stops and I'm convinced they're about to go at it in front of the children. The Golds are still with us in the living room. They watch but don't seem that surprised. I'll bet they've seen it all before.

Sophie jumps up. Positions herself in front of Mike. Her voice is bordering on shrill. "Is that enough, Margo? Or do you need more?"

I want more. I want a hell of a lot more.

"We're good," I say, picking up my phone. I turn off the recording app.

It was too good to be true. Sophie's a friend but she used me. I was naïve to think this was anything other than a strategic move on their part. *Stupid.* The Drummonds want me to put out a safe, lukewarm article and I can only assume it's to remove the opportunity for an exclusive, which might make some of the media back off. Maybe they think it's okay to use me like this. Maybe they justify it to themselves by thinking about the payday that I'll enjoy.

Can't polish a turd, that's what they say. There's no way I can spin the material to make it more interesting. I know what people want to know and I didn't get it. The Drummonds are media savvy after all these years and they know what they gave me.

Nothing.

"Thank you so much for doing this," Sophie says. She stands up, throws her arms around me and holds on like she's a constrictor. I feel her body shivering. Meanwhile, I'm as stiff as a board.

I break off the embrace. Step back. Still, she doesn't seem to notice that something is wrong.

Screw it. I'm not letting them off that lightly.

"What about a photo?" I ask.

Sophie's polite smile fizzles out. "I'm sorry, Margo. It's just too soon for her. We did explain beforehand."

Edward crosses the room. He walks past Mike like he doesn't exist.

"My granddaughter's been through enough," he says. "She's still got a life to live when this racket dies down."

Mike shakes his head. "It doesn't matter. Sooner or later, it's going to get out there. You ever hear of the internet, Edward? Once you put a photo online, it's there forever."

"I don't give a damn," Edward says, his nostrils flaring. His eyes are still locked on me. "No pictures."

Mike glares at the back of the old man's head. "She's my daughter."

"STOP IT!" Sophie yells in a voice that could break glass. Everyone stops what they're doing. A horrific silence lingers in the living room, then Sophie, without saying another word, storms out. Her footsteps recede upstairs.

I stand there. Mouth open like I'm waiting to catch flies.

I just so happen to look over at the TV. Darcy's still sitting with her arm wrapped around Lola. Watching Disney cartoons.

19

SOPHIE

"Sophie?" Mike asks walking into the gloomy bedroom. "Are you okay?" He stops behind me and starts massaging my shoulders.

"Wow, Soph. That tense?"

"Can you blame me?"

I stand at the window, longing for some daylight in the room. The curtains are drawn, just in case some opportunist managed to get past security and is perched in a tree in the back garden, camera at the ready, waiting to steal a photo from inside the Drummond house.

"I'm sorry," Mike says.

I glance to my right. The bedside drawer on my side is open and we both know that's where the pills are. I don't even bother to hide it from Mike anymore. Just like he doesn't hide the whisky bottles. Just like he doesn't come home at a normal hour.

"I shouldn't have run out like that. Is Margo still here?"

"She left."

"Bugger."

"She won't write about it."

"That's not what I'm worried about, Mike. I'd like to keep the few friends I have left in the world. Not push them away. Not make them uncomfortable to be around me."

I turn around, placing my head on his chest. It's warm – so warm it feels like hot lava flows in his veins. His heart pounds against me.

"I feel like such an idiot."

"It's my fault," Mike says, pulling me in tighter. "You'd think after all these years that I'd be able to handle Edward better."

I lift my head off his chest.

"You'd think after all these years he wouldn't be such a snob."

"True. He's no saint either, is he?"

I know what he's doing. "Mike...don't."

But Mike's got that look on his face. He needs the emotional catharsis. To let it out in the dark and quiet of the bedroom because he can't do it out there. Not in front of Dad. Not in front of Mum.

"We all know what Edward likes to get up to with his young lady friends. And when I say young, I mean *young*. Maybe I should've mentioned that to Margo. What a dirty old bastard the great Edward Wallace is."

His voice trembles with rage.

"Oh God," I say, taking a step back. "Please, Mike. Not now."

Mike's teetering on the edge of another outburst. Then, his eyes cool. He holds his hands up. "Sorry. He's just such a fucking *prick*."

I nod but I don't want to think about any of that right now. Or ever. Everyone in the inner circle knows that Dad's a serial cheater. Even the twins and Maria know it, I think. And he does like younger women. *Much* younger. He's in his seventies, for God's sake. It's a dirty, disgusting Drummond secret that no one talks about. Maybe we should but the thought of discussing it with anyone turns my stomach.

With any luck, it's all in the past. He's not exactly a young buck. He's got ailments.

Mike notices the bedside drawer half-open. He sighs.

"Are you self-prescribing again?"

"Please don't lecture me."

He nods. "I'm not. But we can't let it become a problem again, Sophie. She's back with us. We got her back and we have to try for her sake. We have to get back to who we were before the nightmare started. For all of them."

"And for us?"

"Yes. Of course."

We've said the words before so I'm not holding out much hope. Our problems are so deep-rooted and in Mike's case, with the gambling, they predate Darcy's disappearance. My dependency issues or 'self-prescribing' as Mike puts it, go back to university. There was always a magic pill to keep me awake. To keep me calm. Mike's drinking did get a lot worse after Darcy went missing. After the press labelled us child killers. On top of all that, he's got a complex about marrying into money.

I walk over and close the bedside drawer. Then, I turn around.

"It'll get better after Margo's article is published," I say. "The media will gradually lose interest. Something else will happen in the world and they'll move on. We'll go back to work and the kids can go back to school. Then, we can concentrate on what Darcy needs."

"Right."

We embrace again. I stay there, locked in Mike's arms, knowing that closing the bedside drawer isn't much of a statement. I should flush the pills down the toilet. All of them.

But I've no intention of doing that.

20

MARGO

For the next three days, I lock myself in the house, writing the article.

It's awful.

It's so bad that all I can think about is getting it over with. Nonetheless, bad *will* sell, at least this time. There's plenty of interest from my growing list of contacts. It's a story about the Drummonds. And that's hot right now. Even if it is vanilla journalism.

While I'm writing, I live off coffee, snacks and Uber Eats deliveries. That, and about four hours of restless sleep a night. My back is stiff from too much sitting. I download one of those apps that reminds me to get up every twenty minutes and walk around for a bit. I ignore it and, after about a day and a half, delete it.

This article needs all my attention. Not because I think I've got something great. It's because I know I haven't.

Still, the tables are turned and that feels good. The bigwig editors are pitching me for a change. Selling themselves and their publications, trying to convince me why they're the best fit for the exclusive. I've become their favourite person in the world. Gift hampers clog up the downstairs hallway. Flowers. Chocolates. Champagne bottles that only the world's strongest man can lift. These are resourceful, cunning people. They want that exclusive Drummond interview more than anything else right now. Mum's been complaining about the constant deliveries. About the lack of space in the hallway. You'd think she'd be happy that I was getting somewhere. That, in financial terms at least, I'd hit the jackpot.

Sophie's called three times since the interview. At first, she was all apologies for the horrific atmosphere inside the house and for storming off at the end. I told her not to worry. The second call was to ask about the article. About its progress so far. I was vague. The third call was to ask if she could read it. I told her I wasn't finished but even if I was, I've got no intention of letting the Drummonds see it. That wasn't a condition and besides, she's got nothing to worry about. It's watered-down garbage.

In the end, I go with one of the big newspapers. Why the hell not? I wish I had the sort of bank account that would allow me to give it free of charge to *The Big Issue* or something a lot more worthy than tabloid trash, but I don't.

I get paid. The interview goes out.

Then, I sleep for a couple of days. I sure as hell don't read it.

There are hundreds of emails waiting for me when I finally check back in with the world. To my surprise, I'm asked to do a Zoom interview live on one of the major breakfast TV shows. Live? Holy shit. I catch a glimpse of my reflection after two days of mostly sleep. There's a bird's nest growing on my head. I've seen mummified corpses that look better. And they want me on TV? Seems like the article has gone down pretty well despite its lack of substance. Damn, I must have spiced it up better than I thought. Maybe I should write fiction.

I decide to roll with it. Go on TV and embrace the publicity. Raise my profile.

I'm well paid for the additional interviews too. TV and podcasts mostly. A large chunk of that change goes to Mum. Since moving back in with her, I haven't been able to chip in with expenses as much as I'd like. Now I can. I buy overdue birthday presents for my niece and nephew. Some clothes for myself. For Mum. The rest I put away, knowing fine well that my fifteen minutes of fame won't last.

I give myself a night off following an interview with a New York-based true crime podcast. It's heaven. I'm in my bedroom with the door closed, watching a Nordic noir show on Netflix. Drinking hot chocolate. Eating crips. Trying to forget all about Darcy Drummond. What I forgot to do, however, was turn my phone off.

It rings on the bedside table. If looks could kill, my iPhone would've exploded.

"Fuck."

I pick it up.

"Hello?"

"Margo!"

"Who's this?"

"It's *so* good to hear your voice."

I sit bolt upright, grab the remote and pause the film. I know that voice, even though my brain is sluggish and the name doesn't come right away. "Who's this?"

A donkey-like guffaw in my ear. The penny drops.

"Steve?"

"Did you forget about me?" he says in a mock-serious tone. "Oh Margo, that hurts."

I wish I *could* forget.

Steve Driscoll, ex-boyfriend. He was a rebound. For a while at least, being with Steve was better than being alone. He's not much to brag about – an overenthusiastic gamer who lives for conspiracy theories. Works as a traffic warden Monday to Friday to fund his internet and fast-food addiction. To make things even more embarrassing, Steve was the one who dumped me. I think it started with an off-hand comment I made about 9/11.

"What the fuck do you want?" I ask.

I stare at the static image on the TV screen. It's what you'd expect from one of these Nordic Noir things. A bunch of freezing cold cops standing around the ice staring down at a body that's literally turned blue. Looking at the dead body on TV makes me think about Trevor and Hattie Burton. About what happened in that house.

"How have you been?" he asks.

I'm not in the mood for his friendly banter. It's bullshit. I know he's trying to soften me up for something else yet to come. "Fine, until you called. What do you want?"

"Saw you on TV the other day," Steve says.

Bingo.

"You're looking good, Margo. Bloody hell, you're looking really good. Did you finally get that gym membership?"

"Piss off."

"I mean it."

"I mean it too. Piss off. We've got nothing to talk about."

The nerve of the prick.

"Do you think I'm stupid?" I ask.

"Eh?"

"You heard me. Do you think I'm stupid?"

"Take it easy, Margo. What's wrong? Time of the month, is it?"

"Bye, Steve."

"Wait! I just want to talk. I know I messed up last year."

"I couldn't care less about last year."

Honestly, I don't know what I ever saw in the guy. Heavy smoker. Rhino breath. Okay, he was pretty funny sometimes. I've always liked a man who could make me laugh. I suppose he was easy to be around when he wasn't wearing his tinfoil hat and ranting on about fake moon landings and Princess Diana's murder at the hands of the Royal Family.

"Can we just talk for a while?" he asks. "I've missed you."

"Nope."

"This is important. It's about the Drummonds. This is something you *have* to hear."

"Steve–"

"Hear me out, Margo. C'mon, just give me five minutes."

"Why should I?"

"You're the face of this story right now. You need to look closer at Mike Drummond. I think he's–"

I end the call before the conspiracy theories begin. I can't take it. Is this the price of my fifteen minutes? Whackos and ex-boyfriends crawling out of the woodwork? Steve's voice is the last thing I want to hear on my night off. There's more than enough speculation about the Drummonds and how they were involved in their daughter's disappearance. I guess some people have nothing better to do with their lives.

"Margo?"

The floorboards creak. There's a brief knock and the door opens. Mum's head leans through the open doorway. She's got Velcro rollers in her hair, inspired by a video she saw on Tik-Tok. Yes, my mum is on Tik-Tok. She's even a content creator and some of her recipe videos are pretty good.

"Who was that?"

"No one."

"Didn't sound like no one."

"It was Steve," I say. "That loser I went out with for ten minutes last year."

"Did you hang up on him?"

"Yep."

There's a stony look on her face that reeks of disapproval. "It's not often a man asks you out these days, Margo."

My jaw drops and I'm back to catching flies. "What? He didn't ask me out. He only got in touch because he saw me on TV and he knows I'm getting paid. That's the sort of man you'd like me to start dating, is it?"

"Don't take that tone of voice with me."

I groan. Why do I feel like a teenager? Maybe it's because I'm back living in my childhood home. God, I have to get out. I wish Dad was still alive. He always understood me a little better.

Mum shrugs. "Well, you can't live here forever."

"Thanks for your concern about my love life," I say. "And about my living situation. I'm actively looking for accommodation."

A lie. But I'd get on it as soon as I had the energy.

Mum shakes her head, then walks away. *What the hell?* I hear footsteps descend the stairs as she goes back to the living room. She turns on the TV. The muffled sound of the ten o'clock news. What was that about? That's how grateful she is, even after I just deposited thousands of pounds into her bank account a couple of days ago. God, I have to get out. Put a deposit down somewhere. My own place.

But what if the money dries up again?

I can't go back to my old job. They wouldn't have me anyway. Not after all those names I called the boss on my last day. Those aren't the sort of names that one forgives in a hurry.

The living room door opens and the TV is suddenly louder. Mum yells up to me from downstairs.

"Margo! I'm making you a cup of tea. Want to watch the ten o'clock news with me?"

It's like the previous exchange didn't happen. I don't want to go downstairs but I know that Mum appreciates a bit of company at this time of night. I stare at the TV screen in my bedroom, wondering if I'll ever find out who the body on the ice is. And whether it ever gets warm in Iceland.

"Coming."

Five minutes later, we're sitting on the couch with tea and biscuits. She won't say as much but I think Mum regrets what she said upstairs. Maybe she was hungry. *Hangry*. Who knows? She's being nice to me now. She even said, not for the first time, how well-written the Drummond article is. We watch TV in silence. Something about rail strikes. There's a war in the Middle East and immigrants are fleeing the carnage.

I look at the terrible images onscreen but I'm thinking about the article. Selfish, I know, with all that's happening in the world. I can't forget how bad it is. Will it come back and bite me on the backside when I pitch something new?

Well, Margo, that last one you wrote was a bit thin. Wouldn't you say?

"Nothing about Darcy tonight then?" Mum says, staring at the TV.

"No."

"I wonder how she's getting on."

"Who?"

"Darcy."

I look at Mum. She's relaxed in her armchair, sipping tea and watching a woman announce the regional weather forecast. "What do you mean?"

She shrugs. Keeps her eyes on the map of the UK, covered in rain clouds and single-digit temperatures. "Och, nothing. Just wondering about the impact of all that isolation on a child. She didn't grow up around other children. Poor thing won't have developed any social skills."

I think about Darcy in that house. Watching cartoons. The social anxiety disorder.

"It won't be an easy transition," I say, picking up the remote and lowering the volume so Mum can hear me. "I don't know what's going to happen in terms of school or college. She clings to cartoons, to fairy-tale narratives. Simple notions about good and evil. Maybe it's how she copes with what happened at...the end."

"What did happen?"

"I don't know all the gory details. Not judging her, though, if she's involved in their deaths. It had to be self-defence. They were planning to get rid of her."

Mum's chewing on a biscuit. "That family need some peace and quiet to get on with their lives."

That was true. There were so many different people going in and out of the Drummond house – psychologists, psychiatrists, social workers, police and doctors – that it was impossible for them to get back to a normal routine.

I look at Mum.

"Weird though, isn't it?"

"What's that?"

"I keep thinking about what Darcy did. Going back to that house after overhearing what the Burtons were planning to do to her. She had a chance to get out. Why not run?"

"God knows. She's going to need a lot of therapy."

"Maybe. It's just–"

I hear my phone ringing upstairs again.

"Steve," I say, looking up at the ceiling. I fire an imaginary gun in that direction. "Still think he's the man of my dreams, do you?"

She narrows her eyes. "Don't be so quick to push him away. You're running out of time."

"Thanks, Mum."

I take my tea upstairs with the intention of telling Steve Driscoll where to shove it. I grab the phone. Sit down on the bed.

"What do you want, Steve?"

"Is this Margo Martin?"

The voice is disguised by some kind of software. It's a deep, distorted gurgle from Hell. Not unlike the sound of a robot talking underwater.

"Who is this?"

The silence drags on. For a second, I think the robot voice is gone. Then, it crackles in my ear again.

"I want to talk to you about Darcy Drummond."

I press the phone tight against my ear. "What do you mean?"

"There's so much you don't know."

"About?"

"About this story. About Darcy."

Again, a lengthy pause makes me think the call is over. I'm about to hang up when the voice comes back. The crackle. An exhale. This time, it's straight to the point.

"I know who took her."

21

MARGO

I get up off the bed and close the bedroom door. For good measure, I turn the key in the lock and sit back down on the bed.

The phone is still tight against my ear.

"Are you still there?"

"Congratulations on your big story," says the distorted voice. Because of the software, it's impossible to tell whether the compliment is genuine or not. It's almost funny. Some kind of voice tech that makes the caller sound like something out of a horror film. There's something demonic about it. I'm spooked but whatever else this is, it's interesting.

"Steve? Is that you? Is this your plan B?"

No answer.

"Hello?"

"You don't know me."

"Well, in that case, why don't you introduce yourself?"

"My name doesn't matter."

"It matters to me. How did you get my number? Why, if

you want to be taken seriously, are you hiding behind that voice-changing software?"

"None of that's important."

The cold shiver down my spine tells me this isn't Steve. The Drummond article is out there. My name and face are out there too. How hard is it for someone with the know-how to get my private phone number? What if my address has been leaked? We've already had people at the door, mostly in a professional capacity. But I don't want anyone else showing up without an invitation.

Shit. Not this guy.

"I want to confirm what you already know," the voice says. "Deep down. That none of this is what you think it is."

"None of what?"

"The Drummonds."

I hear a noise downstairs. Mum's just walked into the kitchen and switched the kettle on for a second cup of tea. That's good, as long as she doesn't come up and ask me if I want a top-up. The dishwasher door slams shut. She walks back into the living room.

"What about the Drummonds?"

"They're hiding something," the voice says.

"Care to elaborate on that? You say you know who took Darcy. Why don't you just come right out and say it?"

I can hear him breathing. Assuming it is a *him*. He's hesitating in response to the question. This is the first time it feels like I'm talking to a human being and not a piece of technology.

"Are you still there?"

"Don't let your friendship with Sophie Drummond cloud your instincts."

"My instincts?"

"Yes."

"I have no idea what you're talking about."

"I read your story in the newspaper. It's remarkably dull."

That one hurts. I guess there's a part of me that hoped I was being overly self-critical of the article. But this guy's just nailed it. My worst fears. Honest criticism.

"Fuck you."

Who is this guy? I wonder if it's just another conspiracy nutter like Steve. A full-time contrarian. Someone whose life is so devoid of meaning that he spends all his time disagreeing with established narratives just to get a response from people. Just a troll on a crusade of nothingness. There are so many people out there who hate the Drummonds, and it doesn't matter that Darcy's return has been legitimised by scientific testing. That her belongings were found in the Burton house. She's home and yet, still, the wackos will seek out a way to torment them.

"Who are you?" I ask. "Why don't you turn your silly voice off and speak to me like a normal human being?"

No answer.

"I said, who are you?"

"Someone who's trying to help you get what you want."

"What do I want?"

"The real story. You want the truth about the Drummonds, don't you? About what happened thirteen years ago on that beach. Most of all, you want the name of the one who took her."

"The Burtons took her."

"Are you sure?"

"I wasn't there. But if it was someone else, just tell me."

"I don't want to *just* tell you. I want you to find out for yourself because you've already taken the first step, at least in your mind. You know something's wrong with the story, don't you?"

"Do I?"

"Listen to my voice. I'm the confirmation. I'm the one urging you to listen to your instincts. If you do that, you'll find the real story that's buried underneath the lies. That's what you want, isn't it? The truth?"

"That someone else took her off the beach?"

"Yes."

"And that same someone else gave her to the Burtons?"

"Exactly."

A bead of sweat trickles down my face. I don't recall turning the radiator on and yet it's boiling.

"The Drummonds are hiding something," the voice says.

"So are you, mister."

There's a crackling noise down the line. It sounds like paper rustling in my ear but it's my mystery caller laughing.

"I'm a Good Samaritan."

"No," I say, perched on the edge of my bed. "You're a crank caller. You're a timewaster who saw me on TV and went digging around for my contact details. I'm still not convinced this isn't you, Steve. Whoever you are, don't call this number again or I'll report it to the p–"

"Hattie's picture book."

I almost drop the phone.

"Hattie's picture book," he repeats slowly.

He's talking about the picture journal that Hattie kept over the last few years of her life. Darcy told the police that Hattie kept a picture book of her favourite memories. Sophie told me about the book during the interview but it didn't make it into the article. I hadn't seen any of the drawings. It didn't fit into the story. The police still had the book, Sophie told me. Most likely, the Drummonds would get it when they were finished. But how many people in the world, at this moment in time, know that book exists? The Drummonds. The Wallaces. Me. The police.

"What about it?" I ask.

"Have you seen it?"

"No."

That crackly laughing again.

"The police have it," I say. "I can't just walk into the police station, pretend it's a library and ask to borrow it."

"The police *had* it."

"Okay. Where is it now?"

"Don't you want to know what really happened?"

"Yes, I do."

"Go back to the Drummond house," says the voice. "Ask Sophie if you can take a look. And do take a look, Margo, take a very good look at what's hiding in plain sight. Because if you do, you'll discover the seed of a real story."

22

MARGO

The phone call bugs me for the rest of the night. Despite my best efforts to forget about it, Robot Voice has well and truly managed to stir the pot. I try to watch TV but I can't concentrate. I go to bed and end up staring at the ceiling for the rest of the night.

He knew about Hattie's picture book. How could a crank caller know about that? The book's existence isn't public knowledge, at least not yet. So, who the hell was that guy? That keeps me staring at the ceiling when I should be asleep. Is he a police officer, trying to keep his identity anonymous? But why? It doesn't add up somehow. The other possibility is worse. That the caller comes from inside the Drummond family circle.

Fuck.

What *did* happen on that beach thirteen years ago?

Am I turning into a conspiracy nut as well?

I get about three hours' broken sleep. Despite that, I feel fresh the next morning. Fresh and restless. I know I have to do something. I can't just sit around the house watching British *Judge Judy* rip-offs. But what do I do? I can't just go back to Castle Drummond and ask to see the picture book. At least, not yet. Not so soon after the interview. I've also got zero desire to go back there after the way it ended last time.

So, what else can I do?

What's useful?

I could borrow Mum's car. I could drive to Glasgow and visit the Burton house. It's something I've wanted to do for curiosity's sake, and while it might not yield much in terms of results, it's a way of getting closer to this story.

The Burtons. Somehow, I have to get to know them better.

Okay. I'm doing it. I'm going to Glasgow.

I get up and take a shower. The warm water makes me sleepy again and, after getting dressed, I go downstairs, drink two cups of black coffee and eat some toast and hummus. Mum assures me she doesn't need the car today so, after making an excuse about visiting a friend, I set off for the M8.

Mum's car is a second-hand Fiat Panda. It's been a while since I've driven and, once I get onto the motorway, I'm like an old lady in the slow lane. Too many cars. Too fast. Shitting my pants is putting it mildly. About halfway to Glasgow, I realise that I've typed the wrong address into my phone for the Burton house. Doing my best not to crash, I make the correction.

So far, it's going well.

I'm in Glasgow an hour later. Driving gets easier the more I do it. I take a slip road off the M8, following the red arrow on Google Maps which takes me along the M73, M74, then past Hampden Park on my way to Cathcart.

I wasn't expecting to be this nervous.

What am I trying to prove? Am I here because the Drummond article has left me feeling like a fraud?

Real story, Robot Voice had said. *Find the real story.*

Sophie's my friend. Then again, she used me to put out a safe, fluffy article that didn't probe too deeply into Drummond affairs. At least, I think she used me. Good old Margo. She's just grateful for the break. Well, safe stories might be good for my bank account, but not for my long-term reputation.

Friends don't do that.

I'm well within my rights to investigate further.

I find the street not long after Hampden Park. It's quiet-looking. A true crime cliché. After parking near the main road, I take the short walk to the bottom of the street, which is a dead-end. I pass several rows of terraced houses. It's the very last house on the street, number thirty-three. That's the one I'm looking for. Trevor and Hattie's house. Well, it used to be. There's a flimsy barrier of yellow police tape on the fence, informing the public not to enter the premises.

I stand on the kerb. It's a gloomy-looking house, not much to look at. But this is where Darcy spent most of her life.

Why?

Who brought her here? Was it really Trevor and Hattie or did someone else hand her over to them?

It's a depressing thought. A little girl stolen from her family. Locked up behind that white door with the arched window. Growing up with no other children to play with. Cartoons her only friend.

I hear voices on the street and realise that I'm not alone. *Of course*, I think. *This house is famous now.* I turn around and see a young man and woman in their early twenties standing on the road. Facing the house. The man takes photos while the woman talks quietly into a microphone. Looks like they're recording a podcast. We exchange polite nods and go about our business.

I walk a little. Take a look around.

Turns out it's not a dead-end after all. Yellow police tape blocks a narrow alley that runs alongside the Burtons' house and continues onward to the neighbouring streets. A lot of people have been here. I see piles of fresh and withering flowers heaped up in the alley on the side of the house. A handful of teddy bears are propped up too, not unlike the one that young Darcy is holding in the famous photo that was all over the news back then. Cards. A banner that reads 'Welcome Back, Darcy'. Children's dolls, which seems an odd choice considering that Darcy is now seventeen.

I'm not sure how I'm supposed to feel. Not sure it was worth the time it took to come over here. If anything, I feel depressed. Creeped out. The horror of it all seems that much closer. Is this what standing outside a haunted house feels like?

I wander off. There's a slight incline on the walk back towards the car and my legs feel sluggish all of a sudden. It's like the sleepless night has finally caught up with me. This is why people go to the gym. To make the exercise that day-to-day life throws at you feel easier. *One of these days*, I tell myself. I walk slowly, taking in the surroundings. There are a few residents in their gardens. Doing chores. Talking to neighbours over the fence, glancing down towards the house. *The* house. They must be fed up of people like me and the true crime podcasters gawping at the Burton house.

"Morning," says a male voice from across the street.

I look over and see a thirty-something man leaning over

his wooden fence. He's younger than the other neighbours I've seen and seemingly less hostile to strangers. There's a pleasant smile on his face. He even gives me a wave.

I cross the road.

"Morning."

"You're the reporter," he says. "Aren't you?" He's got an accent that sounds a lot like Manchester. His face is flushed from the gardening work he's been doing. An open binbag sits on the path behind him, spilling over with weeds and grass. I see trimmers. A brush. Gloves. Looks like he's been busy.

"What reporter would that be?" I ask.

He runs a hand through his hair – a floppy, unwashed Beatles haircut.

"Saw you on The Breakfast Show, right? Talking about Darcy Drummond. You're the one that interviewed the family. I read it in the papers."

I flinch. Then, I smile and try to steer him away from the article. "That's right. I'm Margo Martin."

He offers a hand over the gate. "Tom Webster."

His face folds in a sudden apology.

"Hands are a bit sweaty."

"Honest work," I say with a smile.

We shake hands over the gate. Despite his slim build, he's got the grip of a silverback gorilla and I'm relieved to get my hand back.

"Hey," I say. "I'm trying to find out some information about the Burtons. What they were like, that sort of thing. You know? Don't suppose you can help?"

He nods.

"You're not the first person to ask."

"I'll bet."

"You writing a book or something?" he asks. "A follow-up to the article?"

"Not sure yet. Depends on what I find out."

He wipes the back of his hand over his sweaty forehead. "Fancy a brew?"

"A what?"

"Cup of tea. Come inside and we'll have a chat about it."

Wow, Tom's a fast worker. I don't particularly want to go into the house but it's clear the other neighbours won't be so forthcoming with their time this morning. And I feel like this trip has to be for something.

"Sure," I say. "Tea sounds good."

He nods towards the house. "I've only got herbal. That okay?"

"Perfect."

"C'mon then."

Tom opens the gate and I follow him up the driveway, dodging the binbags and work tools that litter the path. We go into the house, making small talk about what he's doing outside. General tidying, he calls it. Things he's been putting off for weeks. As soon as I walk into the house, I can smell weed. It's enough to make my eyes water but I don't think Tom's even aware of it anymore.

He points to a door on the right. "Living room. In you go and I'll put the kettle on. Is peppermint tea okay?"

"Fine," I say, trying not to get stoned.

I walk past three guitar cases on the hallway floor. As I take the right into the living room, I hear the kettle boiling in the kitchen.

Jesus, that smell. Feels like the entire house is high.

It's a pretty drab living room. Dull colours, tired furniture shrivelling up slowly. Tom's a bachelor, I'm sure of it. Ageing musician, if I had to guess. Not quite ready to let go of the rock-and-roll dream even though it ditched him years ago. Maybe I'm wrong. Maybe he's got a wife. Kids, dogs, cats and whatever. But it's quiet in here. Very quiet. Few photos. The weed and guitar cases hint of a man living alone.

How did he end up in Cathcart, I wonder?

I peel back the blinds while I wait. We're almost directly opposite the Burton house. The two podcasters are still across the street, taking photos and recording. Some of the neighbours are still eyeballing them. Making sure they feel unwelcome. Someone else comes along. A dark-skinned woman pushing a buggy with a sleeping toddler inside. She pulls a fresh bouquet of flowers and places them on the other side of the gate. She stops for a moment and, with her head bowed, it looks like she's praying. Then, she turns the buggy around and walks back up the street.

The Burton house is a shrine.

"What was your name again, love?" Tom says, squeezing through the gap in the door with two scalding hot cups in hand. He offers one to me and I take it. "Sorry, I'm absolutely awful with names."

"Thanks. It's Margo."

"Margo! Of course. Sorry about that, love. Never forget a face though. Sit down, Margo, take the weight off your feet."

"Thanks."

I take the sad-looking couch while Tom flops into the armchair. Those twin sweat patches on his underarms are growing fast. I can't smell anything over the weed but I wish he'd open a window.

"So," I ask. "How long have you lived in Scotland?"

"Ooh, about four years. Nearly five."

"What brought you here? Work?"

He smiles but it's not a happy smile. His eyes dart to the floor and when they come back to me, the light is gone. I've touched a nerve.

"A woman brought me here. But she's long gone and it's the work that keeps me here."

He laughs.

I nod towards the window.

"So, how's it been these past two weeks?"

He slurps at his tea. Gives a lazy shrug of the shoulders. "I know this much, love. The neighbourhood is in a state of shock."

"Really?"

"Oh aye. It's just...the Burtons? Kidnappers? I mean, bloody hell. And not just kidnapping anyone, but Darcy Drummond of all people."

"Hard to believe?"

"Try impossible. They say it's the quiet ones you have to watch, though, eh? They weren't bloody wrong."

Impossible. There's a jolt of electricity in my body when he says it. Without knowing it, that's the word I've been waiting for. I try not to show my excitement but when I drink my tea, it goes down so fast that I lapse into a temporary coughing fit. Classy as always – that's me.

Tom looks puzzled. "Y'alright, love?"

I nod. Slap my chest and when I can speak again, urge him to continue. "What do you mean by impossible?"

"Those two over there? It's hard to imagine, that's all."

"Go on."

"I just can't imagine 'em ever doing it. Kidnapping a child on a public beach and carrying her away before anyone saw 'em? Them two? I can't even imagine 'em running. Then again, I guess normal rules don't apply when you've just kidnapped a child."

"Did you ever see Darcy?" I ask.

He leans back in the armchair. Narrows his eyes. He's giving this one some serious thought.

While I wait for an answer, I look at several framed pictures sitting on the mantelpiece. There's a younger and fresher-faced Tom up there, pictured along with his mates at legendary UK music festivals such as T in the Park and Glastonbury. They look like they're having the time of their lives. Eighteen, nineteen, twenty years old. I picture this guy back then, travelling far and wide to go to Oasis gigs and every music festival under the sun. Maybe that's where he met his Scottish girlfriend. I doubt living alone in Cathcart was part of the dream back then.

"Honestly," he says with another lazy shrug, "I don't remember ever seeing her. There are lots of kids running up and down this street. I wouldn't have paid much attention even if I did see her. But sounds like she didn't get out much."

"What about the Burtons? They didn't mix much? Chat to neighbours?"

"Nah," Tom says. "Kept to themselves, those two. Come to think of it, getting a good morning out of Trevor and Hattie was like squeezing blood out of a stone."

"Right."

"Another drink, Martha?"

"Margo. No, thanks."

"Shit. Sorry, love. How about something to eat?"

There's a hopeful look in Tom's eyes. He probably invites every eligible woman into the house, hoping that sparks will fly. I glance at the festival photos again. Wondering where all Tom's mates are now.

I finish the last of my tea and put the cup on the table. Then I stand up.

"Long drive back to Edinburgh."

I don't miss the flicker of disappointment in his eyes but Tom proves to be a gentleman. He thanks me for the chat and it's sincere enough to be heartbreaking. He sees me to the door. We say a quick goodbye and I walk to the top end of the street, ignoring the sullen glances of the neighbours.

I sit in the car for a while without turning the engine on. Staring through the windshield. There's a feeling I can't shake.

The kidnapping. There's so much that doesn't make sense. Now we know it was the Burtons, and still something's not right. Tom is right to doubt his neighbours' capabilities. From what I know, Sophie, Mike and the three kids were sitting close to the water's edge that day on Bournemouth Beach. Whoever grabbed Darcy had a lot of work to do before the coast was clear. Sure, it was super crowded. They still had to be fast. Really fast. Were the Burtons really up to it? Were they capable of lifting a child off the beach and getting her away quick enough before Mike and Sophie noticed she was gone? Anything's possible if you're desperate enough. But it's not convincing.

I start the engine and the old Panda makes a grinding noise. She resists. There's a whirring sound like an electric motor turning. I turn the key again and, thank God, it starts. I don't want to break down here.

That creepy, distorted voice echoes in my mind.

The Drummonds are hiding something.

Maybe I'm as nutty as Steve and all the other conspiracy

fruitcakes out there. Maybe I'm right. Maybe they're all right too. Or this could be nothing. It could just be me trying to overcompensate for writing a shitty article.

And yet, as I drive away from Cathcart, I'm convinced that someone else was involved in Darcy's kidnapping. That someone else picked her up off the sand that day.

Someone who knew her.

23

SOPHIE

It's a miracle.

I look around the dinner table and tonight, I see a normal family.

This is what Mike and I have been waiting for since Darcy's return. Well, since she went missing. It's Friday night and we're all here, eating Chinese takeaway. All seven of us. Chinese food is Maria's favourite and we're gathered around the table celebrating her outstanding year at school so far. Like all the kids, she's been working from home recently but we've been in close contact with her teachers and Maria's recent grades have been outstanding. She makes it seem so effortless, and now she's at that point where Oxford is the inevitable next step. Or Cambridge. Whatever she wants. We won't push but I'd be lying if I said I hadn't envisioned her future a hundred times over.

"I propose a toast," Mike says, lifting his glass of wine off the table. His second of the evening. "To Maria. To the next doctor in the family."

I hold my glass up and clink it off Mike's. Then, I look at

Maria. "And sweetheart, I'm sure you'll make a much better doctor than your mum."

Mike winks. "Hear, hear."

My God, I'm enjoying myself. I've almost forgotten what it feels like to be without constant anxiety. If only Darcy would smile. I know she's uncomfortable, bless her heart. But we're doing okay. The television is off for a change. No cartoons. More importantly, Dad isn't here to wind up Mike, and because of that, it's a completely different atmosphere.

This is what we need. No outside interference, just us learning how to be a family together. I wish I had the guts to tell my parents to back off. It's too early to tell if Margo's article has dampened the enthusiasm of the media presence outside the house.

I hope so.

I take another sip of wine. Already, the alcohol is going to my head and I'll happily let it. We're trying. We're really trying here. I haven't opened the bedside drawer and Mike hasn't been going to the casino in Glasgow. We'll gladly take quiet lives. Boring lives. Our children need us.

Maria sips her water. She doesn't drink Coke like the others, believing it'll make her put on weight and that she'll end up a bad runner. She values her place in the school cross-country team too much. I tell her the occasional treat is okay. The stick insect influencers on social media, however, are more persuasive than her mother. Maria's smart but she's still a young girl. I can't imagine how hard it is for them these days with all the noise coming from the internet. *Wear this. Don't eat this. Do this. Believe this. Don't believe that.* We do our best to filter it but there's only so much we can do.

"I don't know if I want to be a doctor," she says.

Mike shoves a forkful of rice into his mouth. He talks and

chews at the same time, something that Dad never fails to criticise. "You can be whatever you want, darling. Just be sure to make lots of money. Okay?"

He rubs his thumb over the tip of his index and middle finger. The 'money gesture'.

Maria frowns.

"Nothing less than a billionaire," Mike says, "and your granddad will think you're a failure. You've got Wallace blood in you. Don't you forget it."

"Mike," I say, smiling.

Seems like two glasses is more than enough these days.

Mike nods an apology. "Sorry."

I look over at Darcy, desperate for eye contact. She's barely touched her food but she keeps running her fork through the rice and tofu, giving the impression that she's eating like everyone else.

"Everything okay, sweetheart?" I ask. My voice is different than it would be for the other kids. More formal. "Do you want anything else?"

"No, thank you," she replies.

She's miles away. Probably back in *that* house. The thought of her in there pulls me back to darkness. I want to kill those people all over again for what they did to my daughter. My firstborn. She can barely look me in the eye, for God's sake.

Another sip of wine.

"How about a toast?" Mike says.

Tom gasps. "We just had one!"

"Yes," Mike says, looking over at the twins. "You're absolutely right, son. We just did. Silly me."

Jusht did. Shilly me.

He pours himself a third glass of wine.

"This is good," Mike says, setting the bottle down. "This is really good."

His face is flushed. Looking at him, I feel a tight, pinching sensation under my chest. I hope he slows down but this isn't the time for a confrontation. We're celebrating.

"A double toast for Maria," Mike says, raising his glass yet again. "Well done, sweetheart. We're so proud of you."

We make the toast. Everyone except Darcy. She's barely touched her Coke although I know she loves the stuff. She can't wait for dinner to be over. To get away from us, to go back to the TV, either in the living room or the big Samsung we installed in her bedroom. I look at her across the table. She's lifeless. Like a robot that's been unplugged.

She's here but I haven't got my daughter back. Not yet.

I look at my family. It's incredible how much Maria and Darcy resemble one another. They both look so much like I did at their respective ages. There's been an instant dislike between them from the get-go. I wonder if Maria has felt side-lined since Darcy's return. Hopefully, this dinner reminds her of how much we love her. She understands, I know she does. It's such a bizarre situation. Darcy's always been this gigantic shadow living with us for so many years. For so long she was a photograph, and now she's here. Flesh and blood.

They're siblings. And yet it's so effortless with Darcy and Lola. Guess it can't be like that for everyone. The twins are still awkward around her too.

Maybe I just want too much too soon. I want everything to be perfect now while reality has different plans. Darcy coming home is just the beginning of a long reintegration project. We've still got so far to go.

"Nick," I say, noticing the way he's picking at his food. "Eat up, please."

"I'm not hungry."

He's the classic, huffing teenager.

"Do you want to play video games after this?"

He snorts in disgust, but he eats when he sees that I mean business. Mike pours himself another glass of wine and I want to kick him under the table. I can feel the anxiety bubbling up inside me. Still, I cling to my smile and look at Darcy throughout the course of the evening, hoping that something will come back.

It doesn't.

Dinner ends. I start gathering the dishes. Mike and Nick offer to help, but I smile and tell them to stay put. They offer again and I *insist*. There's a huge sigh of relief when I take them through to the kitchen.

I close the kitchen door, putting my back against it. I need something for what's bubbling up inside me. Even a cigarette would do but I don't have a pack of those stashed in a bedside drawer upstairs. I do have the pills.

No. I can't.

Just be a good mum, I remind myself. *Keep going.*

I'm loading the dishwasher when I hear the scream.

"What the–?"

I'm paralysed for a few seconds. Then, I hear another scream and snap out of the nothingness. I'm running towards the kitchen door, pulling it open and sprinting down the hall. As I run, I envision all the worst-case scenarios. Mike on the floor, clutching both hands to his chest. Fatal heart attack. Eyes bulging. Face burning red. One of the kids choking. Their little eyes turning to me as I run in, desperate for a saviour.

I hear someone on the stairs. I turn my head and Mike's thundering downstairs, buttoning his trousers. He must have gone to the bathroom, leaving the kids alone.

"What's going on?" he yells.

I gasp.

"No idea."

I push the door open and the scene inside the dining room is like something out of *Mad Max*. The twins are on their feet, backs to the wall. Their faces white with shock. Lola's dropped to her knees in the corner of the room, tears streaming down her face. They're watching Darcy and Maria rolling around the floor, throwing hard punches. I see the wild look on their faces. The intense loathing. It chills my blood. Now Darcy is on top, pinning Maria to the floor.

"STOP!" Mike yells, overtaking me as we run towards the table.

My legs freeze up. I see the knife in Darcy's hand. I scream and my voice is unrecognisable.

"Darcy, no!"

A sudden thought comes to me. Darcy killed Trevor Burton. She stabbed him to death inside that house.

"Mike, the knife!"

Mike drags Darcy off her sister, holding her back as she struggles to get back to the fight. Her arms and legs flail. Thank God she drops the knife. I pick a tearful Maria up off the floor, pulling her away as I prioritise putting distance between the two girls.

The look in Darcy's eyes. Like she wants to rip Maria's head off her shoulders.

"Enough!" I yell.

"What's going on?" Mike repeats, looking back and forth

between the two girls. His chest is heaving and he's badly out of breath. That's one way to sober him up.

No one answers.

"Your father asked you a question," I say in a firm voice.

Darcy points an accusing finger at Maria. "She called me stupid."

Maria gasps. Her cheeks are blazing red as she shakes her head. "I didn't."

Darcy keeps stabbing her finger in Maria's direction. "You said I was stupid because I didn't go to school. Because I was home-schooled by *them*."

I frown. "Maria? Is that true?"

"No. She's a liar."

Darcy spits in Maria's direction. "You're the liar."

"Darcy," I say, eyeing the fresh puddle on the floor. "We don't spit in this house."

"She's a headcase," Maria says. "She attacked me for nothing."

The twins say nothing. I don't want to put them on the spot. I let go of Maria, satisfied she's not going to lunge at Darcy. With that done, I hurry over to the corner, drop to my knees and scoop the wailing Lola into my arms.

"It's okay," I whisper in her ear. "It's over. It's just a silly fight."

"Go to your rooms," Mike says. He looks more confused than angry. "Both of you. And stay there until we say otherwise, got it?"

He looks at me as if to say, *is that okay?*

I watch Darcy as she walks out of the dining room, her head lowered. And there was me thinking that Maria was the jealous one. Was it insensitive of us to celebrate Maria's scholarly achievements like this? I should've known that

Darcy might have insecurities about her home-schooling. Why didn't I think of that?

I still see the knife in her hand.

God knows, we'll keep trying. But one thing is glaringly obvious. We don't know this young woman. We knew her once as a little girl, the one frozen in all those famous photographs, but we don't know who she's become in her absence.

What she's become.

24

MARGO

I get back to Edinburgh around mid-morning. On the way back to Mum's house, I fill up the car with petrol as a thank you for letting me borrow it. Once I'm back in the house, I pour myself a glass of water in the kitchen and go upstairs. I close the door. Lock it. Collapse onto the bed with a sigh.

My head's still spinning. A dull ache forms at my temples and I close my eyes to forget. Just for a second.

The scratch of a key in the lock. I hear Mum opening the front door. I lift my head off the pillow and a quick glance at the clock beside my bed tells me I've napped for four hours.

"Oh shit."

I throw myself off the bed. My concrete limbs are sluggish and weak. The headache is still there, pulsing at the temples. Feels like I'm hung over without the fun of being drunk. With a hoarse groan, I stagger out of the bedroom, into the landing, and lean over the oak bannister at the top of the stairs. I feel like I've been run over.

"Hi."

"You up there?" she asks.

"No, this is just a recording of my voice that I prepared in case you decided to call up to me at some point in the future."

"Don't get cheeky with me."

Mum's standing at the foot of the staircase. She might be getting older but her resting bitch face is still up there with the best of them. Hand pressed against her hip. I feel like I'm twelve and late for school.

"Were you calling me for a while?" I ask.

She nods. "Have you got cotton wool stuck in your ears?"

"I was asleep. You just came back, didn't you?"

"I've still been calling."

"I was asleep."

"I gathered that much."

"And yet you kept calling. So, what is it? Where's the fire?"

Mum lets out an exasperated sigh but her face relaxes a little. "I was going to ask if you wanted to go to the cinema later. Remember that Tom Hanks film we were talking about? It starts in a couple of hours. We can make it into town if you get a move on."

I nod. "Glad you didn't wake me up for anything important."

"Well," she says, "I need to know if I'm making dinner or not."

I let out a loud yawn. My brain feels like sludge. "Can we do it another night? How about this weekend?"

"Are you working tonight?"

"Kind of."

"Are you sure you don't want to go?" she asks. "Might take your mind off work."

I can see that Mum really wants to go and, on any other night, I'd just suck it up and give the old girl the company. But I'd be terrible company. This Drummond thing has well and truly messed with my head. Maybe it's because Sophie's a good friend and this investigation, if I can call what I'm doing an investigation, feels like skulking around behind her back. But it won't let go. Intuition keeps calling me back to the battlefield. I need to know who my mystery caller was. I also need to take his advice and look at Hattie Burton's picture journal too, even if it means pissing off Sophie and Mike with the request.

Three words are doing laps in my mind.

Something isn't right.

"We'll go at the weekend, okay? And we'll have dinner before the film – my treat. How does that sound?"

Mum nods. "Aye, that's fine. Are you alright?"

"Just a little tired."

"Aye. Well, go back and sleep if you need to. Sorry I woke you up."

"It's okay."

I go back to my room and sit down on the bed. The curtains are pulled over, shutting out all the unwanted light.

Sophie's my friend. But I *need* to see that picture book. Robot Voice thinks there's something important in there that I should see. Something that will turn the lights on. What was it he said? Something like, *you'll see what's missing.*

Ah, shit.

I stretch out on the bed like a starfish. God, I wish that Drummond article wasn't out there circulating under my name. It's really bugging me. An article that so many people all over the world have read. *Crap by Margo Martin.* Translated into a gazillion languages. *La mierda. La merde. La merda.* The lukewarm nature of the piece eats away at me, as does the fact that the Drummonds used me. They knew I'd be grateful and that I wouldn't rock the boat. Wouldn't ask the hard questions. Press harder for a photograph. They played me.

Now it feels like I've killed my career with one article. That's impressive, even for me.

I close my eyes. That distorted voice plays like an endless echo.

Don't you want the real story?

I hear Mum switching on the TV downstairs. That loud sighing noise she makes when she flops onto the couch. Legs up on the coffee table. She turns the volume up too loud. Little things take me back to being a kid in this house. Damn. I wish Dad was still alive to sit beside her. I know she misses him more than anything even though she doesn't talk about him much. It's hard seeing all the photos.

I wish I'd given Dad something to be proud of before the stroke. It wouldn't be this. It wouldn't be the Drummond article because he'd have seen right through it. Told me the truth, that it was a watered-down piece of crap. And that I was capable of so much more.

"Fuck it."

It's not too late to save my journalistic soul. That is, if I commit to this. To the real story. I've got a lot of work to do. *One more chance, Margo.*

I open my laptop. Create a blank document on Word and say the first line out loud whilst typing at a furious pace.

"How can I get more information about Trevor and Hattie?"

I stare at the blinking cursor. No matter what, I don't allow myself to get frustrated. I wait for the moment to pass.

But I'm waiting a long time for inspiration to strike. Downstairs, I hear the muffled sound of the weather forecast.

I turn back to the screen. That blinking cursor is taunting me.

Trevor and Hattie Burton. Who were they? What do I know so far?

Not a lot.

They were extremely reclusive people with no other family members. None that have come forward anyway, and what's the likelihood of anyone in their right mind declaring their kinship with a couple of child kidnappers? No children, siblings, cousins – nothing. I'll assume that the rest of the neighbours in Cathcart know about as much as Tom. Doubt they'd talk to me even if they did know something.

The only person who can tell me anything about Trevor and Hattie is Darcy. But Sophie isn't going to let me talk to her anytime soon.

What she might do is let me look at Hattie's picture book. That's what Robot Voice thinks I should see. I just need to ask, and say nothing of the strange phone call.

My mobile rings beside me. I almost knock the glass of water off the bedside table as I reach for it.

"Hello?"

"How's it going, gorgeous?"

I groan. "What do you want, Steve? I'm really not in the mood to talk about the man on the grassy knoll."

"Very funny," he says. "Thought I'd give you a chance to reconsider that drink."

"I'm busy."

"Doing what?"

"Shaving my head."

"C'mon," he says. "One drink. What's the harm?"

"Nope."

"Still working on the Darcy Drummond story?"

"Bye, Steve."

But he's fast.

"I thought the Drummond interview was all done and dusted," he says, speaking like it's a sprint. "Why are you still working on it? Is there a follow-up? Did you find something else out?"

That's a lot of questions.

"You think I'm rich, don't you?"

"Eh?"

"You think I'm rich after the interview, don't you?"

"That's cold," Steve says. "I don't want your money. Bloody hell, Margo. This is so much bigger than money."

"What's bigger?"

He sighs and it sounds like I'm trying his patience. "We both know there's something not right about all this, don't we?"

It frightens me how much Steve's words are also my words.

"Goodnight, Steve," I say, ending the call.

"It's him. It's Mike D–"

I put the phone on do not disturb. Then, it's back to the laptop and blinking cursor. Even before I opened the Word document, I knew what I had to do. I'm not getting a sit-down interview with Darcy Drummond anytime soon. That leaves the picture book. I have to see it and I won't feel guilty asking because, at the end of the day, Sophie used me.

I can't forget that.

But maybe I can return the favour.

25

MARGO

I hate to say it but Sophie's looked better.

"Hi, Margo."

"Hey Sophie," I say, doing my best to sound cheerful. "Good to see you."

"You too."

She's standing at the front door, yet to invite me into the house. It's like there's a courtesy lag or something. That's not like Sophie. No makeup on, which also isn't like her. Ruffled hair. Eyes not quite focused. She glances over my shoulder and gives a half-hearted wave to the security guard standing on the driveway. There are only a couple of security guards here now. The round-the-clock press vans are gone. There are no crowds, only a handful of people scattered up and down the street who may or may not be journalists still chasing that elusive first photograph of Darcy. They could also be filmmakers, podcasters or curious citizens.

All the curtains are still closed in Castle Drummond. The house remains a fortress.

"Did you text?" Sophie asks, looking confused. A hand

fumbles around her jeans pocket, as if searching for her phone.

I shake my head. "No, I just took the chance you'd be here."

"Oh."

"I just need to talk to you," I say. "Won't take long."

Sophie gives a sluggish nod. Slowly, she pulls the door open. I smile, work my way through the gap, and we plod down the hallway towards the living room. No sign of Miss Snotty-Pants today.

"Are you okay?" I ask, following her. She doesn't seem to hear me at first. "Sophie? Is everything alright?"

We stop beside the spiral staircase. She turns towards me, a tight-lipped smile on her face. "Fine. What can I do for you, Margo?"

Okay.

"Umm...you thinking about going back to yoga anytime soon?"

She frowns like I just spoke backwards. "Yoga? Oh right. We're just waiting for this...back to normal."

"You sure you're okay?"

"Fine."

"Getting enough sleep?"

"Too much."

I tilt my head to the side. My tone of voice is still pleasant chit-chat. "You sure about that?"

The fog clears from her eyes and for the first time since she opened the door, Sophie's looking at me with something that resembles clarity.

"Margo."

"What is it?"

"I feel like I'm losing my mind."

I'm not certain I heard her right. She whispers so low that it cloaks the words. Why is she whispering all of a sudden? I look around the hallway, expecting to see a face at the entrance to the living-room. Mike. Edward. Darcy. But we're alone. I put a hand on Sophie's shoulder. She's rigid. Feels like I'm comforting a mannequin.

"Did you say...losing your mind?"

She nods.

"What do you mean, Sophie?"

There's such a despondent look on her face that I think she's about to collapse, curl up in a ball on the floor and sob her eyes out. Instead, she makes a slight hand gesture, sweeping the hallway.

"Nothing's changed."

"What?"

Her lip trembles. "Things were supposed to get better when she came back. But everything that was broken is still broken. More so, I think. I can see how silly it was now. Thinking everything would just magically fix itself."

I take my hand off her shoulder. "It's early days."

She shakes her head. The eyes still clear but welling up. "We're a mess. Mike's constantly battling the feeling that he's not good enough. Not rich enough. Maria and Darcy are at war with one another. The twins are scared of Darcy. I think I am too."

She buries her face in her hands.

There's a creak on the stairs. I look up and see Tom standing on the top step. He's watching his mum, a look of concern spreading across his face. I smile, trying to reassure him.

"Hey."

He looks at me but doesn't speak.

"No school today?"

He shakes his head but keeps looking at his mum. "We haven't been going."

"Oh, that's right. Well, you'll be back soon when all this dies down. Don't worry about your mum, Tom. She's just tired."

Sophie takes her head out of her hands. She nods in response to what I'm saying but she can't even bring herself to look at her son.

"C'mon, Sophie," I say. "Let's sit you down."

With a hand on her back, I lead her into the living room. The cleaners must have been in this morning because, as always, it's the perfect showroom. I can still smell the cleaning chemicals. It's neat but sterile, kind of like the entire house. Maybe I'm just jealous. After all, Sophie and I are about the same age. She's here while I'm back with Mum, sulking in the bedroom like a teenager.

The TV is on, of course.

Darcy and Lola have their backs to me. I don't know if they heard us coming in.

I force Sophie to sit down but she's restless and is back on her feet seconds later. She offers me tea or coffee and I refuse. She's unsteady on her feet and I don't like it. *The Lion King* gets louder across the room. The reunion of Simba and Nala takes over the Drummond living room.

Lola giggles. Glances over her shoulder. Sophie doesn't even seem to notice that the TV is too loud. She falls into the armchair again. Looks like she might fall asleep.

"Where's Mike?" I ask.

"Out."

I struggle for something to say.

"You must be looking forward to getting back to work."

She shrugs. *Okay,* I think. *Straight to the point it is then.* Do it before Sophie falls asleep on me. Whatever the hell meds she's taking, she's taking too much. I should say something to Mike when I see him. Unless he's drinking. In which case there's little point trying to get sense out of him. I've seen Mike drunk.

"The Burtons," I say.

Sophie shakes her head. "Hmm?"

"The Burtons."

"What about them?" she asks, her eyes narrowing.

I pull the chair in closer. Talking just loud enough for Sophie to hear but not so loud that my voice reaches Darcy's ears. The TV is still deafening so my words are shielded.

"What sort of people were they?"

Sophie heard that all right. She looks at me like I've just peed all over the carpet. "What sort of people were they? Kidnappers, for God's sake. The scum of the earth."

I nod. "Something's bugging me about them."

I have to repeat that line to get a reaction.

"What?"

"Well," I say, ignoring the fact that she's clearly not comfortable. "I'm trying to profile them. Sorry, I should've explained. Given you some context."

Feels like Sophie is staring through me.

"There might be a follow-up article," I say. "I'm talking to some editors and I'm just doing a little digging around, you know. I want to understand the Burtons as people. Understand what could make them do such a terrible thing."

"How the hell should I know?" Sophie asks.

"I know. It's just–"

I'm digging a hole. Fuck it. I might as well dig deeper. I raise my voice, making sure I'm heard over the TV.

"What about that picture book?"

Light flickers on and off in Sophie's eyes. "What about it? It's just a book of nonsensical scribbling."

"It's here?"

She nods.

"You were so helpful," I say, hands clasped, resting on my lap. I'm a picture of innocence. This isn't easy and I have to remind myself that she used me to put out that watered-down article. "Giving me that first interview. Now there's a chance of a follow-up. More focused on the Burtons than you guys. This could be great for my career, Sophie. It'd be so helpful if I could glance at the book. Just five minutes, that's all I need."

The rope-like veins on Sophie's neck go taut. "It's just doodles and scribbling."

"Can I see it?"

Holy shit. It feels like I'm drowning in quicksand.

Eventually, she stands up. A brief nod of the head. There's something unnerving about the way she's smiling at me.

"Always happy to help your career, Margo. It's in Darcy's room. I'll go get it."

26

SOPHIE

The dosage is too high. I'm a doctor, for God's sake. I have no idea why I keep doing this to myself, self-prescribing too much.

I should know better.

I *do* know better.

I'm standing in Darcy's bedroom. The curtains are closed and I feel trapped – not in this room, not in this house, but in my own skin. My eyelids feel like they're weighed down. My feet are sinking into the floor. I wish I could pull the curtains open, unlatch the window and breathe in some fresh air. But I can't because there might be someone out there waiting to take photographs.

I have to stay in the dark.

"C'mon," I whisper to myself.

The self-medicating has to stop. My children need me.

Darcy's room needs some colour. I know she hasn't been back long but there's no personality in here. No posters on the wall, no indication of who she is or what she's interested in. Maria's room, on the other hand, is full of athletics trophies, debate team awards, and she has at least two posters of her favourite pop stars on the wall. We've offered to redecorate the room for Darcy. She shrugged. Gave the impression she couldn't care less. I still remember her bedroom in the old house. Bursting with light and colour. So many toys that we didn't have enough space to keep them all. She was our firstborn and we spoiled her beyond belief.

I never thought it was possible to love someone like that. But that's how I loved Darcy.

It's how I *love* her.

The media showed no mercy in the aftermath of her disappearance. The coverage was vicious. I still can't believe the viciousness of their vendetta against us. Mike and I became punchbags for the world to let out all their negativity. All their hatred. Their envy. And boy, did they let it out.

"She's back," I say to the ghost-like figure in the full-length mirror. I know that she's back. What I'd give to *feel* it.

I walk over to the wardrobe. Slide the mirror door open, reach up and take Hattie Burton's picture book off the top shelf. It's unspectacular. Black moleskin cover, about two hundred blank pages with childish scribbling from start to finish. It's only here because Darcy wants it to be here. Personally, I'd have binned it. Or burned it.

What does Margo think she'll find in here? And who's asking to see it? A journalist or a friend?

Who cares what Trevor and Hattie Burton were like? My daughter is a stranger to me and all she does is sit in front of the TV and watch cartoons. She should be ready to take on the world. Instead, there's nothing in her eyes when she looks at me. Everything is a comparison to the angel we lost and I know that's not fair on this version of Darcy.

Where is Mike now? He should be here with me and his

children. We're cooped up inside this house and yet, somehow, he still manages to sneak off and then he's gone for hours. Why are we behaving like she never came back?

What am I doing?

Oh yes, the book. I have it. It's in my hand.

I walk out of Darcy's bedroom, the book tucked under my arm. A thick fog has settled in my mind but I walk towards the sound of cartoons.

27

MARGO

I look through the book, trying my best to ignore Sophie, who's watching me like a hawk.

I'm also trying to ignore *The Lion King* in the background. Lola giggles constantly while Darcy is a silent statue of a teenage girl. She doesn't laugh. She doesn't move. What I'd give to be in a quiet space looking through Hattie's book at leisure. To be able to take notes. To have a coffee to help me focus.

I flick through the pages.

Sophie needn't worry. I have no idea what I'm supposed to be looking for and the only reason I'm here is a phone call that might have been a prank. She's right about Hattie's book. It's just a series of childish scrawls. Artistic gibberish. Spilled out memories. Still, I try to make sense of it. A frequent visual of the early pages is the image of a couple holding hands. Stick figures. Wild hair. Sometimes they're standing in a large field of grass with a yellow smudge in the sky. Sometimes they're staring at a big screen – a TV or cinema screen? Standing in front of the Eiffel Tower or maybe it's Blackpool Tower. Holding hands. It *must* be Trevor and Hattie. Their courting days. Notably, there's nothing before Trevor. What about Hattie's childhood? Were there no memories worth keeping? Did life start when she met Trevor?

Darcy told the police that Hattie was afraid of losing her memory. That they didn't have many photographs to look back on and that's why she started sketching in this book. I know what they did was awful but man, that's kind of sad.

I keep looking. My eyes adjust to the crude style and I pick out moments from their life together.

The wedding day. The white dress. A room full of empty seats.

I look up and Sophie's eyes leap away. She sits forward on the chair, then back again. Crosses her legs. Uncrosses them. The Valium (if that's what she's on) is wearing off. It's like she's on amphetamines now.

"Everything okay?" she asks.

Her voice penetrates my concentration. But I smile. Give her a polite nod of the head. Back to the book. Away from the early sketches, turning my attention to the middle and end parts. The lines and colours become even less polished. The drawings are frantic. Sophie keeps talking and I get the feeling she's trying to distract me.

"We should really throw it out," Sophie says. "But Darcy wants to keep it. For some reason."

The Lion King blares in my ears.

"Right."

I don't want to talk. And yet I'm starting to feel like this visit was a waste of time. I can't see a damn thing in these pages. *I've been fooled. It was a prank.* But I force myself to browse from start to finish again, hoping that something will leap out at me.

I shift in the seat. There's a hot, pinching sensation at the back of my neck.

Scribbles. More scribbles and, still, nothing catches my eyes. Is it me? Or is there really nothing here? If nothing else, I feel like I'm getting to know Trevor and Hattie. I see more than two shuffling old people losing their minds. The journal is a document to their youth. Love hearts everywhere. The childlike imagery is powerful. I feel another jolt of sympathy for the woman and her fear of forgetting.

Once again, the mood changes. It's a book of two halves and the joy of courting is over. Black suns appear in Hattie's skies. Clouds. Rain that looks like falling daggers. A woman with dark, curly hair appears a lot. I assume it's a self-portrait.

Sophie's pretending to browse through her phone. If I sit here for much longer, she'll probably start turning off the lights.

I can't drag this out for much longer. I wouldn't dare go back to the start either. I open the pages at random. Nothing. Again. Nothing. One more time and I land about halfway through the book.

I stare at the centre, in between pages.

"Shit."

I look at the kids. Then Sophie.

"Pardon my French."

"Something caught your eye?" Sophie asks.

I'll say. I run my finger over the ragged edges of a missing page. How did I miss that? It's subtle and I must have been skimming too fast to notice. It's the only thing in the book that's out of place.

There's a rush of excitement. I turn back to the page before the one that's missing. It's nothing special. A drawing of a car on the road. A cloud of smoke billowing out of the exhaust. Another yellow blob of sun in the sky. What does it mean? Trevor and Hattie are on the move? They're going somewhere?

My heart's racing.

"Margo?" Sophie asks. "Is everything okay?"

I hold the book up, turning it around so that Sophie can see the ragged edges of the torn sheet.

"There's a page missing."

Sophie's eyes remain foggy. Either she's still feeling the pills or she doesn't share my excitement. "So there is. Maybe Hattie Burton did it."

I mean, it's possible.

"Can I ask you a question, Sophie?"

I'm still trying to keep my voice down and make myself heard over the sound of the TV. Not easy, but I don't want Darcy to overhear this.

"Of course," she says.

I point to the book. "The Burtons. Do you really think they were capable of grabbing Darcy that day? Getting her through the crowd?"

Sophie's face gives nothing away. "It was busy. They didn't have to be quick. They had to be clever."

Fair point.

"Still, you guys only took your eyes off Darcy for a second."

"Maybe they were fitter back then."

I shake my head. "The police did find some photos in the house from around that period. Just a few, unframed loose snapshots in the bedroom drawers. I don't know. They really don't look capable of grabbing a child, steering her through a crowd and doing all that before the alarm is raised. Sure, it takes cunning. It also takes a good dose of physical fitness. And as you know, it was hot as hell that day."

Sophie narrows her eyes. I don't like the way she's looking at me.

"What are you getting at, Margo?"

It doesn't add up, Sophie. That's what I'm getting at. The more I think about it, the less convinced I am that Trevor and Hattie Burton took your little girl off the beach. Sure, she ended up with them. But there were others involved in her kidnapping. I'm sure of it.

My mystery caller wasn't a prank.

"Nothing," I say.

I close the book and hand it back to her. And, after a quick goodbye, I get the hell out of Castle Drummond.

28

MARGO

The Uber drops me off at the end of the street. I thank the driver (who mercifully stayed quiet on the way back from Morningside) and now I'm walking towards Mum's house. I'm about thirty seconds away when I see a tall, fidgety shape lingering beside the gate.

Oh shit.

The pulse throbs in my neck. There's no one else around and the late afternoon gloom is anything but comforting. The houses are quiet. Curtains shield the windows and the prospect of short days is coming as the Northern Hemisphere tilts away from the sun and towards winter. I think about making a sharp U-turn and getting the hell out of Dodge. Walk back towards the main road, sticking close to the streetlights.

That's ridiculous. What the hell am I running from?

The Drummond thing. Just because I'm asking a couple of questions, it doesn't mean the CIA want to throw me in the back of a van.

I walk to the house, trying to project confidence.

A voice calls over from the gate. "Margo?"

I stop. There's a combination of relief and irritation.

"Steve?"

"Aye, it's me."

He emerges from the dark, oblivious to the fact that he almost gave me a heart attack. Steve blends in well with the dusk, his black jacket and matching jeans clinging to his lanky frame. He's still got a slightly ape-like walk. Chin whiskers. That's a new one. His boyish face, even in his early forties, doesn't suit facial hair.

"How's it going?" he asks. There's a smug grin on his face. Like he just one-upped me by catching me outside the house.

"What the fuck are you doing standing outside my mum's house?"

"Been waiting for you."

"Waiting for me? Are you stalking me or something?"

He shrugs. "I knocked on the door earlier. Your mum said you were out. Said you'd be back soon so I thought I'd wait."

"How long ago was that?" I ask.

"I don't know. About twenty minutes ago."

More like three hours, I'll bet.

I glance at the house. The curtains are pulled over but I see the pale glow of the living room light seeping out at the sides. I can even hear the TV turned up too loud. Confirmation that Mum's hearing is all over the place.

"I'm surprised she didn't invite you in," I say.

He laughs and shoves his hands in his pockets like he's cold. "Actually, she invited me in for a cup of tea. Nice that she still remembers me."

I glare at the house. Then at Steve. "She still remembers the cockroach infestation in the kitchen last year."

"Wow. Still a charmer, eh?"

"What do you want?"

That's Steve's cue to take a step closer. He lowers his voice like the next-door neighbour might be down on all fours, eavesdropping behind the tall hedge. Knowing what I know about Mrs McCormack, she might be doing just that.

"I've been thinking about the Drummond situation," Steve says.

It feels like someone's pulling at a tight knot inside my chest. I hold both hands up. "Don't go there, Steve."

There's a horrified look on his face. "Are you serious?"

"You heard. Why are you even bothering me? We're not friends. We're not anything anymore, okay? You're just a guy blocking the pavement."

He glances around the neighbourhood. Looks like he's genuinely wary of something. Or someone. "It doesn't make sense, Margo. You know that better than anyone."

"What?"

"The official narrative."

I play dumb because I don't want to be on the same page as this guy.

"Official narrative?"

His eyes light up like a Christmas tree. "That Trevor and Hattie Burton grabbed Darcy off that beach."

I glare at him. "Steve, is there anything you want to tell me?"

"What?"

"You called me twice the other night, didn't you? First time, I hung up on you. Then you called using voice-disguising software."

Steve frowns. "Eh?"

"You heard."

"Margo, why would I disguise my voice?"

I don't have a good answer.

"What did they say?" Steve asks. There's a hint of desperation in his voice. I feel like I've just poured petrol onto a fire. "The caller?"

I say nothing. There's another thing that makes the caller unlikely to be Steve. How would he know about Hattie's journal? Unless there's a leak somewhere and news of the journal's existence made it into the tinfoil hat community.

Whoever made that call, it wasn't Steve.

He's not letting go either. He's got that manic look in his eyes. The thrill of the chase. "What did this caller tell you about the Drummonds?"

"Nothing. Forget it."

"Forget it?"

"It's none of your business."

He nods in a smug, I-told-you-so manner. "That's okay. I know anyway. They're telling you the same thing I've been trying to tell you. Right? Look closer at the Drummonds if you want to find the real kidnapper."

"Nope."

His eyes are shimmering. "There's a BIG story here, Margo. Don't you feel it? Of course you do. You're so much better than that lightweight Drummond-friendly article you wrote. C'mon. What about the *real* story?"

His hands are up.

"Listen, okay? There's been a lot of talk online."

"Don't start with that bullshit."

"Hey, will you just shut up and listen to me for a second? I'm not talking about the usual websites and forums where any moron with a Wi-Fi password can peddle any old garbage. I'm taking about...*premium access.*"

I almost burst out laughing.

"There are some very smart people on these pages, Margo. I'm talking borderline genius. Radical, in the truest sense of the word. It's scary and they provide genuine insight, *alternative* insight, probing narratives we're all supposed to accept."

I point to the gate. "I'm cold. Are you finished?"

His body deflates like a beach ball. Reluctantly, he takes a backwards step, never taking his eyes off me. "The Drummonds used you. You know that, don't you?"

I clench my jaw.

He reaches out like he's about to put his hand on my shoulder. Something stops him and his arm shoots back like a strip of retractable measuring tape. He's so intense it's comical.

"I can help you figure out what really happened to Darcy."

"Is that right?"

"Someone else took her off that beach. We both know that, don't we?"

It's not his words that bother me. It's the realisation that this creep and I are thinking along the same lines. Theories about the Drummonds have existed for years. Some are close to credible but most are outrageous nonsense. The 'someone else took her' line has come and gone. But now it's back and it's very sticky, at least in my mind. Steve is mirroring my own suspicions like he can see what's going on inside my head. Does that make me a conspiracy nut now?

"Mike Drummond," he says. "You want to be a good journalist? Take a closer look at Daddy."

"Why would I do that?"

"C'mon," Steve says, his upper body twitching like he's a sprinter on the starting blocks. "Don't play dumb. He's a serious gambling junkie. I mean, *serious*. And it goes way back to before Darcy went missing."

"Did the boys on premium access tell you that?" I say. "It's not exactly news that Mike's got issues."

"Margo, his debts are legendary. We're talking–"

"Steve," I say, cutting him off. "About five minutes ago, I asked you a question. I'll ask you one last time. What do you want?"

"I want us to help each other," he says. "I want us to be a team just like we used to be. Most of all, I want the *truth*."

I cringe.

"Steve," I say in a calm voice. "That family has been through hell. Leave them alone."

"Mike Drummond's gambling again," Steve says. "He's back at the Riverside in Glasgow. You should see the state of him, Margo. You think he'd be happy, wouldn't you? Having just got his daughter back after thirteen years."

I arch my eyebrows. "Life's more complicated than that."

He takes a step closer. I think he's going to reach for me again but he doesn't. Lucky break for him. "C'mon. Why don't we go into town and grab a bite to eat? Talk it through. I'll pay for the food even though you're loaded."

I walk past him and unlatch the gate.

"Night, Steve."

"C'mon," he says, his voice cracking. "This is *real* journalism."

My throat clenches as I walk up the path and shove my key in the door. He's still there at the gate, watching me like a hawk.

"Next time you see him," Steve says, "ask him outright what happened that day. Watch him squirm in his silk underwear."

I close the door and put my back against it. Mum doesn't hear me come in over the TV and it's just as well. I can't move. I can't breathe. The hallway spins like a fairground ride and just for a second, everything goes black. I'm out on my feet with the words *real journalism* ringing like a distant bell in my mind.

I SORT MYSELF OUT. Grab a glass of water from the kitchen and have a brief chat with Mum. She's quiet tonight. She's on her chair, feet on the table as usual. She doesn't ask what I've been up to and I'm grateful because I don't have the energy to explain or the will to lie to her. I'm hungry but all I can be bothered to make is a peanut butter sandwich which I take upstairs to my room with a cup of green tea.

I sit on the bed. The sandwich goes untouched and the tea is forgotten.

How far back do Mike's problems go? How bad did it get? And is there really a connection in all that to Darcy's disappearance?

The conspiracy nuts would love to see me struggling with this. They can't be wrong all the time, though, can they?

"What the fuck is wrong with you, Margo?" I say.

Having lost my appetite, I take the food and tea back downstairs. I say goodnight to Mum, then I get ready for bed. *Early night for me*, I think, trying to trick my mind, which is nowhere near ready to switch off. I brush my teeth, moisturise, then I'm under the covers. It goes as expected. I toss and turn but it's no good. I'm wired and the Drummond thing won't let go.

To hell with it.

There is something I could do.

I turn on the light. It's not even half past nine. I throw back the covers, get up and get dressed in a scruffy sweater and jeans combo. Insomnia chic. I close my bedroom door over. Then, I creep downstairs like a naughty teenager. The TV is on and it's loud enough for me to go unheard in the hallway. Sounds like she's watching a documentary about the Royal Family. She doesn't even like the Royals.

Oh Mum, I think.

I grab the car key off the hook. She won't notice it's gone, I hope. She'll be straight to bed once she's tired enough.

Once again, I feel like a teenager. It's like I'm sneaking out to meet a boy.

Hurrying outside, I unlock Mum's car, start the engine and back out the driveway. With any luck, Mum won't look out the window before she goes to bed and notice that her car is missing. Maybe I should text when I get there. Just to stop her from calling the police.

I follow the sign for the M8 and travel west to Glasgow. That's where the Riverside Casino is. I hope that's where Mike Drummond will be too.

It's a forty-five-minute drive. Once I reach Glasgow, I plod around the city centre trying to get my bearings. Finally, I park just off Argyle Street. I lock the car, then it's a short walk south towards the river.

The streets are quiet. A light rain falls.

A quick left onto Jamaica Street, then right at the Broomielaw, a major thoroughfare that runs adjacent to the north bank of the River Clyde.

The Riverside Casino is straight ahead. This is where Mike likes to spend his evenings. It's no secret to anyone who knows the Drummonds. Across the street, there's a late-night café. Not a lot of people inside. I walk in, order a black coffee and take a seat at the counter by the window. I've got the perfect view of the casino entrance.

I sip the coffee. It's not very good but my body welcomes it.

An hour passes before I see Mike and, holy shit, it's worse than I thought.

29

MARGO

It's almost midnight as the casino bouncers throw Mike onto the street.

It's gentle as far as these things go. The two hulks in black suits working the door aren't being overly aggressive, although they are standing a little too close to Mike, blocking the casino entrance in a way that looks like, *I dare you*. Mike won't dare. He isn't a wild-eyed drunk. His hands are up. Looks like he's apologising. Most likely, telling the bouncers that he'll be on his best behaviour if they'll only let him back in. The body language is classic. Submissive. Someone who doesn't want to be perceived as a threat.

One of the hulks shakes his head. Mike talks some more, then, with a casual shrug, gives up. He descends the steps and sort of falls off the kerb, his feet narrowly missing the camber as he lands on the road. He's a drunk mimicking sober. Hands shoved in his pockets. There's an indifferent expression on his face even though he's swaying from side to side. Mike's usually so well groomed but his shirt is hanging out at the waist. He glances at his big gold watch about three times, as if not sure what to do with himself. He laughs at some private joke. Then, the hands go back in and out of the pockets.

People stare. They're starting to recognise him.

I get up, leaving my coffee on the counter. I push the café door open and feel the drizzle on my face as I walk outside. Traffic check, then I hurry across the street. Mike's on wobbly feet in the middle of the Broomielaw as I grab him by the arm. He spins around at warp speed. Looks at me and there's no recognition in his eyes. In fact, it looks like he's about to yell all kinds of obscenities at me. That's the street kid, the one buried under the expensive clothes and jewellery.

Then, a flicker of recognition.

"Margo?"

"Hi, Mike."

He looks around in a panic, as if expecting to see Sophie standing across the road. Just the thought of it makes him look sober again. "What are you doing here?"

"C'mon," I say, dragging him away from the oncoming traffic. Some of the cars slow down for us. Others beep their horns and whizz past.

"You need coffee," I tell Mike as I steer him towards the pavement.

A van driver blares his horn at us as we cross the street. Hand gestures are made on both sides. Mike's about to yell something but I lock my arm tight around his and escort him off the road. I feel the eyes of Glasgow all over us.

We hurry into the café. The light from the ceiling feels like an attack.

I send Mike to a table in the corner and leave him there

while I order two black coffees. I'm flying on caffeine and adrenaline. Might as well keep the wings flapping.

There's a small scattering of customers. Glasgow's lonely souls. Fortunately for us, most of them are lost in their phones and paying no attention to anything else going on.

I sit down, tucking my wet hair behind my ears.

The coffees arrive quickly. Steam spirals from both cups and I thank the server, then push Mike's coffee across the table towards him. He looks at it like it's a cup of oil.

"Drink it," I say. "You need to sober up before you go home."

He takes a sip and pulls a face like it is oil. Then he leans into the table, looking across the street at the casino with the longing of an addict.

"I was on a real winning streak over there. Believe it or not."

"Everyone's on a winning streak," I say. "Until they start losing."

He laughs. "No, really. I was doing good tonight."

"Is that why they kicked you out?"

He turns away from the casino. Looks at me for a second, then lowers his eyes to the table. "You saw that?"

"I saw enough."

Mike braves the coffee again. "Yeah, well. I might have said some things I shouldn't have. It's no big deal."

He looks at his watch. My gut instinct tells me he's figuring out how long he can leave it before trying his luck with the bouncers. I hope I'm wrong.

"What are *you* doing here, Margo? Are you following me?"

"Not exactly."

"Not exactly?"

"Mike," I say. "I need to ask you some questions."

"For an article?"

"No. For curiosity's sake."

I lean forward across the table. Hands clasped. "How long does it go back?"

Mike's head flinches like I just landed a stiff jab to the temple. "Eh?"

"You're a gambling addict, Mike."

"Woah. Margo–"

"How long does it go back?"

Mike's about to protest but instead, he falls back into the chair. There's a sigh of defeat. He picks up the coffee cup and looks down like he's thinking about drowning himself in there.

"You know one of the best things about being drunk?"

I shrug. "The hangovers?"

He smiles. "Nope. It's the forgetting. For a few hours at least, I get to forget that the world knows so much about my life. About my failings."

"How long, Mike?"

He's still looking at the coffee. "Goes back to when I was a teenager. I was gambling before I was old enough to drink. That's what we did. A bunch of poor lads who dressed up and hustled our way into casinos for fun. We had nothing to lose either. But when we won...oh boy."

"I know things are hard at home right now," I say.

"Sophie told you that?"

"She did."

Mike's face shrivels up. "Aye," he says. "It's not what we expected, you know? Everything was supposed to just fix itself when we brought her home."

"Not realistic, is it though?"

"No."

I think about Steve's wild-eyed insistence that Mike had something to do with Darcy's kidnapping. And yet, there's not a shred of evidence against Mike or Sophie. People have been looking at them for years, accusing them of killing their child, willing them to be caught out, but it's all speculation. I'm not going to fall in line with Steve and his merry band of nutters. Not if I can help it.

"You're supposed to be the happiest man in the world," I say. "Didn't you read the papers?"

He nods. "I feel sorry for her."

"Why?"

Mike talks through gritted teeth. "After everything she's been through, Margo. That poor girl deserves better. It's always been strained at home, and that's what she's come back to. Strain. Tension. Weakness. Sophie's family sticking their noses in where it isn't welcome."

"Edward's hard work," I say.

The light from the ceiling makes Mike's skin look old and waxy. "They're horrible people. It's a different world, Margo. Old money. Privilege."

"I wouldn't know."

He laughs. "You're better off, believe me. Makes me wonder, though, if Darcy wasn't better off with the Burtons."

"You don't mean that."

Mike chews on his bottom lip. All the while, he keeps glancing at his giant wristwatch. "Nah, I suppose not."

"Is that why you're still chasing that once-in-a-lifetime jackpot?" I ask. "That's the only way you can compete with the Wallaces, right?"

I've never talked to Mike like this before. So frank. Tonight, it feels easy.

"An architect's salary is a good one," he says. "But it doesn't go far in my family."

"Not if you piss it away at the casino."

He nods. "Fair enough. I don't know why I'm like this. I love Sophie. I didn't fall in love with money."

His face hardens.

"I wish Edward would die."

He looks at me.

"Does that shock you?"

I shake my head. "Not really. I know he belittles you at every opportunity."

"He thinks his money makes him untouchable," Mike says. There's a grimace on his face. "I admit – he can be a charmer on the outside, but he's an evil old bastard."

"Don't hold back."

Mike doesn't hesitate. "Are you aware of the things he's done?" He leans across the table and the reek of whisky almost knocks me out cold. He lowers his voice to a whisper that almost escapes me. "Dirty old bastard likes younger women."

I sit back. "I've heard the rumours."

Mike looks at me. Shakes his head. "Not just rumours."

He looks around the café. Satisfied that no one's looking at us, Mike digs his phone out of his pocket and puts it on the table. I watch as he unlocks and scrolls to photos. He opens an album titled 'X'. Slides the phone closer to me.

"A screenshot," he says. "Taken from a forum."

"What's this?"

"Read it."

I take the phone, click on the image and zoom in. It's all text. A comment from a rusty-looking forum with a pale blue background. The comment was written by someone with the username 'Daisy'. The headline for the discussion is 'Rape Survival'.

I look at Mike.

Mike recognises that I'm about to speak. He shakes his head. "Read it."

I pinch the screen to enlarge Daisy's comment.

Hey, everyone. It's 1.41am here in London. I am so glad to be with you all tonight. It's good to know that I can reach out to other likeminded souls even when I'm hurting like this. Physically. Mentally. Spiritually. And all this pain because of a man, a rich man. All because of what he and his friends did to me. I'm scared to say his name anywhere, even here in a safe space. Fuck it, I will. I know that there are others on this forum who've hinted at the same man. Edward Wallace. He lives in Edinburgh. This man is a rapist.

I'm sixteen years old.

Mike shows me a few other screenshots taken from the forum, which he says no longer exists. Daisy's comment inspired a few others to come forward with their own stories. The subsequent discussion spares no detail when it comes to what Edward and a group of other men allegedly did to her at certain organised parties. It's graphic. Maybe it's the caffeine but I start to feel a little jittery.

"You get the picture," Mike says.

"Yep."

I slide Mike's phone back across the table. There's a sudden desire to wash my hands. "Has Edward ever been–?"

"Caught? Reprimanded? God no. As far as anyone in the

Wallace family is concerned, it's all filthy lies concocted by gold-diggers. And as I mentioned, that website no longer exists. It's amazing what money can do, isn't it?"

"So we don't know what became of Daisy? Or the others?"

Mike drinks the last of his coffee. His hand remains on the cup, soaking up the surface heat before it's gone. "God knows. I only hope they managed to get on with their lives."

"How did you find out?" I ask.

"About the forum?"

I nod.

"I think I was pissed off with him one night," Mike says. "Ended up browsing the internet, looking for dirt on Edward. I'd heard the rumours. Typed in the right keywords, I guess. God knows how many websites he's had taken down. Sick bastard."

"Why'd you keep the screenshot?" I ask.

Mike doesn't miss a beat. "Edward's obsessed with my failings. Well, here's a tangible reminder of his."

"Allegedly."

"Aye."

He wipes the back of his hand over his mouth. His stubble grates, harsh like sandpaper. Mike stares into empty space and when he finally talks, I'm not sure he's talking to me. "All I ever wanted was the sort of fuck-you money that would liberate us from Edward. I'm good in there. I know I can do it. But God knows that trying has gotten me into a lot of trouble."

I feel a flicker of excitement.

"What sort of trouble?"

"Long story."

"Try me."

"Not tonight. There's not enough coffee in the world for that story."

I fall back into my chair, disappointed. Light rain taps against the window. Radio-friendly pop music crackles out of the speakers. The door opens and a curly-haired woman walks in, closing her umbrella before she's fully inside. As she lingers there, she looks over at our table and I think I see a flicker of recognition in her eyes. It looks like she's going to come over and say – *are you Mike Drummond?*

Then it's gone. She walks to the counter and orders a takeaway tea.

I point my thumb across the street. "I don't think the casinos are going to make you a billionaire, Mike."

He smiles and drums his fingers on the table. I think the caffeine has given him a second wind. "I've been close, Margo. I've been so close."

"To billions?"

Mike shrugs and I don't take it as a yes.

"Whatever. You're not close now, are you? They just kicked you out and I doubt it's the first time either. Why don't you take the hint, Mike?"

His eyes burn as he looks towards the casino. "I'm good mates with Stu, the owner. I'll get back in."

"Go home to your family."

Mike's attention is back on me. The light catches the grey bags under his eyes. "I can't go home."

"You can and you should."

He nods like he agrees. Then he glances at his watch. Then, across the street. It's like watching an addict whose fix has been delayed. This isn't the Mike I know from the posh house in Morningside.

"Can I ask you a question, Mike?"

"Shoot."

"Did you look at Hattie's picture book?"

His face wrinkles into a frown. "Aye, I had a quick look at it. Can't say I was too impressed."

"One of the pages has been ripped out. Did you notice?"

His facial expression is neutral. "Is that right?"

"You don't know anything about that?"

"Me?"

Even now, he's only half-listening. About seventy percent of Mike Drummond is already across the street and back in the Riverside Casino. Shooting for the stars.

"Do you really think the Burtons were capable of grabbing Darcy on their own?"

"I have no idea what they were capable of, Margo."

"Of course," I say. "I'm just asking questions."

Mike chews on his bottom lip. "You don't think all those questions have been asked before, Margo? Like a million times? Read the books. Watch the documentaries. Sophie and I have been the prime suspects for years, at least according to the tabloid rags and everyone else who'd gladly profit from our worst nightmare. Even now they're saying we paid off the lab for a positive DNA test."

Mike stands up, zipping his jacket to the neck.

"Fuck them. Fuck all of them."

He points at the empty cup.

"Thanks for the coffee."

I stand up with him. "Forget the casino, Mike. C'mon. I'll give you a lift back to Edinburgh."

There's a pained look on Mike's face. He knows what the right thing to do is and yet he gives me a wave, then walks out. I take my coffee back to the counter at the window. As I slide onto a stool, I watch Mike cross the street and, sure enough, after a brief conversation with the two hulks, he's allowed back inside.

"Oh, Mike."

I should be in bed sleeping. I'll drive home as soon as I've finished my coffee. In the meantime, I check my phone. Three very long texts from Steve pop up, listing all the reasons that Mike's a suspect in the Darcy kidnapping.

I groan. There's no way I'll get any sleep tonight and, if I'm honest, I don't want to go home. Not just yet. I order a green tea, then sit at the window, watching the bright lights of the casino. The river is a black giant flowing behind it. On the street, a blur of people goes back and forth. It's the relentless churn of late-night Glasgow.

I'm dozing off when Mike appears at the casino door again. I sit up straight. Sort myself out. I glance at my watch and realise it's been three quarters of an hour since our conversation ended.

"What the fuck, Mike?"

He's not alone. There's a woman hanging onto his arm. Tall, blonde and statuesque. Covered in fake tan and, if I have to guess, I'll guess she's a pro. She must be freezing in that skimpy red dress. They're laughing like maniacs. Clinging onto each other for dear life as they descend the stairs and stagger along the pavement. Fuck. Mike's eyes are spinning – I can see that from across the street as well as I can see the fake tan. He doesn't even have his jacket on.

They walk away from the casino.

A lot of people are looking at them.

Oh boy, I think to myself. *The shit's going to hit the fan tomorrow.*

30

SOPHIE

Dad stands behind me in the living room, reading out the morning headlines on his phone. He's saved them all.

As if I haven't seen them already.

"*Gambling addict Drummond leaves casino with hooker!*" he barks in a voice that's loud enough to take the roof off. "And what about this one? *Family man Drummond's big night out in Glasgow.*"

Mum reads the next one. She's been scrolling through Google News on her iPad. Her voice is quieter but with no less disgust. Her porcelain-white skin looks like it's about to crack. "*Mike Drummond's gambling and sex shame revealed!*"

My parents are driving me crazy. Literally batshit crazy. Having them both here reading the headlines out loud to me is the last thing in the world I need right now. What next? Will they go on social media and read every single post?

My head is splitting.

"How could he do this to you?" Mum says, pacing the living room. Her cheeks are blazing red and her lips pursed.

"He's weak," Dad says, lowering his phone at last. "He's always been weak."

That last part. The way Dad says it and the way his face folds into a sour grimace of disapproval. Like he's blaming me for falling in love with Mike. For bringing him into this family. He turns around. Picks up one of the trashy tabloids he brought with him. Holds it up like a footballer holding a trophy. Mike's all over the front page, photographed leaving the Riverside Casino with a scantily clad woman whom Mum calls 'a professional'.

This all happened last night.

Mike hasn't come home. Hasn't texted. I have no idea where he is.

My parents' voices merge into a dissonant drone. I long to self-medicate. But...the kids. Someone has to be strong for the kids. They're in their rooms, all of them, and they know that something's wrong. They also have access to the internet.

I haven't even stopped to think about how this has made me feel. What concerns me is that I feel nothing.

Jimmy and Mary Gold came over this morning to help with the children. Our former employees would've seen the headlines early. They didn't call. They turned up at the door first thing this morning, asking if we needed help. The look on my face was all the answer they needed. Jimmy's upstairs now, playing with Lola. Mary's in the kitchen making smashed avocado for breakfast. I can smell the basil from here. God, I miss the old days when the Golds lived with us. Jimmy as night-watchman and Mary the cook. They were staff, friends and family wrapped up as one. It feels like a lifetime ago.

"I've failed Darcy," I say. "She wasn't supposed to come back to *this*."

Dad takes my arm and guides me to the armchair. "He's racking up debts again. You remember what happened last time, don't you?"

How could I forget?

I'm sitting down. Looking up at Dad who's like a giant towering over me. My voice sounds small – a whisper in the void. "This is a blip. We're just...exhausted."

Dad leans over me and I smell the citrus in his aftershave. He squeezes my shoulder. "He's weak. Darling, I tried to tell you all those years ago. Remember?"

I say nothing.

"I mean, where is he now? He should be here at your feet, grovelling for forgiveness."

"Still lying with his slut," Mum says. "That's where he is."

All the voices. I want them to stop. Then, I'll open the bedside drawer. Empty the bottle. Sleep it all away.

"Do you trust him?" Dad says, his eyes burning a hole in my head.

I'd be stupid to say yes and yet I still do. Mike *is* weak. He's a gambling junkie and a borderline alcoholic. But he's the only person in the world who understands what I've been through. And *I'm* weak too, although Dad never talks about that.

"Do you trust him?" Dad repeats.

I look at my parents and I realise that something else is going on. There's something strange about the way they're standing side by side. Stiff and formal.

Do you trust him?

"What's going on?" I ask.

It's Mum who inches forward. Her feet are so quiet it's

like she's floating across the living room. "You *do* remember what happened last time?"

"Yes."

"It got way out of control, Sophie darling. Mike put himself in serious debt with serious criminals. For God's sake, someone attacked you in the street. The kids were... how shall I put it...threatened."

My body tenses just thinking about it. "I remember."

"And then it stopped," Dad says. He clicks his fingers as if to exaggerate the point. "Just like that."

"I remember that too."

Dad comes closer now. He takes Mum's hand and squeezes tight like it's some sort of cue to proceed. Their unblinking eyes are all over me. "And what happened next?"

"We went to Bournemouth," I say. "We went to Bournemouth and Darcy was kidnapped."

"Darcy was kidnapped," Dad repeats.

My stomach lurches.

I find myself thinking about Hattie's diary. Someone *did* tear a page out of the book and I remember the way that Margo was banging on about Trevor and Hattie being incapable of escaping off that beach with Darcy. She sat right here in this living room, implying that someone else was involved.

I shake my head. The rattle of machinery in there gets louder.

Dad's fists are clenched at his sides. "That son of a bitch was involved." He leans over me. It feels like the entire house is leaning over me and blotting out the light. "Think about it, darling. Just think about it and you'll see what we've always seen – that there's a connection between Mike's debts and

Darcy's disappearance. We don't know all the details but there *is* a connection."

I sink deeper into the armchair. Dad's still talking but his voice fades into the dark corners of a waking nightmare. And in that same nightmare, I remember three small coffins sitting on my doorstep.

A warning from Mike's creditors.

31

MARGO

I walk along Argyle Street in the early afternoon drizzle. An old man in a flat cap is selling newspapers. His pitch is sheltered under the awning of retail behemoth Marks and Spencer. He smiles and I return the gesture. The shouty newspaper man yelling out the headlines seems so archaic. Still, in the digital era, it's not without its charms.

I look at the headline pinned to his stand. Or at least, I see the words that matter. *Mike Drummond. Gambling. Sex. Junkie. Debt.* Luring the paying customers in like flies to shite.

Here I am, back in Glasgow. I'm still not sure I'm doing the right thing. Mike's a big boy who can make his own decisions and there's no reason for me to feel guilty about what he did last night. But I do. I knew that Mike was an easy target for freelance photographers. Stalking him, hoping for a drunk Mike shot and getting something much better – a drunk Mike shot with a high-class sex worker on his arm. I should've tried harder to stop him going back into the casino. I might have been able to persuade him to come back to Edinburgh with me. Mike's the one who messed up, but in a way, I feel like I did too.

That nagging sense of guilt put me on the train from Edinburgh Waverley to Glasgow Queen Street. I have to do something to make it right. With the rain easing off, I take a left, heading away from the crowds on Argyle Street and back towards the casino which, according to my watch, opened seven minutes ago.

I walk inside, wincing at the scent of cleaning chemicals. Looks like I'm the first customer through the door today although customer isn't quite the right word considering my intent isn't to spend money. Cut glass chandeliers hang from the ceiling. I read once somewhere that chandeliers were a common feature in casinos because they were intended to create a dazzling atmosphere, fuelling the gambler's sense of delusion and thus encouraging them to spend large sums of money. I don't know about that. Then again, it works all the time. Look at Mike Drummond.

The floor is a tasteful blend of red floral carpet and wood. I walk towards the bar where a young man stands so motionless it looks like he's waiting to be switched on. My heels clack as I cross the wood.

"Afternoon," the bartender says, coming to life.

"Hi. I'm looking for the boss. Is he in?"

"You're looking for Mr Docherty?"

"Would that be Stu Docherty?"

He nods. "Yeah, that's him."

"He's in?"

"Sure, I think he's in the office. I'll go and check if he's available. Who shall I say is looking for him?"

I smile. "Just tell him it's a friend of Mike Drummond."

If eyes could smirk. "One moment, please."

"Thanks," I say, watching the bartender go.

He walks across the vast casino floor, disappearing behind a panelled door. I wait with my elbows propped on the counter, wondering if Mike's been home yet. I need to check on Sophie later. God knows what Edward and Liz have been filling her head with this morning. There's no excuse for what Mike did, of course, but Edward and Liz are the last thing she needs. The gloating. The I-told-you-so. The constant pecking at her ears.

I wonder if she wants to save her marriage.

Welcome home, Darcy. By the way, Mum and Dad are getting divorced. Which one of us do you want to live with?

Damn, the casino is quiet at this time. Still, the lunchtime customers will be on their way, and I try to imagine what sort of people want to spend their lunch hour in a casino.

People like Mike.

I hear the panelled door open. Footsteps and hushed voices approach from behind. I turn around, watching as the barman and the manager walk towards me. The barman gives me a smile, then slips around the counter. He starts moving glasses and bottles around. Doing a little cleaning. Acting like he's busy in front of the boss.

"Can I help you?" asks the manager.

Stu Docherty is about forty. One glance is all I need to know that the man has got a serious addiction to tanning beds. His skin falls somewhere in between bronze and tangerine. He's slim, well-dressed in an expensive-looking suit.

He smiles after his question. The man's teeth are so white that I should've brought sunglasses.

"Mr Docherty?"

"Call me Stu," he says, thrusting his orange hand towards me. I shake it and wonder if my hand will glow in the dark tonight. "What can I do for you?"

"My name is Margo Martin."

"Of course. The famous journalist."

Famous? A smile breaks out on my face and I hate myself for it. Am I famous? Or is this guy laying on the charm thick?

"That's me."

"I liked your article."

My jaw tightens. "Thank you."

"Can I get you something to drink?" Stu asks, gesturing towards the bar. "On the house."

I wave the offer away. "No, thanks. I won't keep you long. I just want to talk to you about something."

"For which publication? Website?"

"Oh no," I say. "This isn't a professional visit. Don't worry about that. I'm here as a family friend to the Drummonds."

Stu nods but doesn't look surprised. "Okay."

We relocate to a four-seater table near the bar. As we sit down, I hear the door open and the sound of voices and footsteps coming closer. I glance over my shoulder. Three twenty-somethings, dressed in slick suits and good shoes, have entered the building. Clean shaven. Bottle tans. Looks like the bankers' lunch hour getaway. They head straight for the bar.

Stu gives them the once-over. Then he looks at me. "How can I help you, Margo?"

"I'm sure you're busy," I say. "So I'll get straight to the point."

"Please do."

"I want you to put a lifetime ban on Mike Drummond. Force him to stop him coming in here and destroying his family's life."

Stu frowns. "If he can't come here, he'll go to another casino."

The way he says it.

Mansplaining prick.

"That's out of your control," I say. "But it would be a start. This is Mike's favourite haunt and you own the place, don't you?"

Stu crosses his legs and flicks a speck of fluff off his suit trousers. Already, I'm getting the impression he's bored. "I co-own it. This one here and another casino in Edinburgh, one in Aberdeen and London."

I don't recall asking him for a list.

"Mike's gambling has to stop," I say. "I'm sure you've seen the headlines this morning."

"I know all about Mike's gambling," Stu says, a smarmy grin emerging. "But when all's said and done, Margo, he's a grown man and he can do whatever he wants with his money. *His* money, yeah?"

"So, you don't care?"

"It's hardly my place to intervene. If I take an interest in Mike's private life, does that mean I have to follow up on everyone who comes in here? Make sure they get a taxi home? Fix them a hot chocolate? Tuck them in and tell them a story?"

I clench a fist under the table. What I really want to do is ram it into Stu's orange face.

"He's an addict," I say. "Quite often, intervention is required with addicts. And yet you let him in here every other night. Even last night, he got back in after being thrown out. I guess Mike's got a lot of money to spend, eh?"

Stu shakes his head. "I've known Mike a long time. He's doing okay. Last night was a blip."

"He's doing okay? Are you serious?"

Stu glances at the trio of customers loitering at the bar. Then he leans a couple of inches over the table. His eyes narrow and he lowers his voice. "You think it's bad now? You should've seen him back in the day."

"Go on," I say.

"What's that?"

"Tell me how bad it was back in the day."

He glances around the casino and it seems like he's checked out of the conversation. I wonder if I'm keeping him away from the tanning salon.

"I've known Mike for years," he says, suppressing a yawn. "We go way back to my first casino in Edinburgh. The one on Leith Street. Mike's always been cavalier, to put it mildly, and that was long before Darcy went missing."

"Stu, if you know how bad it was, you know how bad it could get again. Right?"

There's no reaction on Stu's face. His voice is a Glaswegian monotone that sounds like it was pre-recorded on downers. It's only the sight of his lips moving that convinces me otherwise. "Everyone lets off steam in their own way. I don't think Mike would be a lot of fun to be around if he wasn't allowed out to play."

It feels like I'm talking to a brick wall.

"You know Mike, right?" Stu asks.

I nod.

"Then you know all about his money hang-ups. The poor slum kid who married into the Wallace family."

Stu's phone lights up on the table. He glances at it, decides the notification isn't important enough and flips it over. "Ever been a poor council estate boy who married into one of the wealthiest families in the country?"

"Can't say I have."

"Me neither. Sounds good, doesn't it? Like one of life's lucky breaks and yet Mike carries it around like a cross on his back."

"How bad was it?" I ask. "Back in the day."

Stu backs off, holding up both hands like I just pulled a gun on him. "I think I've said quite enough."

I break out my best shit-eating grin.

"How would you like me to include you and your business in a follow-up story about the Drummonds?"

"Come again?"

"I'm good at digging, Stu. It's my job. If I start digging around here, what will I find?"

There it is. A pinprick of doubt appears in Mr Orange's eyes, and it's beautiful.

"Dig away," he says, slowly leaning back in the seat. "You'll find a trail of successful and legal business practices."

I cling to my evil grin. "Cool. Maybe I'll start with the sex worker that Mike left with last night. I'm sure it won't be hard to track her down. I wonder what she'll tell me about this place. About what goes on in the back rooms."

Stu sits forward. "I don't know much about Mike's history."

"But you go way back," I say. "You've had a front row seat and I'm sure you and Mike have had more than a few late-night chats over a nightcap. Mike's talkative when he's drunk, isn't he?"

A squeal of laughter from the bar. The drinks are in and

the bankers are loosening up while the casino begins to hum. More customers appear. Various staff members walk back and forth, taking up position at the tables. Frank Sinatra's voice trickles out of the speakers at low volume. Soon this place will be in full swing.

"What do you want to know?" Stu asks.

"Tell me about Mike's past. About the old gambling problems that put the new ones to shame."

Stu checks his nails for so long that I think he's trying to catch his reflection in them. I have to admit, they're impeccably manicured. Certainly put mine to shame. Finally, he looks up. "Two words. Astronomical debts."

"Go on."

"Millions."

I hold my poker face despite the whooshing sensation in my gut.

"Millions?"

Again, I notice Stu looking around the casino. Eyeing the customers. He shifts around in his seat constantly, fidgeting with the lapels of his jacket.

"I never said any of this. Okay, Margo? This conversation didn't happen."

I almost laugh out loud but okay. I'll play.

"What conversation?"

He nods. "It got bad for Mike. Really bad."

"How do you know this?"

"You're right," he says. "Mike *is* a talkative drunk. And he'll confide in anyone after a few too many drinks."

Stu runs a finger down his lapel. Looks like he's checking for dust.

"And?"

He shoots me an impatient glare. "Mike's always had a great job. Great salary too but it wasn't enough to fill the gaping hole inside. That poor bastard thinks he reeks of the gutter. Of the slums. Edward Wallace did that to him."

"That's why he gambles," I say. "It makes him feel like a winner. Plus, there's always the chance of hitting the jackpot."

Stu gives a dismissive wave of the hand. "It's a pipe dream. Mike's a decent enough gambler but if you aim that high you're going to have to be exceptionally fortunate or rack up a hell of a lot of debt trying."

"He kept losing?"

"Sure did. And he kept coming back."

I shrug. "Okay, so he borrowed money. Where? From you? From the casino?"

Stu smiles on one side of his mouth. "No. Lending money isn't my business. He took a loan from some very... unscrupulous people."

"Loan sharks?"

"Correct."

"You know these people?"

"Not personally."

I nod. "And he lost all that money too?"

"He lost it big time."

I exhale. My throat's dry and I wish I'd taken that drink. I think about asking for a glass of water but I don't want to interrupt the flow of conversation.

"What happened?"

Stu studies my face like there's an exam coming. I wonder if he thinks I'm testing him. That I know this already and want to see if he's bullshitting.

"What happened?" he says. "The moneylenders wanted their money back with interest. That's what always happens. Mike didn't have it. Threats were made against his life but sometimes the best way to make people sit up and take notice isn't to threaten them. You threaten their family."

I try to keep my poker face. "They went after–?"

"That's right," Stu says, cutting in. "Sophie was mugged in Edinburgh city centre. In broad daylight. Did she ever tell you that?"

"No."

"Did she tell you that three child-sized white coffins were sent to the house?"

The cold shoots down my spine. "Shit."

He nods. "I'll take that as a no."

One of the lunchtime customers laughs manically in the background and it sounds like madness from another world seeping into our conversation.

"I'm not talking about small-time moneylenders," Stu says. "These weren't the sort of people working out the back of a van handing out fifty-pound notes to junkies who couldn't pay their electricity bill. This was big time. Highly organised. No matter what, you paid these people back."

I'm speechless. Literally. Nothing comes out of my mouth.

"Then," Stu says, "it all stopped."

"What stopped?"

"The threats. The intimidation. It stopped. It all went away. Poof."

My voice is a hoarse croak. My throat, as dry as a desert. "Let me guess. All this happened approximately thirteen years ago?"

"Bingo. One minute, Mike's family was in grave danger. And the next, they weren't. Make of that what you will."

I feel lightheaded.

"I need to get back to work," Stu says, pushing his chair back. "But it's been a pleasure talking to you, Margo."

There's a dazed smile on my face as I zip up my jacket. He offers his hand across the table and I take it. "Thanks for the info."

"So, you're a friend of the family?" he says.

"That's right."

"Will you be going to visit anytime soon?"

"Maybe. Why?"

"Mike left his jacket in the cloakroom last night. Our lost and found stuff tends to vanish if it's left lying around too long. And after last night, I don't think we'll be seeing Mike around here for a while. It's an expensive coat."

"Right," I say, still feeling like I'm waking up from a dream. "I can take the jacket back."

Stu's already walking away. "Thanks. I'll go get it."

He comes back a few minutes later and hands over the jacket. It's long and bulky, sort of like a pea coat. It's heavy and not the easiest thing to carry around but I take it. It's a good excuse to check in with Sophie and see how she's doing. It does mean I'll have to come up with a reason for being at the casino in the first place. Fuck it, the truth will be a lot easier.

I thank Stu for his time and assure him I won't be writing about the casino anytime soon. With the coat folded under my arm, I walk towards the exit, only stopping for a slip of folded paper that falls out one of the many pockets.

I pick it up. Notice that one of the folded sections is

peeled back about an inch. That's all I need to see the colours. It's all I need to see that this is a drawing.

"Holy shit," I say.

I stand there, blocking the casino doorway. Staring at the slip of paper in my hand. I know what it is without unfolding the rest of it.

I *know* what it is.

It's the missing page in Hattie's diary.

32

MARGO

The sound of a blaring car horn almost gives me a heart attack.

I stop in the middle of the road.

"Sorry," I call out.

The woman in the red Tesla is glaring at me through the windscreen. She makes an impatient sweeping gesture with her hand, brushing me off the road. I lip-read a barrage of swear words. After a second apology, my legs remember their purpose and I make it across the road in one piece.

It feels like I'm floating. Ever since walking out of the casino, I've been looking at the sheet of paper that fell out of Mike's pocket.

I can't think straight.

I need a drink. That and to get myself off the streets before I walk in front of another car.

"C'mon," I tell myself. "Get a grip."

I walk on autopilot back to Argyle Street. My skin feels like it's burning underneath my clothes. A tight pinching sensation flares up at the back of my neck. And on my chest.

Feels like insect bites. Feels like I'm under attack. God, it's so busy. Hordes of people walk past, unaware of the turmoil swirling around inside me. I'm falling. I can't seem to remember the layout of the city centre.

Eventually, I stumble upon the Admiral Woods pub on Waterloo Street. It looks quiet so I go inside. I'm met with the sound of the Manic Street Preachers on the radio. It's a newish place by the looks of it. Feels a little too polished around the edges. No wear and tear. No scars on the table. Too shiny. Like a new pair of shoes that hasn't been taken outside yet.

I get my shit together, at least enough so I can order a white wine at the bar. I thank the young woman at the counter, then take my drink over to one of the booths. Away from the window. Away from the street.

My palms are sweating. There's a horrible ringing noise in my ears that I can't shake off.

I take off my coat and throw it down on the bench along with Mike's jacket. Then, slowly, as if handling sensitive explosives, I place the ripped page on the table in front of me. I start to unfold it.

The pub door opens and I almost jump out of the seat.

"Fuck."

A grey-haired man with a wild shock of white hair walks past my table and orders a pint of Tennent's Lager at the bar.

I compose myself.

Back to the sheet of paper on the table. The edges curl upwards, exposing the creases. I slide my fist over the surface, flattening the page out as best I can.

There's no doubt about it. This is the missing page from Hattie's diary. That aggressive, childlike scrawl is unmistakable. The imprecise colouring. Squiggly lines. It's the work of an unsteady hand and yet despite the poor craftmanship, it's easy to understand what the image represents.

I drink. Then, I study the picture.

I see the yellow blob of sun hanging in the sky. It's a common feature in the journal, almost as if Hattie puts it there on auto-pilot. The sky itself is a hazy scribble of blue, and the golden-brown sand at the foot of the page intermingles with a choppy sea that's made up of a series of waves with pointed shark-fin tips. There are lots of pinkish swirls on the sand. People. Lots of stick arms and legs poking out of them. It's crowded, just like it was in real life that day on Bournemouth Beach.

Two people in the foreground. Bigger than all the other stick people filling up the beach. This is the centrepiece image of Hattie's beloved journal and I think I know why. One of the stick people is handing over a smaller stick person to the other one. A child.

I focus on the stick man handing the child over.

Another sip of wine.

It's a generic drawing of a man with a mop of brown hair. It could be anyone in the world if not for the giant dot of yellow beaming on the man's wrist. It looks like a miniature sun. But it's a watch. It's Mike's gold watch.

"Oh shit."

Those watches are his trademark. They're big, oversized and disgusting. Just another symbol of Mike's pathetic need to belong with the Wallaces. *I'm rich! I'm someone.*

"Mike tore it out," I whisper.

I finish the wine, get up and order another. Back at the table, I try to put the pieces together. Darcy wanted Hattie's picture journal back for whatever reason, so the police hand it over when they're finished with it. Mike saw it. He looked through it in a panic. He saw *that* page and ripped it out, most likely intending to burn it at the first opportunity. The police must have dismissed the drawings. What about Sophie? Probably too drugged up to the eyeballs to notice. Or maybe Mike tore out the page before anyone else had a chance to look through the book. And why would Sophie be looking for anything? There were no mysteries left to solve. Darcy was found. Her identity was confirmed through DNA testing. Trevor and Hattie were dead. What was the point in looking at childish pictures?

I look outside onto Waterloo Street. Traffic is steady. Everyone that walks past looks like they haven't got a care in the world.

The mysterious caller put me on to this. I'm fairly certain it wasn't Steve. So, who was it? Who wants me to point the finger at Mike?

I fold up the sheet of paper. Put it in my bag. The wine feels like arsenic swirling around in my guts. A thought occurs to me. What if Stu texts Mike and lets him know that I've got his coat? That's not a comforting thought.

Mike knows that the drawing is in his pocket. He'll go batshit crazy when he realises that he left the coat at the casino. That makes me a problem.

One more glass of wine, I think, turning back to the bar.

For medicinal purposes.

33

MARGO

I turn off my phone once I'm back in the house. Seeing or talking to anyone else right now is the last thing I want. My head's all over the place and I need time to think. Fortunately, Mum's out of the house for a few hours, having tea with friends, followed by a library stop late afternoon.

The curtains are pulled in the bedroom. I'm standing in the gloom, listening to a car driving slowly up the street. The engine growls and fades. A bird scurries across the roof. The flapping of wings explodes outside the window.

I'm on edge. My hands twitch, my pulse throbs and the constant sensation of falling keeps me off balance.

I think about Mike in the café last night. Was I really sitting across from the man who handed Darcy over? Were the conspiracy nuts right all along? I recall the way that Mike showed me those forum screenshots about Edward. Was Mike, perhaps feeling the walls closing in, trying to create a diversion?

Look at Edward. Look at what a monster he is.

Well, Edward might be a twisted old shit. He might deserve to get his dick tasered for what he's done, but right now I'm looking at Mike. That *is* the gold watch in Hattie's drawing. I'm sure of it. Mike always thinks that someone is looking at him and I've no doubt he would've taken his best and most eye-catching bits of jewellery on holiday to Bournemouth. It certainly caught Hattie's eye.

My phone rings on the bedside table. The noise almost stops my heart. Fuck. I thought I'd switched it off but turns out I couldn't even manage that simple task. What the hell is wrong with me?

I pick it up, not recognising the number on the screen.

Ignore it, says the voice in my head. And yet, I know I can't. I hit the green button and jam the phone against my ear.

"Hello?"

"Margo, how are you?"

My heart gallops at the sound of Mike's voice.

I sit down on the bed. Maybe I fall. Mike never calls me. I try to talk but it feels like my tongue is swollen in my mouth.

"Mike, is everything okay?"

Stupid question. He's all over the news for the wrong reasons.

Despite this, he sounds bright and chipper. A little hoarse. "Oh yeah, no worries. I messed up but this might be the wake-up call I need to get my act together."

"How's Sophie?"

"Getting there."

"Are you back at the house?"

"I am. It's tense but...we're working through it."

I stare at Mike's coat hanging over the back of my chair.

Hattie's drawing isn't in his pocket anymore. It's in my handbag and I've got no idea what I'm going to do with it.

"What can I do for you, Mike?"

"Heard you went to the casino earlier."

Oh shit.

It feels like there's an electrical short circuit in my heart. I suck in a lungful of stale bedroom air and push my back against the wall. Fucking Stu, orange-faced bastard. He told Mike and now Mike knows I've got his jacket. He's an addict but he's not stupid. He must be wondering whether I've found what was in his pocket.

"Yeah, I did."

He laughs but it's forced. "What did you go there for?"

My hands are shaking. "Listen, Mike, I'm Sophie's friend. And I'm yours too for that matter. I feel bad about letting you go back into the casino last night. I should've dragged you away kicking and screaming."

"It's my mistake," he says. It's the first thing he's said that sounds genuine. "You're not responsible."

"Still," I say. "I should've tried."

The hoarseness creeps further into his voice. "Stu says you have my jacket."

All this heat from the media and his family, I think. *And you're worried about a jacket?*

"I have it."

"Appreciate you picking it up, Margo. Saves me the embarrassment of going back there. I'll drive over to your house and collect it. How does right now sound?"

I nearly fall off the bed.

"Can it wait? It's...not that cold outside, is it?"

What a stupid thing to say. I'm even blushing.

Mike laughs. "But you *are* home right now, aren't you?"

There's a jolt of panic. I throw my legs over the side of the bed and stand up. Did Mike follow me from the train station? For all I know, that was his car I heard driving along the street a few minutes ago. Was it? Is he parked outside the house right now, fully aware that I'm home alone?

"Margo?"

The phone slips in my sweaty grasp. "What's that?"

"You okay?"

The fucker's toying with me. "I'm fine."

"Great," he says. "Oh, there's just one other thing. It's awkward but...well...I have to ask."

"Okay."

"I saw the guy who took those pictures last night. The ones that are all over the internet of me leaving the casino."

You and the sex worker.

"What about him?"

Mike exhales in my ear. "He looks a lot like that guy you used to go out with. The one we met at Mick Johnson's pool party. Remember?"

Mick Johnson's pool party was the first 'posh' party I'd been to at Sophie's invitation. It was an indoor pool, of course. Scotland, for God's sake. It was in St Andrews. I can't believe I took Steve to a fancy house like that but I did. And somehow, Mike remembers him.

"What are you saying, Mike?"

"Every good reporter has their photographer. Isn't that right?"

"I see. Do you really think I was working last night? Do you think I recorded our conversation too?"

Mike sighs down the line. "No, I don't. That was out of line. I apologise, Margo."

I've known this guy for a while but right now it feels like

I'm talking to a stranger. *Enough of this bullshit*, I think. I want to ask him – *were you involved in Darcy's disappearance?* I want to scream and make his ears bleed.

"Shouldn't you be with Sophie right now?"

"I will. Right after I stop by your place."

"Don't."

"Sorry?"

The words trip over my tongue. "Don't go to my Mum's house, Mike. I'm not there and neither's the jacket. Listen, I'll get it back to you soon. Don't worry, it's safe."

"It won't take–"

"Bye."

I hang up before he can say anything else. Then, I hurry over to the bedroom window on shaky legs. I peel back the curtains, wince at the light and see a few parked cars. A woman dressed in activewear pushing a pram. No sign of Mike's fancy Audi.

Fuck, my heart's in my throat.

I stare at Mike's jacket. The phone rings again but I ignore it. Instead, I go downstairs and check that all the doors are locked.

34

SOPHIE

Mike's home. I can hear him now, rattling around in the bedroom. He's making a racket like he's turning the house upside down.

We haven't talked. Instead, we exchanged frosty glances across the living room. Neither one of us has the energy for a confrontation right now and that's not a good idea while the kids are in the house. The *I-can't-believe-what-you've-done* argument will have to wait. Thank God my parents have gone home. Mike seems agitated, almost as if he's the one who woke up to see tabloid pictures of his soulmate leaving the casino with a sex worker. This wouldn't have been a good time for Dad to provoke him.

What's he doing in the bedroom?

Is he looking for something?

I hope he's not in major debt again. I literally feel sick when I think about the people who came after us before. Nightmares still plague me from time to time. With all that in mind, the fact that Mike slept with another woman seems trivial. It's not, but I'm trying to prioritise my children's safety.

Jesus, Mike.

He's ransacking the bedroom up there. Definitely sounds like he's looking for something. Money?

"Mum?"

I turn around and, to my surprise, Darcy's standing at the living room door. I didn't hear her approach. This is the first time I've seen her long blonde hair tied back into a ponytail. She's dressed in a black t-shirt and blue jeans with white trainers on her feet. One hand is thrust deep into her pocket. The other is holding on to a tall glass of water. She's looking up to the ceiling, towards our bedroom.

"Is Dad okay?" she asks.

I manage a smile for her. "He's fine. He's absolutely fine."

"What's he doing?"

"Umm, I'm not sure. I think he's looking for something."

This is the most animated I've seen Darcy since we brought her back from the police station. Usually, she's a cross-legged statue sitting in front of the TV. Sleeping in the bedroom, her door locked. Not now. It's her eyes, I think. They're so bright and alert. It's like she's woken up all of a sudden after being asleep for weeks.

"I'm sorry," she says.

"For what?"

"For what he did to you."

I want to go to her but she's inching out of the door and into the hallway. Even if this is only a flying visit, it's our best interaction yet.

"I'll be okay, sweetheart," I say. "Thanks."

Darcy walks out but before that, she raises the glass of

water in her hand. "I'll go check on him. He might be thirsty."

I nod. "I'll be in the kitchen," I say. "If you need me."

"Thanks."

I'm listening to Darcy on the stairs when I'm interrupted by a chirp from the phone in my pocket. Darcy's footsteps recede to a whisper on the upstairs hallway. When I can't hear her anymore, I take the phone out my pocket and see a text waiting from Margo.

I read it twice. As I do, an uneasy feeling rises in my stomach. Feels like a knot being tightened.

> Where are you? We need to talk about
> Mike. Urgent.

35

MARGO

It took me almost an hour to pluck up the courage to text Sophie. I edited the text about a hundred times. Read it aloud. Deleted it. Rewrote it. Edited it. An hour, no kidding.

All the while, I kept waiting for a car to pull up outside the house. The driver's door slamming shut. Mike's urgent footsteps coming up the garden path. A polite knock on the door followed by fists pounding on the glass.

It didn't happen.

At least, it hasn't happened yet. But Mike's on the way, I can feel it.

That's why I have to get to Sophie first.

We've arranged to meet in the city centre in an hour. We'll sit down in Princes Street Gardens and I'll tell her about Hattie's picture in Mike's pocket. Shit, I'll tell her straight that I think Mike was involved in Darcy's disappearance. That it's connected to his gambling. To those staggering debts he racked up. It won't go well. This will be the end of my friendship with Sophie. I don't expect her to nod along and agree that, yes, somehow the man she loves gave up their eldest child because it was that or Sophie and the other kids were dead too.

Or...who knows?

Maybe something will click for Sophie. Despite the horror of this revelation, maybe she's always had her suspicions but kept them buried deep down, her rational mind unable to accept it. The family were in serious danger back then. Sophie got mugged. The kids were threatened. And then it all just stopped.

But I'm not an idiot. It's going to be painful. Most likely, Sophie will call me crazy and walk away.

Still, I have to say it.

Outside, the low growl of another car on the street. They all seem to be moving in slow motion. My blood runs cold until it recedes into the distance.

Mike's on to me. He knows I've found the missing page, I'm sure of it. He'll have called the casino, asking Stu if the cleaners picked up a piece of paper off the floor. He might have driven over there to check. And when he couldn't find it, that's when he knew it was still in his jacket pocket.

The house has never felt smaller. I need to get outside. The weight of Mike's dirty little secret is too much.

A sudden knock on the door nearly kills me. I clamp a hand over my mouth.

Did someone creep up to the door?

I walk on my tiptoes, stopping at the top of the stairs. Crouching to a half-squat, I stare down at the front door and make out a blurred figure on the other side of the frosted glass. Is it him? Did he park somewhere else and walk to the house?

What the hell do I do?

Another knock.

"Parcel delivery."

It's a woman's voice.

I almost pass out with relief. Okay, where did *she* park because I never heard the van? Damn it. Looks like Mum's been ordering stuff on Amazon again. Her life's never been the same since she discovered online shopping.

That knock took a year off my life. Swear to God.

I gulp a lungful of air, then walk downstairs and open the door. The delivery driver smiles, and why not? She has no idea. I sign for Mum's package and as she turns back down the garden path, I look over her shoulder. Do a quick check. Every parked car on both sides of our little street – do I recognise it? Is there a silver Audi anywhere? What if Mike's using a rental today to fend off reporters?

It would be easier for him to use a rental. I envision Mike laying out the plastic sheet in the boot. Patting it down. Smoothing out the wrinkles with his gloved hands. Leaving just enough room to fit a tiny female journalist in there. Knock me out. Wrap up the body, then take a drive to the coast.

"Shut up," I bark at myself.

I put the parcel on the floor for Mum to find later. Then I back away, my nerves shredded. The thought of going out terrifies me. The thought of staying in is worse.

I have to do this for Darcy. The girl is traumatised and potentially fucked for life. She's a wreck of a child in a young woman's body, staring at cartoons instead of engaging with life.

And all because of Mike.

Right now, I'm the only person that can expose him. I know it but Mike knows it too. It's a race against time.

I have to go.

I've got to get to Sophie before he gets to me.

36

MARGO

I did it. I'm outside at last. A nervous wreck, looking over my shoulder every few seconds as I hurry towards the bus stop. I'm still not sure if I've seen too many movies or if I've got good reason to think someone's after me.

I've already checked the Uber situation and the wait is too long. I'd rather keep moving. Wait in a public bus stop. Hopefully there'll be other people waiting for a bus to the city centre.

I lock the front door and walk down the garden path. Open the gate. Close it. Turn left and from there it's a short walk to the bus stop. Every little noise is like a plane crashing out of the sky. Voices. The flapping of bird wings. Machinery chugging along in the distance. Everything feels like an attack.

I'm okay until I see someone step out of a car that's parked up ahead. It all happens so fast. A hunched figure crosses the road towards me. It's a man. He's waving his arms.

"Margo!"

It's Steve.

"My God," I say, narrowing my eyes. I'm about to unleash hell when I see his face. It's red and puffed up on both sides. There's a jagged gash above his left eye that's leaking blood. His posture upon approach is stooped, one hand clamped against his ribs. He looks at me with a glazed expression.

"What happened to you?" I ask.

He talks through gritted teeth. Pain in every hard-fought syllable. "Mike Drummond. That's what happened to me."

There's a cold wriggling sensation in my stomach.

"What?"

Steve's swaying. I reach out and grab him to stop him tipping over.

"I think you need to go to a hospital."

"No."

"At least sit down then."

He shakes his head and then starts to talk like it's a race. "Crazy bastard jumped me. God knows how he found me but he did. Jumped me from behind. Knocked me off balance and before I knew it, I was down on the pavement. Taking punches. Kicks to the head. *Be careful who you take pictures of.* That's what he said while he was killing me. What if I've got brain damage?"

No one will notice, I think.

"So, it was you taking photos last night?"

He gives me a sheepish look. "Is that really the pressing concern here, Margo? I've been assaulted."

"I guess I should be thankful," I say. "Thankful you didn't sell any photos of me helping Mike across the street. Or of us drinking coffee together."

Steve shrugs. "I'm gathering evidence."

"You've been stalking the guy. Waiting for the perfect photo opportunity. Well, I hope you got paid."

"It wasn't like that," Steve says, rubbing his swollen jaw. His words are thick and slurred. It's almost comical. "This is bigger than that. This guy's a scumbag. He has to be brought to justice for what he did."

"How do those photos help do that?"

Steve's swaying again. "They reveal his true character."

I can't handle this right now.

"Steve, maybe you should back off, okay? Head injuries are no joke. You shouldn't even be driving, for God's sake."

There's a noise behind me. I spin around and see one of the neighbours pushing his wheelie bin to the edge of the curb for emptying.

"Bit jumpy," Steve says. "Aren't we?"

"I have to go," I say.

Steve dabs a finger over his eye. He looks at the blood on his fingertip and winces. "There's something else you should know, Margo."

"What?"

"Mike Drummond thinks we're a team. He thinks we're working together – that you're the writer and I'm the photographer."

"He said that?"

"Pretty much."

I groan like I'm the one who's beat up. "Why are you here, Steve? What do you expect me to do?"

Steve raises his wheezy voice, a hand still pressed to his ribs. "Margo, enough of this bullshit. You have to see this guy for what he is. He's scum. A monster. He gave his daughter away like a piece of used clothing!"

My already shredded nerves aren't getting any better.

"We're not safe," he says, grimacing in response to a jolt of internal pain. "That's what I came here to tell you. To *show* you. Drummond's a loose cannon. He'll do anything to stop the truth coming out about Darcy. And that means keeping us silent."

My head tilts to one side. "Us?"

"He thinks we're a team."

"We are most definitely *not* a team," I say, sidestepping the hunched figure of my ex-boyfriend. "Now, if you don't mind, I've got to–"

He grabs my forearm. His face is red and twisted with pain. "This guy's dangerous. We need to stop portraying him as a distraught father."

I feel the weight of the neatly folded slip of paper in my jacket pocket. All that matters right now is getting to the city centre and telling Sophie what I've discovered. This is none of Steve's business. It's not something for him to brag about on his forums or whatever to his incel pals. If this is true about Mike, it's a tragedy. And it'll probably break Sophie. But she has to know. She has to see the drawing and come to her own conclusion about whether Mike's hiding something or not. After that, she can do what she wants. But I'll have done all I can.

I pull my arm out of Steve's grip.

"I need to go."

"Margo, wait–"

This time, I walk past him. "Get that cut looked at."

I ignore Steve's ongoing protests and set off towards the bus stop. I walk quickly, crossing the road as a silver transit approaches. Shit. I envision it skidding to a halt beside me at the kerb, the side doors sliding open and a pair of rough hands pulling me inside.

Get in here, you interfering bitch!

The van whooshes past.

I keep walking. One foot in front of the other, that's how it's done. That's how I'll get there. Where is Mike now? He's under a lot of strain with today's headlines but being a gambling junkie and an alcoholic are things he can come back from. He can't come back from his involvement in Darcy's kidnapping. That's the sort of thing they'll bring back public executions for. And if they can't put a literal rope around his neck, they'll kill him in other ways. Crucifixion by media. Either way, he's finished.

He needs that drawing. He's got a tiny window of opportunity to get it and keep me quiet.

I think about Steve's pulpy face.

What will Mike do to me?

There's a squeak of brakes behind me.

Fight or flight kicks in. I'm about ready to break the world record in sprinting when I turn around. Sophie's head pokes out of the passenger side window of a silver Audi. But it's not Mike's car. Edward is sitting behind the wheel. Looking at me through the windscreen like I'm some strange, undiscovered species of animal.

My legs almost give out.

"Sophie?"

I walk over to the car. "What are you guys doing here?"

Sophie tries to smile but something's wrong. Panic fills her eyes. Her skin is so white it's translucent. She gets out the car. Walks toward me.

"Have you seen Darcy or Mike?"

"No. Why? What's happened?"

Sophie's haunted eyes look through me. Her chest rises and falls like a runner's at the end of a gruelling workout.

"Darcy's gone. She's not in the house and we can't find her anywhere."

My mouth drops open.

"Darcy's missing?"

Sophie nods. "Mike's gone too. He came back to the house after...well, after everything that happened, and now he's gone too. The pair of them have just vanished."

I feel numb.

Edward lowers his window and thrusts his head towards the gap. His wispy grey hair flutters in the breeze, exposing the grim countenance. The solemn, blue eyes. "The bastard's taken her. He's finally cracked under all the pressure."

Sophie shakes her head. She keeps looking at me. "We don't know anything yet."

Edward's not finished. "We know this much. Darcy hasn't left the house since she came back. And there's blood on the floor in the living room."

"Oh shit," I say, looking back and forth between them. "Blood?"

"A couple of drops," Sophie says. "It might have nothing to do with–"

"Have you heard from him?" Edward says, cutting his daughter off. "Sophie said you were at the casino today. Have you spoken to Mike since then?"

I nod. "He called earlier. I have his jacket. He wanted to come over to the house and pick it up but we didn't arrange anything specific."

"Margo," Sophie says. Stretched to her full height, she dwarfs me. "Why did you want to meet me today? You said it was urgent."

I nod again but I can't talk. I can barely think straight. This is too much. I think Edward's right. Mike *has* cracked under the pressure. This latest scandal has tipped him over the edge. He's already beat up Steve, for God's sake.

I thought he was coming for me.

But...this?

Why would he take her?

Something occurs to me. What if Darcy remembers what happened on that beach thirteen years ago? It's possible. She wasn't a baby – she was four. It must have been highly traumatic but she could retain those memories. What if she knew all along? Maybe she didn't tell the police about Mike's involvement because she wanted...what...what did she want? To confront her kidnapper, her *real* kidnapper, face to face when she was strong enough? Could that be it? Did she want to look her father in the eye and ask why?

Maybe she confronted him today. Perhaps this casino incident emboldened her somehow. Or maybe she was fearful that Mike, after yet another colossal fuckup, wasn't going to be around for much longer.

Maybe she went for it. Sat down beside him and started asking the hard questions. If so, I'm the least of Mike's problems.

That's it.

Darcy remembers what he did.

She confronted him at some point today and that's why Mike grabbed her. He panicked. He has to keep her quiet because he's finished if this gets out. All I have is a picture. But Darcy has memories.

Oh fuck.

This time, Mike won't be handing her over to child traffickers.

This time, he'll have to get rid of her.

PART III

The Hostel

37

THE GIRL

Redhall House is cold and empty. It used to be a children's home and now, years after its official closure, it's been left derelict, fenced off and boarded up.

It's perfect.

Perfect for what we have to do.

From the outside, it looks like such a grand old place, and yet the building has been left to rot. Grass grows long in the surrounding grounds. On the inside, paint peels off the walls and surfaces are littered with dirt and dust. There's graffiti everywhere. And that's not the worst of it. Redhall House carries a controversial reputation and, before its closure, it was investigated as a place where children were mistreated. Orphans. Troubled children. They came here and were supposed to feel loved.

Still, I feel safe in here.

I found Redhall House via a BBC news report about abandoned buildings in Edinburgh. Right away, I knew I'd found the perfect place. It's only a five-minute drive from the Drummond house.

I walk over to the chair in the centre of the front room. The man sitting there is stirring awake, again.

"Can you hear me?" I ask.

I pull the tape off Mike Drummond's mouth. It makes a delicious tearing sound and Mike twitches and gyrates like he's receiving the fatal voltage in an electric chair. Then he stops. The glassy eyes stare up at me. His voice shakes.

"Darcy. Why...are you...doing this?"

He looks at the knife in my hand. Then he sees the blood on his arms. I've already cut him several times and now I press the tip against Mike's left forearm. I find an unspoiled patch and rake the knife across the surface.

Mike screams.

"No one will hear you," I say over the noise.

Each *plop* of blood lands on the floor. When the screaming stops for good, the dripping continues like tiny claps of thunder.

"What...did you give me?" he asks.

I straighten up. Stare across the room at a sunbeam and the dust particles floating silently inside it.

"Think," I say. "It wasn't that long ago. You were in the bedroom making noise. I knocked. Then I came in and offered you a glass of water. For your hangover. Remember?"

His foggy eyes stare into space, trying to remember. "I..."

Doesn't matter. I remember. Mike was so grateful for that glass of water. Most of all, he was grateful that he still had a friend in the house after the way he'd humiliated the family. And not just any old friend, but his long-lost daughter.

Of course he took the glass. Didn't suspect a thing.

I didn't give him too much of Sophie's ground-up pills –

just enough to make him sleepy. Afterwards, I stayed with him in the bedroom, waiting for the powder to take effect. Fortunately, no one else in the house was in a hurry to come and visit Mike. Still, it took too long for my liking. It was time to get things happening and my nerves were playing up bad. Eventually, though, he flagged. His words were slurred. Shoulders drooped. He tried to sit down on the bed but before his legs gave out, I grabbed his arm and led a groggy Mike downstairs. I knew the kids were in their rooms and that Sophie was in the kitchen. I had one shot to get him out of there without being seen.

"There's something I want to show you," I whispered in his ear.

He tried to talk.

I pressed a finger to my lips. "Shh, it's our secret."

We walked downstairs. He was happy to follow. No one interrupted us as I unlocked the front door and led Mike outside. We hurried down the long and winding driveway, all the while keeping the hood of my sweater over my head, just in case any photographers were lurking nearby. At least we had the trees shielding the house from the street.

"Where are we going?" Mike asked.

I didn't answer. Mike was starting to get heavy. After unlocking his Audi, I pushed him into the passenger seat. Leaned over and fastened his seatbelt. *Click.* Then I climbed in behind the wheel and started the car.

I stared at the front door. Waiting for it to open. I expected to see Sophie running towards us at any second.

Nothing happened.

Mike turned groggily towards me. "You can drive?"

"Yes."

"Where...are...we–?"

"Just relax. We're going for a drive."

My driving skills are basic. I've got no license and only the memory of a few occasions behind the wheel, driving rich men's cars around the car park at rich men's parties. Racing other girls for the rich men's amusement.

YouTube videos had also refreshed my memory of how to drive.

I lowered the handbrake and backed out of the driveway like a nervous learner. Mike fell asleep beside me and began to snore, a sluggish drone in my ears. I put the car into drive. My foot grazed the accelerator. The Audi glided down the street. One last look at the house in the rearview mirror. The tip of the Drummond roof disappearing behind a line of horse chestnut trees, their autumn colours showing.

I did it. I got us out.

I gripped the wheel and followed the route to Redhall House. The one I'd memorised on Google Maps. I drove at an unremarkable speed, never straying too fast or too slow. Taking in a series of deep breaths, holding and releasing. Keeping that wheel steady. Concentrating on nothing except the journey.

A police car stopped beside us at the traffic lights. I didn't look. My eyes were fixed straight ahead until what felt like an hour passed and the lights turned green. The police car drove off ahead of us. I followed at the same, inoffensive speed.

"Soon be there," I said to the sleeping Mike.

I told myself that another part of the plan was over. That I didn't have to pretend to be Darcy Drummond anymore.

Still, this was no time to pat myself on the back. There was a lot of work to do. We reached Redhall House and I almost wore my arms out dragging Mike out of the car. I discovered that the only way to get inside the building was through a solitary window at the back that wasn't boarded up. It took all my strength to pull Mike around the back and squeeze him through that gap. Fortunately, he was slim enough to fit. He took some cuts on the way in though. The window ledge was littered with glass fragments. I got cut too. But we were in and, with beads of sweat dripping off my brow, I dragged him by the arms to the front room. There was just enough light around that side of the house to see, a flock of sunbeams seeping through the cracks in the boarded-up windows.

I found the chair, the rope, and tied him up.

And now here we are.

I check the rope that's holding Mike to the chair. The knots are good. I practiced knots like those long before walking into the police station in Cathcart and telling them that I was Darcy Drummond. Strong knots were always going to be a part of the grand finale.

I pull hard. The rope claws at his skin, cutting off blood flow, and I know for a fact he's not going anywhere.

"Please," he says. "Stop...this."

"Shh. Quiet, Mike."

I show him the knife in my hand. He might recognise it. I took it from his oversized kitchen with its soft lighting and fancy, modern appliances. So much stuff. No one will miss a little knife.

I walk around the room and Mike watches my every step, his arms bloody like props from a horror film. The adrenaline is still flowing and I don't think he feels the pain yet. His eyes shimmer with fear.

"Who are you?"

I stop. Turn to face him. "Well, guess who I'm not!"

Mike doesn't hesitate. "Darcy."

"That's right."

Mike's chest heaves up and down. His breathing is a series of ragged gasps that sound like the end of him. "Who...are...you?"

"What does it matter?" I say, stepping towards the chair. "Who is anyone? We're nothing but the stories we tell ourselves. And what kind of story is this, I wonder?"

Mike yells in an ear-splitting roar that takes me by surprise. I didn't know he still had it in him. "Enough!" He frantically twists his head around, trying to follow me as I circle the chair. "What are you talking about?"

"Others will come."

"What...others?"

Mike flinches when I put a hand on his shoulder. My hand slides down the arm towards the wounds and I give it a squeeze. His blood hits the floor.

Plop-plop-plop.

He makes a gurgling noise in his throat.

"Okay," I say, letting go.

I laugh, pat him on the shoulder and then whisper in his ear. "I guess we have time."

His head jolts from side to side in a desperate bid to make eye contact with me. "Time...for what?"

My voice fills with the excitement of a child. "For the truth, of course."

"The...*truth?*"

I start to circle the chair again. This time, I stop directly in front of Mike. He looks at me like I'm an evil giant. "Why don't you stop squirming and relax?"

He eyes me warily.

"Don't you want the truth?"

"About...what?"

"Oh, you silly man."

He yells. "About what?"

I make him wait.

"About what happened to Darcy."

38

W here do I begin, Mike? Will I start with all the nights I cried myself to sleep in that place? Or how about we go back to before I was kidnapped? Before my life in the hostel.

That okay with you?

Don't worry, we'll get to Darcy.

As for me, I grew up in a poor neighbourhood in the east end of Glasgow. Snap! Same as you, Mike. It was a rundown estate with the usual eyesore buildings and teenage gangs running wild. Hard faces. Broken bodies. Police and ambulance sirens were our equivalent of birdsong. If I'd been older, I could have probably smelled the hopelessness in the air. Mum brought me up alone, working two cleaning jobs in two separate office blocks in the city centre. I never met my dad. There were a lot of single-parent households in that estate. But I was happy, despite all the problems. I had Mum, even though she was tired all the time, and I had so many friends to play with. Vicky, Alan, Jill – those are just some of the names I remember. We were inseparable. We spent so much time in the local playground that we might as well have lived there. It didn't have much – a filthy old chute, a see-saw, a rusted climbing frame and two groaning swings that never went high enough no matter how hard you pushed. But it was home.

The playground was encased within a wire fence. You could see it from the living room window of our house. That's how close it was.

I should have been safe.

All I remember is the blissful sense of innocence. Not in a silly, sentimental way with the blinders of nostalgia. It really was like that. We were poor, but so what? We had everything else going for us that wasn't money. And what did I really understand of money as a child? Mum never let me think that we were poor.

It was the perfect childhood until that day. The day the silver van pulled up outside the park.

I recall only fleeting glimpses. The grey, cloudy sky and the excited screams of children and someone shouting 'higher, higher' to whoever was pushing them on the crappy swing. It was just another day.

I saw the van pulling in at the side of the road, just opposite the playground. Didn't think too much of it. What did I have to worry about? This was the same road I had to cross to get back to the house. About a three-minute walk if I was dragging my feet. As far as I know, there were no adults watching us in the playground. We didn't need supervision. We were so close to our homes that we didn't need or want our parents, big sisters, big brothers or babysitters watching over us.

I was sitting on the bench when I saw the man and

woman standing outside the playground. I had no real thoughts about what age they were at the time. I was twelve and every adult looked old to me. Fifties. Sixties. Something like that. They stayed close to the outer fence but never came in. They smiled. They waved. Called some kids over and exchanged words through the gaps in the fence. I heard later from a girl called Alison who spoke to them. She said they worked in a charity shop and that they were driving around the city, handing out old toys and games they couldn't sell.

I didn't get off the bench.

Still, they had their eyes on me. I didn't know it at the time but I was exactly what they were looking for. Tall and slim. Blonde hair and blue eyes.

My best friend, Jill, also talked to them for a while. She wasn't classically pretty so I don't think they wanted her. They could've snatched her up that day and bundled her into the back of the van. Jill wasn't too street smart. But I understand why kids like Jill were drawn to 'friendly' adults. We didn't all come from happy homes, you know? Some of us longed for a smile from a grown-up instead of a clip round the ear. Or worse.

Like I said, the man and woman came to us with smiles.

Nothing happened that day. After about twenty minutes of talking to kids, they got back in their silver van and drove away. They came back two days later. I think that was a Friday. They had toys and games on their second visit, and because of that first visit, they were a familiar face. They worked on building trust. Again, nothing happened. Some of the kids got toys and games and sweets.

I wasn't interested. I didn't talk to them.

They kept coming back and the kids loved them. They must have known that the best time to pull up outside the playground was in the two-hour window after school. The parents were out of the way, preparing dinner. The playground was always busy at that time. It was like we all went in there to shake off school.

You see, Mike, these people are clever. They have all sorts of tactics going on when it comes to grabbing children. In this case, the man and woman were patient and kept coming back. They used their cunning to build trust. Some kidnappers use other young people to recruit kids. These kids work in shopping centres, at public events, outside of school, and especially nowadays on social media. Most traffickers don't need to kidnap outright. They're your friend before you know anything is wrong. Young people are impressionable. Traffickers know this. If someone trusts them, they don't have to try.

Eventually, the man and woman did grab me. I fell for their tricks like everyone else but it was worse for me because I was the target. One day, I started talking to them like everyone else and they'd been showing up for so long that I didn't think twice when they told me about the secret stash of toys and books they kept in the van. The stuff that was too grown up for the other kids to see.

I was twelve years old.

I remember the foul-smelling rag that went over my mouth and nose. A strong arm wrapped itself around my waist and squeezed tight. I couldn't believe the strength of that arm because those people didn't look big or strong. I kicked and fought. Heard the terrifying sound of the van door sliding shut. Daylight gone. Then I was out. They took me to a warehouse where I woke up several times. It was a massive place with a high roof. The smell of sawdust and smoke was everywhere. If I had to guess, I'd say they kept me there for about twelve hours. No food. No water. Just locked in this tiny room, lying on a hard floor, drifting in and out of consciousness. After that, I was driven to another place. And another. When they took the blindfold off for the last time, I was in a room with three single beds. It was the sort of room that looked like it belonged in a cheap hostel. Grimy walls, tattered carpet. The musty smell of damp. The windows were boarded up and the only light came from three electric lamps sitting on three sets of bedside drawers.

The man and woman from the playground were gone. I wouldn't see my kidnappers again for a very long time.

There was a man in the room with me. Several men in fact, all telling me not to cry. I didn't even realise I was crying. The dark-haired man, well-dressed, with a thick coat of stubble on his face, sat down beside me and told me in a kind voice that my mum had agreed to put me in their care because it was all too much for her. She'd suffered some kind of breakdown and needed rest in the hospital. Lots of rest. In the meantime, the men would look after me. The dark-haired man apologised for the way I was taken but most children won't leave their parents without a fight, not even when it's for the best. It has to be quick. It has to be clean.

And Mum had approved my job with them, he said. Times were tough and it was necessary for me to start contributing. Start saving some money.

Be a good girl, they said. You'll earn lots of money and take good care of Mum when she's better.

The men left and my roommates were brought in.

Two of them.

The blonde girl introduced herself as Rita. The redhead was Emily. They were around the same age as me although I suspected that Rita was a little younger. Her face was pretty but a little odd. There were scars there, like she'd had an accident or something. They were both casually dressed in tracksuit bottoms and t-shirts. We sat on our beds talking for a long time that first night. That kept me sane.

What I remember most of all happened when Emily went to the bathroom. Supervised, of course. Rita hurried over and sat beside me on the bed. She flicked her blonde hair behind her ears and told me she had a secret. Something she'd remembered even though it happened years ago.

She whispered in my ear. Told me her name. Her real name, that is, which she wasn't allowed to even whisper in that place.

I was stunned because I recognised that name.

She whispered again.

The men who own us now, she said, *told me that my name is forbidden*.

39

That's your worst fear, isn't it, Mike?

I saw you and Sophie on TV once, and it's a clip that I saw again on YouTube years later. I saw it recently, in fact. It was taken from one of those horrible breakfast-time shows that send most people back to sleep. You were both sitting on the couch, talking to the host, looking all sad and broken. This was for an early anniversary of the kidnapping. The host asked you both about your worst fear when it came to Darcy's fate.

You answered, because Sophie couldn't bear to think about it. Remember what you said? Your worst fear wasn't that Darcy was dead, you said. It was that she'd been taken to a place where they...*did bad things to her*. Everyone knew what you meant. The possibility of that, you added, gave you nightmares.

Well, you're not going to like this story, Mike.

The girl I knew as Rita was such a small, timid thing. Always looking around with big doll eyes. She was a grinner though. She always had a smile on her face, at least for

Emily and me. I got used to the mature, whitish scars on her face and stopped seeing them eventually. Thinking back, I can't help but think they did plastic surgery on her at one point. Rita never said anything about it. I never asked.

Emily didn't give a shit about much. She'd built up a tough shell that nobody could break and she called Rita Darcy without thinking twice about it. She was a pretty girl, early teens, with the reddest hair I ever saw. Ivory skin. Freckles on her nose and cheeks.

Eventually, I started calling Rita Darcy too. It was our three-way secret.

At first, we all fell in line with the official story. That we were there working for our families. Even when we found out what the 'work' was. We cried. We ached. I don't know how we carried on but we did and it just became life.

Childhood was over.

The girl they called Rita never forgot who she was even though it had been years since she'd been that person. It was still there in her mind. Still, the memory of what happened on the beach that day was a little blurry. Maybe she couldn't remember. Maybe she didn't want to remember, but she was Darcy Drummond. We all knew the story and we all – that is Emily and I – wanted to know what happened.

The poor girl had nightmares. She'd wake up covered in sweat and you could see in her eyes, before she was fully awake, that she was reliving the events of what happened.

She wasn't good with words, at least not when it came to that. But she liked to draw. They let us have paper and pencils and crayons. Darcy lost herself in art.

She drew people. I remember seeing lots of drawings of a tall, golden-haired woman. It was Sophie, I think, but without the drugged-up eyes. This was an angelic, perfect vision of Sophie. Sometimes late at night, when there were no guards around, she opened up our wardrobe, dug her way through a pile of discarded clothes and bags to the back, and carefully took out the only possessions she valued. Three items that went back to her old life before 'Rita'.

1/ A teddy bear called Marvin.

2/ A pink t-shirt with *Daddy's Princess* on the front.

3/ A bucket hat.

She liked to draw them sometimes.

I asked how she'd kept hold of those things over the years. Darcy told me about a family she'd lived with for several years in a remote stretch of land. An older man and woman who had no other children. There was a border collie dog called Arthur. They were nice people, she said. If a little cold. The way she described the place, it might have been an island. Freezing cold. Surrounded by choppy water that discouraged visitors. Very few people living in the area. That's where she went after they dyed her hair and changed her face. Back when the world was looking for her. And somehow those three items stayed with her from the beach to that island. Darcy never let them go. She hid them. Her real name was written in black marker pen on the label of the t-shirt.

Even at a young age, she knew to hide that name.

Darcy told me that several years later she started to play up. She was isolated. Frustrated. Although her old life was a blur, she hadn't forgotten everything. The girl known as Rita became, in the words of her false parents, a 'problem child'. They could change her hair, face, and give her a false birth certificate, but they couldn't erase everything.

This, along with the danger of her true identity, led to her removal from the island. A boat ride followed by a long drive with a man who had a gun in the car brought her to the place we called the hostel. The same place that I'd been taken to. Darcy had been there for about two or three years before my arrival.

Darcy kept those three items hidden unless she was drawing them. Eventually, we moved them to my bottom bedside drawer because sometimes the guards would rummage around in the wardrobe looking for old bits and pieces that had been in there long before we started using it as a clothes dump.

I liked it when she talked to us. She could be a little quiet sometimes but I was always glad when she started to open up a little. Felt like she trusted us. I remember this one night, we were all sitting on our hard beds, long past our bedtime. This was about a year since I'd been snatched. Our little bedside lamps were on. Brick-like mattresses underneath us.

"Who grabbed you?" I asked.

I thought she might describe the same couple who got me at the playground. They were obviously connected to the hostel in some way.

"I've asked her that before," Emily said. "She won't say."

But I had to know. I felt my backside scooting to the edge of the bed.

"Who grabbed you?"

Darcy's head was pressed against the wall. She closed her eyes and I wondered if she was back there on the beach. Four years old, the warmth of the sun on her skin. The sand running through her fingers. Thousands of voices on a summer's day and the deep roar of the waves. And then, a pair of hands. Pulling her away.

Emily shook her head. "You don't have to answer. What does it matter now anyway?"

"It matters," I said. I was about to explain to Emily why it mattered when Darcy's voice cut me off.

"The man," she whispered.

Emily and I exchanged glances.

"What man?" Emily asked.

Darcy wrinkled up her nose, exposing some of those old scars. I'm not sure how old she really was at this point. Thirteen? Fourteen? At that moment, she looked much older. We all did.

"Who grabbed you?" I asked again.

She shook her head. There was nothing after that, just a long silence. And just when I thought the conversation was over, Darcy began to tap her wrist. Her left wrist. *Tap, tap, tap.* Over and over again.

"What does that mean?" Emily asked.

"The man."

"What man?"

Darcy kept tapping her wrist but we couldn't figure out what she was trying to tell us. I took a chance and jumped off the bed. I grabbed Darcy's sketch pad off the bedside drawers and handed it to her. Then I gave her a pen and backed off towards my own bed.

"Don't tell us," I said. "Show us."

It worked. She started scribbling furiously. This went on for ages, and every now and then she'd look up, just to make sure we were still paying attention. When she was finally done, Darcy held up the pad. Showed it to me, then to Emily. I'll never forget it.

"The man."

I was looking at the rough sketch of a beach. The sheet of paper sliced into three segments of sand, sea and sky. A gigantic blob of sun floated in the sky, its shimmering rays beaming down to the sea and sand.

A stick figure stood on the sand, handing something over to another stick figure. A package? Another stick person? Darcy tapped the tip of the pen on the taller of the two stick men. Specifically, at the wrist.

"I don't understand," Emily said.

Darcy looked back and forth between us. Then, she threw herself back into her work. With her head down, she raked the pen on the page and, about a minute later, held it up again for Emily and me to see. Not much had changed. The stick figure's wrist had something on it now. Something that looked like a smaller version of the sun at the top of the page. Rays gushing out across the beach.

Emily squinted. "What's that?"

"The man," Darcy said. There was a pained expression on her face and it was clear she wanted us to understand. She just couldn't bring herself to say it.

I pointed at the notepad. "What's wrong with that guy's arm?"

She shook her head. Very slowly, Darcy was losing the power of speech. If we didn't get it soon, she'd go into her shell.

"Is it a watch?" Emily asked.

Darcy nodded.

"It's a big watch," I said. "Was it really that shiny?"

She nodded again.

I stared at the picture. "The man with the gold watch, is that it? He's the one who gave you away?"

Another nod.

"Who is he?" Emily asked. She was also on the edge of

her bed. Another inch and she'd be on the floor. "What's his name?"

"Shh," I said, pressing a finger to my lips. Emily was getting too loud and we had to be quiet because there were always at least two security men walking around the hostel at night, checking the doors were locked. Making sure the girls were quiet. For all we knew, they were standing outside our door right now.

There was a blank look on Darcy's face. She was definitely on the retreat.

"The man with the gold watch," I said, keeping my voice down. "You knew him, didn't you? You were close."

Her haunted eyes looked at me across the room. I felt them like a punch.

She nodded.

"You loved him?"

There was a strange, whimpering noise. Darcy reached a hand out and turned off her bedside lamp. The room dulled a little. She threw the notepad and pen onto the floor, then turned onto her side. Pulled the covers up to her neck. All I could see now was the back of her head. The long blonde hair, which since her arrival at the hostel had been allowed to go back to its natural colour.

I thought the conversation was over until I heard a meek, ghost-like voice from a million miles away.

"Yes."

40

Antonio was one of the few nice guys working in the hostel.

I was there four or five years before he turned up. He was about eighteen, from Rio de Janeiro in Brazil. Bleached blond hair. Surfer vibes. I don't know what brought him to the hostel, and because he was a bit simple, I didn't know if he fully understood what was going on in that place.

He was kind though. Kind to all the girls but he had a soft spot for me. Because of that he brought us paper, pens and crayons for drawing. As much as we wanted. Turned out there was a shop downstairs, right underneath the hostel, one of those family-run places you could buy pretty much anything – food, drink, stationery, lottery tickets and so on. That was the front for what was going on upstairs. I learned that from Antonio but I don't think he was supposed to tell me.

Were we in a city? A small town? Somewhere rural?

Antonio would sometimes sit beside me when I drew. I

didn't want him watching but I was grateful for the supplies, as well as the sweets and fizzy drinks he gave us. All those little things made a big difference when it came to passing the time. We could do other things in the room besides draw. We had books, an old TV and a DVD player. Some DVDs, not much. Emily liked books and movies but Darcy and I preferred to draw. Antonio would look down at what I was drawing with a goofy-looking smile on his face.

"What are you drawing?" he'd ask in his funny accent. His English wasn't great but he had enough to get by.

"Nothing nice."

But I was letting it all out. I'd make excuses. I didn't want him thinking it was anything serious that he had to report to the higher-ups. Especially the boss, a guy called Sean. That was the man who spoke to me on my first night and told me my mother had had a nervous breakdown. Well-groomed, good clothes and an utter bastard.

Like you, Mike.

There was a lot of anger in me and it came out on the page. Violent fantasies. Like I say, I'd make excuses.

"I remember scenes from films," I'd say to Antonio. "Stabby films. Things I've watched on TV. I just like drawing them, that's all. It's nothing."

"It's bloody," he'd say laughing nervously.

"I know."

I'm sparing you the grisly details, Mike. I hope you appreciate that. I'm talking about the day-to-day details that would make you wince. The *work*. The men who came to visit. And there's something else too. As time passed, many of the girls were taken on outings. What was an outing? Well, we were hired out to special parties. Rich men's parties. We were dressed up. Told to make ourselves look nice.

Perfume, lipstick, nail polish – that sort of thing. But not too much or we'd look too old for their tastes. Then we were put into the back of a van and off we went, a select group of girls from the hostel who were deemed the right type. The prettiest, at least by conventional standards.

I met a lot of other girls at the parties. Girls I never would've met otherwise because we didn't mix in the hostel. At first, we were strangers. Strangers became friends. Over time, friends became sisters and an unbreakable bond was formed. Don't worry, Mike – Darcy never left the hostel. She was far too famous for parties and that was a risk our handlers weren't willing to take.

I don't think our handlers knew who was putting those parties together. Most likely, they dealt with middle men.

Stacey. Jess. Katy. Those were just some of the girls I met. All of us relying on each other to get through the long nights with that old-fashioned music blaring in our ears and the sound of raucous male laughter. It was horrible but the sisters had each other. We'd huddle together in our spare moments, often in the bathroom where it was quietest. Quite often we'd get our hands on a phone – one of the men's phones that we'd lifted from the table. We didn't steal it – they knew we had it. They were drunk, of course, but they knew how untouchable they were, these people. I'm talking about *very important* people. Famous. Powerful. All of that. It's not like we were going to call the police.

Who'd believe a word we said?

But we *were* busy.

It was Stacey's idea to create the forum. She was a bit of a geek and she knew something about the internet and about forums and creating a safe space where we could talk whenever we had a chance to be online. She opened an email account, built several forums on free-to-use platforms, and that was something for us and us alone. The bastards who controlled us couldn't touch us there. We could say anything. We could put it all down. We could scream and shout and tell our stories, which we did at those parties whenever we got our hands on a phone.

And we went to those parties for years and years. We did a lot of talking on the forums.

I was the one who brought up the idea of revenge. I'd thought about it a lot. Especially when it came to certain people who were involved in the parties. With Darcy being where she was and these men living it large, how could I not spend all my time thinking about how to hurt them?

But I'm getting ahead of myself, Mike.

Words will never be enough to make you understand the life we lived. We all fell into dark places sometimes. I was pretty certain that Mum had given me up for dead and, unable to see the point, I tried to end it with a belt and a makeshift noose. Twice. I wasn't the first girl in there to do it. But it wasn't meant to be. Emily walked in and stopped me the first time. Second time, Darcy found me. She panicked and yanked the belt off my neck. Shook the life back into me. I opened my eyes, choking and gasping for breath. She was leaning over me. Saying that everything was going to be all right.

Emily and Darcy. They're the only people who knew what I tried to do.

We became each other's family. We'd eat together in that cramped room. Talk. Read in silence. Draw and watch films. Antonio would come in later in the day, bringing us magazines and cake from the shop downstairs. He'd cut huge slices of cake and hand them to us on paper plates.

Such a sweet boy. You should have seen the way he looked at me.

So, what happens when you can't die? When that option is taken off the table. How else do you ever hope to get out of a place like that? That's how I found myself thinking about escape. Not just for me, but for all three of us. And it was in one of Antonio's late evening visits with cake and sweets, in one of those little acts of everyday kindness, that I saw the potential for a way out.

But it meant doing something horrible. Something worse than any twisted picture I'd ever drawn.

41

We found a way to live in the hostel. We had to. Looking back, it was Hell but you had to live in those flames somehow.

The adults who controlled us were very clever. They knew when to squeeze the girls and when to back off and give us room. Kindness, even if it was fake kindness, was welcomed. It was enough to keep you hanging on from day to day. It was enough to stop me thinking about escape for a while.

There were some moments with my two sisters that came close to happiness. Little things. Just being together mostly, drawing strength and comfort from one another. That's how we lasted years in that place. We saved each other, every day.

But everything went downhill after Darcy became ill.

At first, we thought it was just a cold going around the hostel. Other girls had something too but whatever they had, they got over it. Darcy didn't get better. She was tired and sore. I noticed she was getting skinnier, and there wasn't much there in the first place. We thought it was the flu but still, it didn't go away.

Even getting out of bed became a challenge for her.

A doctor came to the room late one night. Some old guy in a cheap suit with granny glasses perched on the bridge of his nose. The guards hurried him in. The lights went on and there he was, leaning over Darcy's bed, looking at her and listening to the way she was coughing. He listened to her heart. Emily and I sat on our beds, watching. Asking questions, all of which were ignored by both doctor and security guards. Looked to me like the doctor needed a doctor. He was gaunt and his skin was a ghoulish yellowy colour. His clothes reeked of smoke and he was no stranger to coughing himself.

The examination was quick. He left pills for Darcy. Pills for *Rita*. Prescribed rest. Our two handlers that night, Frank and Hugh (who went by the nickname Shuggy), didn't like that, but what could they do? They'd have to report her condition back to Sean, who wouldn't be too impressed.

Escape wasn't an option anymore. I was prepared to live in the hostel for the rest of my life if it meant looking after Darcy. But, as much as I wanted her to, she didn't get better. The slow decline became inevitable. Emily and I stayed with her as much as we could. All throughout that period, we lived with this horrible anxiety churning in our guts. We couldn't sleep.

What was wrong with her?

Why didn't they fix it?

That's my worst memory of the hostel. Watching my little sister fade away to a ghost-like creature. It's the worst by far, and I have a lot of bad memories of that place, Mike. The way she'd sit up in bed, too tired to draw. Too tired to do anything. She was disappearing before our eyes. I begged Frank and Shuggy to go to Sean and tell him how bad it was. This wasn't the flu. Something was eating away at her from the inside. She needed a hospital, not a back-alley doctor with yellow skin.

But there was no chance of them ever taking Darcy Drummond to a hospital. She was so famous, after all. Getting badly ill in that place was a death sentence.

The doctor came back for more late-night visits and left so many pill bottles beside her bed that there wasn't room for anything else. Her drawings disappeared. We protested on her behalf and no one listened. Doctor Yellow Face was useless. His pills, useless. Our keepers were too afraid of who their *Rita* was to get her proper help. She wasn't eating. Emily and I had to force her to drink water.

Then, she was sleeping all the time.

It all happened in less than a month.

I came back to the room one afternoon and got the shock of my life. It was empty. Two thirds empty, to be exact. Lifeless. My side was untouched but all trace of Darcy and Emily was gone. All their things, gone. Their beds had been stripped bare, not even a mattress left on the springs. I must have stood there in the doorway for about five minutes, trying to see if this was real or not. This was a skeleton version of the one place in the hostel that felt like home. The one place where I could forget the aches and pains in my body. The memory of what happened to us over and over again.

It was like they'd never existed. Darcy's drawings were gone. The pills gone. Emily's clothes weren't lying all over the floor, clogging up the place. Just my clothes, neatly folded on my bed. My drawings.

That was the most scared I'd been since the kidnappers grabbed me outside the playground. It was like half of my soul had left my body. And the other half was now an only twin. Forever incomplete.

I pounded my fists on the door. No one came. Then I ran around the room, pulling drawers open, rummaging through the wardrobe looking for God knows what. I did that to the point of exhaustion. Hit the door. Searched the room. All the time, I felt like I was losing my mind. Finally, I remembered the things I'd been keeping safe for Darcy. I pulled open the bottom drawer by my bed and pushed away all my crap. I almost cried when I saw them. Darcy's hat, t-shirt and teddy bear, wrapped up in a plastic bag.

Why was I alone?

Where were my friends?

Antonio showed up after dark that night. I was sitting on my bed, back against the wall, with the light switched off. I had my pencils and paper and I was scribbling but I didn't need to see what I was drawing. I just liked the feeling of breaking the tip on the page. *Snap.* I'd gone through so many and when they broke, I'd just take another one out of the tin. Press down hard on the page and wait for it to break.

The room was so empty and alien to me. It was like a monstrous thing and I couldn't bear to be in there. The thought was unbearable.

No coughing from the other bed.

Where was she?

"Why are you in the dark?" Antonio asked, followed by a nervous giggle.

I didn't answer. He sat down beside me and the bed sank under his weight.

"Where are they?"

I heard him sigh. He tried to put his arm around me and I shrugged it off. Maybe Antonio was the same as the others after all. Have some cake. Here's some crayons. A new DVD to distract you. Now, let me get what I want. They're monsters, all of them.

"Where are they?" I asked, standing up off the bed. "Why aren't they here?"

It was a long time before he spoke in his clipped English.

"Orders from upstairs. Boss thinks it's time to mix things up. Soon, you'll get new roommates. You won't be alone for long. Okay?"

I turned on the bedside lamp. Antonio winced as if I'd just shone a spotlight in his eyes.

"Is Darcy still alive?"

Antonio couldn't bring the shutters down like Sean, Shuggy and the others. He looked scared. He couldn't maintain eye contact. Especially as I raised my voice.

"Where's Emily? Why did they take *her* away?"

He stuttered, repeating what he'd said about Sean wanting to mix things up. It happened, he said. New roommates. Fresh faces. It was on the cards anyway, nothing to do with Darcy's illness. Like I was just supposed to accept that. Forget Darcy? Forget Emily? They'd been my sisters for years.

No, they were doing this because Darcy had died. And they didn't want Emily and me getting angry about it together. Cut ties. Cut all the ties. Move on.

Something snapped inside me.

"Antonio?"

"Yes?"

"Will you do something for me?"

His eyes lit up and he stood up off the bed. He reached for me but withdrew his chimp-like arms when he remembered what happened last time. They flopped to the sides. "Anything. What do you want?"

"Cake. I want cake."

42

I sat alone in the room, waiting for Antonio to come back with the cake. He was only too happy to go downstairs to the shop for me, considering the mood I was in. Before he left, he asked me if I wanted anything specific – chocolate, vanilla, raspberry or whatever.

I told him to get anything. Any kind of cake. And to bring it on the tray like he always did with a couple of Cokes.

The room was so quiet. No more Darcy. No more Emily. I felt hollow, like I'd been carved empty with a dull knife. I knew Darcy was dead. I *knew* it. What I didn't know was what happened. Did she succumb to the illness or was she helped along by our handlers? I suspect the latter. She was a liability to those people. She'd been a liability all those years because she was so famous. And now that she was sick, she was high risk, zero reward. What good was that to the likes of Sean? The girls in the hostel, whether they'd been kidnapped or whether they ended up in that place because they had nothing else, were there for one purpose – to make money.

I didn't know if I was ever going to see Emily again. All I knew for sure was that they wanted us separated in the aftermath of Darcy's death.

Friends, sisters – they could be taken away just like that. No goodbye. No final kiss.

I'd felt anger before but this was something else. This was a fire burning up inside me. A rebirth. I had to feel this sick inside to do what I was about to do. To activate a plan that had been in the works for a long time in the forums I'd created with the sisters.

Revenge.

What else did I have to lose?

Revenge is a purpose. The groundwork had already been laid, not just by me. Like I told you before, Mike, there were other sisters out there and we'd been busy at those parties. Busy birds. Plotting, scheming and dreaming. Conjuring up all kinds of horrors. We had something in the works but it was so big and far-reaching that it felt like fantasy. Like a plan doomed to fail.

But now I had nothing else. That plan, which had been drifting on and off for all those years, became my everything.

Somebody had to pull the trigger.

I was glad to do it. It took the loss of Darcy and Emily to show me that we have no idea what's about to happen next. Life is short.

Might as well give it a go when you can.

There were so many people who had to pay.

Our handlers for what they'd put us through. The man and woman who grabbed me at the playground. The man in the gold watch had to pay for Darcy. I hadn't forgotten about any of them in the plan or in my sick drawings.

I looked like Darcy the most. It *had* to be me who pulled

the trigger and brought this dormant revenge fantasy to life. No more fantasy. Time to make it real. But I had to get out of the hostel to do it. I had to go back into the world and call up the sisters – those who'd gotten out because they looked too old or beat up or they just weren't pretty enough anymore. There weren't many but there were enough.

I could find them through the forums. See if they still had it in them to fight back.

God. There was so much work to do, and this first part was going to sting.

Forward. It was the only direction.

I sat on the bed, cloaked in the dim light. My shoulders and neck were stiff with tension as I waited for Antonio to come back with the cake.

43

"Shut the door," I said to Antonio when he came back.

"Okay."

I patted the bed, urging him to come over and sit beside me. Antonio's eyes lit up because it was the first time I'd ever asked him to come closer, rather than him just doing it. This was an invitation and the mellow lighting only added to the ambience. Clearly, Antonio was in the mood to comfort me over the loss of my friends.

"I don't want to be alone," I said.

The smile stretched across his bronze face. His back touched the door and I heard it click shut. Forks rattled on the tray as he brought the chocolate cake into the room. It was nothing special – a smallish, rectangular block inside plastic packaging. I saw two plates on the tray instead of four and it felt like someone squeezing a giant knot inside me. Darcy and Emily loved chocolate cake.

There were two cans of Coke and the knife for cutting the cake.

"I want to make you happy," he said, nudging my notepad to the side and putting the tray down on top of the bedside drawers. He handed me a Coke. Smiled, then started slicing the cake.

"You made friends with other girls at parties," he said. "Right?"

"Yes," I said, pulling back the Coke tab. The can hissed and I drank.

So Antonio knew about the parties they hired us out to. Maybe he wasn't as naïve about the hostel as I'd hoped.

"You make friends with new roommates. When they come."

That's right. Be a good girl and forget all about Darcy and Emily.

I was done. Done with the lies. Done with being used. How many other girls from poor neighbourhoods had been dragged to the hostel at a young age and told they had to earn money for their broken-down mothers? Made to think they were a burden.

I had to go back to the beginning.

The man and woman who took me. Were they still out there? How long had it been since that day? Nine years? Ten years? Were they still lurking at the edge of a school or playground somewhere, waiting for the next girl? Were they dead? Retired?

I had to find them. The plan we'd been tinkering with for years, if I was serious about giving it a go, required two people to play a certain role. They'd be perfect. I just had to find them, if that was even possible.

Antonio sliced the cake, still wearing that goofy grin on his face. It was the look of a boy who was about to get what he wanted.

"Hope you're hungry."

"I'm always hungry," I said.

"Can I turn the big light on? It's hard to see what I'm doing here."

"No."

"Ha! I'm going to give you a tiny slice for that."

He brought the two plates over, handing me the one with the biggest slice. Still, that dumb grin all over his surfer face.

"Only kidding."

"Thanks," I said. My hands shook as I picked up the little fork.

I could just picture that smile on Antonio's face as he helped Sean and his crew transport a dying Darcy out of the room. As they hurried a confused Emily along. *Get your things, get them now!* Ignoring her protests. He was so proud of himself tonight. Bringing me chocolate cake. One sister dead, one missing but that's okay because...chocolate cake. Still, I ate it like it was my last meal. I ate while Antonio talked with his mouth full about a rapper whose album he'd been listening to all week.

I glanced over my shoulder, making sure the door was unlocked. The key was right there in the lock.

"Are you okay?" he asked.

"I miss them."

"Oh."

"What happened to Darcy?"

Antonio's expression soured. It was like he'd just sucked a lemon. He put his plate down on the bed. Then he stood up and walked over to the boarded window. His feet were heavy on the floor. I saw him glance over at Darcy's bed and wondered what he was thinking about.

"It won't be for much longer," he said.

"What?"

"You being in here. You make money, then you go back to your family."

That's what they'd told him. At some point, however, Antonio must have stopped believing it. Still, he'd keep peddling that line for his sake and mine. Until the inevitable happened and he stopped caring.

I stood up while his back was still turned. Wrapped my fingers around the knife handle and lifted it off the tray. I didn't make a sound. There was time for one final glance at the drawings on my bedside table. At the twisted art.

I could've made a run for it and locked Antonio in the room. That was one option but he would've panicked and made an ungodly racket that would take away the element of surprise. That was one thing I'd need if I was going to get past the other guard on duty that night.

I lowered the knife while the lamplight flickered beside me. Shadows came and went. A moth danced inside the cone-shaped shade and made a scratching noise. I walked forward, slipping my hands behind my back.

"Antonio?"

He turned around. Took a step towards me, letting out his goofy laugh. His arms were outstretched, inviting me in for an embrace. "Is this what you want?"

I stopped.

"Get me out of here."

The silly grin fizzled out. "What?"

"I don't want to..."

He saw the knife.

The colour drained from his face. There was a frantic glance towards the door. He must have seen the key in the lock and realised he hadn't secured the room properly.

Instinct took over. He made for the door.

I stepped in front of him. He stopped.

"What are you doing?"

His voice was boyish. Eyes shimmering with panic. He stammered and the words came out after a few false starts.

"You're safe here."

"Safe?"

"Safe."

"You know what happens to us in here, don't you, Antonio? When they come and get us, you know what's going on, right? We go upstairs, the doors close and we come out a little bit less than before. When they dress us up and put us in the back of the van. You know where we go. I know you do."

"Y-y-you're making money."

His arms were outstretched again. The smile was back. Manic.

"Sean's a good man," he said, wiping a chocolate smear off his mouth. "He's got family. Money. Nice clothes. Good car."

"Is that what you want?" I asked. "Do you want to be like Sean? Or do you want to *be* Sean?"

His eyes rolled back with fear. I knew he wasn't going to help me get out of there. That meant he was in my way.

The light flickered. The moth danced. I lunged forward and Antonio staggered back towards the boarded-up window. Hands up in a defensive gesture. It all happened so fast. I lashed out with the knife, striking downwards in a twelve-to-six motion. Over and over again. He slammed his back against the wall and I found a strength I didn't know I had. This time, I went for the heart or as near as damn it. The knife went in and poor Antonio let out a gasp that didn't sound human.

This time, the blood was real. All my drawings came to life and nothing would ever be the same.

It didn't stop with Antonio. Shug was the other guard working that night, probably sitting in the 'client reception area', which was located near the main entrance. There was a door there that led to a set of stairs. Those stairs led to a back-alley exit and that's where the girls went whenever we were loaded into the van for parties. There was another door on the way down too, and I was hoping that one led down to the shop and, in turn, the street. I'd walked past that door before so many times, wondering where it went.

Time to find out.

But I had to get past Shug. Most likely he'd be in reception, watching the big TV on the wall. That's what most of the guys on night duty did when they weren't patrolling the corridor, listening for any disturbances behind locked doors.

I had to think on my feet. Knife in hand. One thing at a time.

I threw some things into a tattered maroon rucksack that had been sitting at the back of the wardrobe for years. The bag was covered in dust. God knows what poor soul it had once belonged to. I put in some clothes, my notepad and drawings. Darcy's three personal items, the hat, t-shirt and teddy bear, went in there too.

I didn't look at Antonio as I left the room. That I could do without and besides, I knew he'd turn up in my nightmares. Turning off the lamp beside my bed, I stepped outside into the narrow corridor. That was the last time I was in the little room I'd shared with Darcy and Emily for all those years.

I turned the key in the lock. Slipped it into my pocket.

Okay, I thought, staring down the long corridor and inhaling the scent of carpet cleaner. *One step at a time.* That's all it would take to get me out of this building.

I kept on my tiptoes, creeping past the other doors. The muffled sound of TVs on the other side made me think about the girls in those rooms. But this was no time to think about being a hero.

My heart was thumping.

I had to deal with Shug next. That was the obstacle between me and the exit. All things considered, getting past Antonio was simple, the act of killing aside. He had a weakness. Me. He thought nothing of bringing a sharp knife into the room and turning his back on it.

Shug didn't have a weakness. Not that I was aware of. He was twice my size and in a straight fight, I had less than zero chance. The element of surprise was my only throw of the dice and it wasn't going to be pretty no matter what the outcome.

Being so close to freedom, it was terrifying.

I crept past all the closed doors. So many doors. The sound of TV and hushed voices slipping through the walls. The crackle of a loose connection. Laughter. Behind one door, I heard someone make a wailing-type noise. I retained my focus throughout and kept going, making my way down to the end of the corridor.

A right turn. From there, a short walk to reception.

The door was ajar. The sound of a football match on TV blared from inside. I could hear Shuggy mouthing off at the commentators; it sounded like his mouth was full. The rustling of a paper bag, then the sound of crisps being eaten, confirmed this.

"Fucking offside, ref!"

I sidestepped to the edge of the corridor. Tiptoed towards the door with my back up against the wall, never taking my eyes off the reception door.

I stopped. Squatting down, I placed the rucksack on the carpet. My fingers uncurled themselves from the nylon handle with reluctance. Then I straightened up. Once again, I put my hands behind my back to hide the knife.

God, I felt sick.

"HELP!"

I yelled and made sure my feet thundered on the floor.

"SOMEBODY HELP!"

I poked my head through the open doorway. At the same moment, the crowd roared in the football match and the sound hit my ears like an explosion. Shuggy was sitting on the couch, a family-sized bag of salt and vinegar crisps perched on his lap. A two-litre bottle of Pepsi Max sat at his feet.

His eyes bulged with shock. He nearly flipped the couch on its back, such was the violence of him getting to his feet.

"The fuck?"

"There's something wrong with Antonio," I said, twisting my face into a mask of horror.

"Eh?"

"I think he's having some kind of seizure."

Shug's voice shot up an octave. "What the fuck are you doing out of your room?"

I couldn't help it. I grinned, and it must have looked to Shug like a skull leering back at him. Such was the delight I felt in seeing this big dumb fuck in a state of bewilderment. My arms were still rigid behind my back.

I backed out into the corridor.

"Room nineteen," I said. "He's going to swallow his tongue or something."

Shuggy followed me through the doorway. I don't think he was fully aware of what he was doing. "What the fuck?"

"Antonio's going to die if you don't hurry up!"

Shuggy walked past me. I walked with him, matching his step. The knife was tucked away on his blind side. I kept walking with him as we approached the left turn; this sent a message to his lizard brain that I was no threat. That I wasn't trying to escape.

"Is Antonio taking drugs?" I asked.

Shuggy didn't answer my question. I don't know if he even heard it. He was walking faster, and after the left turn back into the main corridor, I fell behind.

He didn't get much further before he stopped and turned around.

"What are you–?"

The first hit was life or death. Side of the neck, targeting that big vein that jutted out like he'd swallowed taut rope. My arm shuddered as I pulled the knife back. Shug's ashen-white face was all twisted up with confusion. He staggered back. Pressed a hand to his neck and then blood spilled through the cracks in his fingers. Panic flooded his eyes and he lunged at me but the effort threw him to his knees.

A dark pool of blood formed on the carpet, spreading out on either side of Shug like wings. I heard the sharp hiss of air leaving his body.

I watched until the end. It doesn't take that long. When it was over, I dodged the blood as best as I could while getting

Shug's phone and wallet out of his pocket. I skipped backwards as the dark stream chased after me.

"Shit."

There was blood on my hands and shoes but it was okay.
I needed Shug's phone especially. Sean's home address or at
the very least his phone number was bound to be in the list
of contacts.

I walked away, pocketing the phone and wallet. It felt like
I was floating.

The TV was still blaring in reception. Someone had just
missed a penalty and the commentator screamed like it was
the end of the world.

I grabbed my bag off the floor. Threaded the strap
through my arm, hurried through reception and unlatched
the door. There was no time to stop. I was a bag of nerves on
the stairs and I felt the cold biting my skin. I outran every
thought that would make a coward of me. *Keep going*, I told
myself. *Keep moving*. The first door I saw was the fire exit and
I didn't know if it would open at the front or back. I had to
get out so I pushed down on the metal bar, released the lock
and shoved the door open. That was it. I was out, sucking in
the night air. The first free air I'd had in a long time.

I was at the back of the building. Wheelie bins leaned up
against the wall, black bags propping up the lids. There
wasn't much else to see. I closed the fire exit over, then
walked a few paces before I found the entrance to the
narrow alley that led towards streetlights and the sound of
traffic.

I walked down the alley.

It still felt like floating.

I stopped on the pavement, directly in front of the
building.

The hostel was nothing more than an ugly block of concrete flats above a convenience shop. From the outside, there was no indication of the suffering that went on in those upper-level flats.

I guess that was the point.

44

L ike Dorothy in *The Wizard of Oz*, I'd been home all the time.

The hostel was in Glasgow. Can you believe that, Mike? All those years, I'd been so close to Mum. I wanted to see her, more than anything, but I couldn't even think about that yet. The sisters had a chance to do something. For ourselves, for Darcy and for all the people who'd been forced to attend rich men's parties as playthings. All the planning and fantasising we'd done over the years – it had to bear fruit.

The girls who got out had started an online forum. I knew the web address (we all had it memorised) but I'd never seen the website. Sure, sometimes we got hold of someone's phone at these parties. Played around with it for a couple of minutes. I learned about Google. About how to use the internet. But we were watched a lot of the time and we didn't want any trace of that website on their phones. That was for the free girls. It was for connecting if we ever got out.

I didn't even know if any of the free girls were still using the website. Maybe they'd given up on all that. But if it was still there, that's how I'd track them down. Let's see how serious they were about revenge.

Come to think of it, Mike, there was more than one website for the free girls. More than one forum, just in case the rich men ever found it and shut it down.

That happened a few years back, didn't it?

I walked away from the hostel. Rain washing the blood off my hands. Antonio and Shuggy were just the beginning for me.

I looked at the signs on the road, recalling place names I'd heard a long time ago. I never thought much about where the hostel was. I knew it was in Scotland because all the handlers and guards, Antonio excepted, were Scottish.

I checked Shuggy's phone as I walked. Navigated my way into his contacts, which featured over a hundred electronic 'cards' for friends, family and colleagues. Shuggy was a lot more organised than I thought he'd ever be. Sean's full name (Sean Callaghan), his phone number and address were filed under 'C'.

Yes.

It was meant to be. And when I was finished with the hostel boss, that would take me on to the next step. Towards finding the two people I'd been wanting to find for years. The playground kidnappers. Sean had to know where they were. Their names.

I wanted them.

The rain fell harder. I wore only a checked shirt with a t-shirt and jeans. Old trainers on my feet. I took shelter under the awning of a restaurant. The card on Shuggy's phone said that Sean lived at an address in Shawlands, located in the southside.

I checked the rucksack. Everything was nice and dry – my spare clothes, Darcy's things and the knife, apart from a few red smears on the blade.

The rain picked up so I found better shelter in the arched entrance to a red sandstone block of flats. It was cold and some old guy walked up to me, a nervous expression on his face, asking if I was there for 'business'. A quick shake of the head and he scurried off down the street, muttering an apology.

I faced the road and felt my heart in my throat every time a car passed. I was waiting for the sharp screech of brakes. Doors flung open. People rushing out, charging at me with lightning speed. Grabbing me. Dragging me away, to punish me for what I did to Shuggy and Antonio.

But no cars stopped.

Rain or no rain, I couldn't hang around. The longer I waited, the more chance the news would reach Sean before I did.

I hurried across the busy road towards a twenty-four-hour petrol station. Walked through the sliding doors and browsed the shelves for a minute, feeling awkward and unsure of myself. I squeezed the ends of my shirt, leaving a wet trail behind me.

The security camera in the corner. I could have sworn it was following me.

The guy behind the counter was about twenty, with a pencil-thin moustache and a bored expression. I walked over that way, clenching my fists at the sides, hoping all the blood was gone.

A thought occurred to me. Was I as famous as Darcy Drummond? Had the world looked for me too?

"Help you?" he asked.

Tinny pop music bled through the speakers. I didn't realise how quiet my voice was until I was forced to speak over it.

"Sorry," I said, starting with an apology for nothing. "Can you help me find this address, please?"

I showed him Sean's address as listed on Shug's phone.

"Have you tried Google Maps?"

"No."

"You should."

The vacant look on my face must have convinced him I didn't have a clue what he was talking about. He took his own phone off the counter. His thumbs tapped away, then he told me that Sean's house was a thirteen-minute drive from the garage.

"Get a taxi," he said. "Or an Uber."

"Uber?"

"Got the app?"

He gave me that pitying look again.

"Want me to call a taxi for you?"

"Thanks."

While I waited for the car to arrive, I bought a small bottle of Coke and some chocolate with Shug's money. Both drink and snack lasted about a minute. Still, it was a much-needed jolt of fuel. As I ate, my mind flashed back to images of Shug and Antonio. They'd never eat anything again. I didn't even know if they had families waiting for them somewhere.

But what about my family?

Who'd cared.

I didn't know if there was enough paper money left for a taxi to Sean's house. I wasn't sure how the credit cards worked either, or if I could use them.

The taxi showed up two minutes later. I jumped in the back and the driver tried to start a conversation. I gave short, clipped answers. I panicked quietly, wondering if this was even a real taxi. Had Sean found out? Had he sent a car to find me?

The driver talked and I squirmed in the back. Feeling sick. Lightheaded. Sweaty palms that stayed sweaty no matter how much I rubbed them on my jeans. Why was this taking so long? Where was Shawlands?

Eventually, we pulled into a quiet cul-de-sac. Few houses. A black cat strolled along the pavement, watching as the taxi stopped beside the kerb.

"Here you go," said the driver.

"Is this it?" I asked, staring through the window. It wasn't what I was expecting.

He repeated the address, I paid and got out quickly. Shuggy had more than enough cash for this taxi and the next one. When the driver asked if I wanted my change, I said no. I closed the door quickly and walked away.

Once the car was gone, I stood on the pavement, ducking the streetlights.

This was interesting.

Sean lived in a quiet, well-to-do neighbourhood with big houses and at least two cars on every driveway. Hard to believe his little slice of paradise was paid for by female slaves. Did his neighbours have the slightest inkling who he was? Were they all monsters too?

A chilly evening breeze grazed the back of my neck.

I stood at the open gate outside Sean's house, facing the driveway. Two SUVs clogged the driveway. The garden was mostly paved, with scattered pot plants at the edges. Curtains were pulled over the bay windows.

I unzipped the rucksack and found the knife. The handle still felt warm.

Unlocking the gate, I walked up the path towards the front door. *Work fast*, I reminded myself. There wasn't a second to lose.

A glance over the shoulder. The street was quiet.

I knocked gently on the door. Too gently, because no one heard me. The TV was low and muffled from inside. I knocked again and this time, I heard a child's piercing voice and the drum-like *thump-thump* of someone sprinting down the hallway. Behind that, the faint sound of a woman yelling for the kid to slow down.

My heart was racing.

He's got a child.

I hadn't even thought about that possibility.

Doubt flooded in. I fought the sudden urge to run, to abandon my plan and call the police instead. But I knew that wasn't enough. And there were certain people who were untouchable. Who were bigger than the police.

Too late.

A dark-haired boy, about five or six, opened the door and my first thought was that he looked so cute in his light blue Spiderman pyjamas. My second thought was that he looked like a mini version of Sean.

A woman's voice from inside the house. Getting louder as she approached the door.

"Robbie, who is it?"

The boy eyed me warily. His tiny voice was hard to hear. "Who are–?"

I grabbed him. Robbie whimpered as I spun him around. Then I locked my arm tight around his skinny chest. He didn't struggle. I felt him go stiff. With my other hand, I put the knife to his throat.

He kept whimpering but didn't scream. I had to get him off the street before someone saw me.

A blonde-haired woman appeared in the hallway with a bottle of water in hand. She wore brightly coloured activewear and her hair was damp with sweat. "Robbie!"

Sean was there a second later. I'd only ever seen him dressed in a blazer and smart trousers in the hostel. That night, he wore a navy t-shirt, crumpled jeans, and he was barefoot.

He stopped dead. I watched as the colour drained slowly from his face.

"Shh," I said to everyone. "Don't make a sound."

45

At four o'clock in the morning, we sat in Sean's car, watching the house across the street. It was still dark and quiet. Even the birds weren't singing yet.

The house was located in Cathcart, about a seven-minute drive from Shawlands. It wasn't as pretty as Sean's house. Not even close. This house was the ugliest one in a row of faded-looking terraced houses that deserved the wrecking ball treatment. The entire street was an eyesore. Litter blew up and down the road like fallen leaves. The smell of cat urine was overpowering.

Maybe it wasn't the houses. Maybe it was me.

We'd been sitting in Sean's SUV for nearly four hours. Everyone was there. I was in the back with Robbie, who'd finally stopped blubbing and calling for his mum. Poor kid. He was innocent in everything except having a pimp scumbag for a father. Sean was in the driver's seat. His wife, Julia, in the passenger seat.

Since our arrival, a couple of cats had walked past the house. Apart from that, nothing else had happened.

Sean glared at me in the rearview mirror. I'd told him to keep both hands on the wheel and, so far, he'd complied. We'd spoken very little. I think Sean wanted his wife and son to think I was a random criminal. That all this was just bad luck.

I leaned forward.

"What do you tell her?" I asked.

I saw the contempt in his eyes. That and a shimmer of panic.

"What's that?"

"What does Julia think you do for a living? Or does she know how you pay for the house? The car. Robbie's Spiderman pyjamas."

Julia's head turned to the side. She was looking at her husband. "What's that supposed to mean?"

Sean shook his head. "Nothing. She's...crazy."

He glanced over his shoulder. Gave his son a weak smile of encouragement. Then, he looked at me, his eyes blazing with fury.

"What do you want from us?"

"This'll do for now."

"Whatever you want, you can have it, okay? Just don't hurt my boy."

"Does she think you work in an office?" I said. "Who knows? Maybe the money is so good she doesn't care where it comes from."

Julia shook her head. "What the bloody hell is she talking about?"

"She's just trying to stir up shit."

I can't imagine what Sean must have thought a few hours ago. The sight of me standing on his doorstep, his little boy at the mercy of one of his slaves. The glimmer of recognition in his eyes. The realisation that this time, he was the one getting fucked. Usually, he'd look at the girls in the hostel like they were *things*.

Not tonight.

I saw the fear in his eyes. I had his life in the palm of my hand and we both knew it.

"Shh," I said, pressing a finger to my lips. Robbie was piping up again with that whimpering noise. "That's a good boy."

Another hour passed. Despite the tension, I heard Julia snoring in the passenger seat. Her head back against the headrest, flopping towards the window side.

Sean glanced at his wife several times over the space of ten minutes. He whispered her name.

"Jools?"

Looked to me like he was checking to make sure she was really asleep. Then, satisfied that she was out of it, his eyes found me in the rearview. His voice a low growl.

"If you touch my boy–"

I leaned forward an inch. "You'll do what? Are you really in a position to threaten anyone right now?"

His neck veins bulged. "How did you get out?"

"You'll find out."

"Did someone let you out?"

"You'll find out."

He looked at Julia, then shook his head. His eyes shone with fear, frustration and anger.

I glanced at Robbie. His head was pressed against the window, his eyelids heavy and closing. Looking at the boy, I felt a surge of pity. He seemed sweet enough but what chance did he have growing up with Sean as a role model?

"This is definitely the right house?" I asked.

I could almost hear his brain ticking over. "It's the last address I have for them. We're not exactly on socialising terms."

"Are they still...active?"

"No."

I saw a bead of sweat trickling down the side of Sean's face. There was little chance of him falling asleep.

"Don't say anything else," he said. "Alright? I did what you said. I brought you here."

"So she doesn't know."

Sean studied his wife's face. His mouth twisted into a frown.

"No."

I stared at the house, waiting for dawn. Waiting for a glimpse of them. I hadn't forgotten their faces after all these years and I don't think I ever could. They'd visited my nightmares plenty of times. They'd smiled. Circled the wire fence around the playground and stalked the children.

"It's alright," I said to Robbie as he stirred in his sleep.

The words felt hollow.

I glanced at the digital clock up front. It was just after five o'clock in the morning. Looking outside, the dark sky showed hints of breaking up. Shards of pink and blue light had appeared in the cracks in between the cloud cover.

"How *did* you get out?" Sean asked.

I pointed the knife at him.

"What happened to Darcy?"

The bastard smiled at me. Then, a quick shrug. "I don't know anyone with that name. Never have."

I fell back in the seat. I felt tired for the first time since getting out of the hostel. My back was stiff. My throat felt dry and cracked. Still, the morning rays found their way into

Sean's SUV and revived me. And the birds were singing at last.

Half an hour later, the front door of the house opened. I sat up. Pressed my face against the cold glass window.

My hands were shaking.

The woman had put on a lot of weight since I last saw her. She took the steps tentatively, like someone in pain, then walked down the garden path and tossed a black binbag into the wheelie bin. I could see her breath in the morning chill. She lifted her head, as if searching for the warmth of the sun.

"Listen," I said to Sean. "Listen good. Whatever you hear over the next couple of weeks, forget it, okay?"

"What do you mean?"

"You'll hear about them. You'll read about them. Forget it. Forget me, forget *this*."

He whispered. "You sick little bitch. What are you planning?"

"That's all you're getting. Forget it or I'll tell the police what goes on in the flats above the convenience shop. One anonymous phone call. That's all it takes."

He shook his head. "Fucking hell."

"All you need to do is stay quiet. No matter what happens. Do that and you can go on living your double life. Okay? You can be a pimp *and* a family man."

"Quiet," he hissed.

"Do we have a deal?"

He gave me a reluctant nod.

I opened the car door and stepped outside. The pinch of a cruel winter was already in the air. Quickly, I tucked the knife into my back pocket.

Sean started the engine and Julia woke up from her

unplanned nap. She looked at me with a fearful expression through the passenger side window. Then, she looked at Robbie in the back.

Sean touched her arm. She pulled it away.

I tapped a finger on the window. Motioned for Julia to open it, which she did no more than an inch.

"One last thing," I said to Sean. I jerked a thumb at the house. "What are their *real* names?"

He glared at me one last time.

"Burton," he said. "Trevor and Hattie Burton."

46

You see now, Mike?

Lies. I made it all up. Everything I told the police that night was a lie. Poppy Burton never existed. I wasn't brought up by two weirdos on a diet of fear and violent newsclips. I wasn't home-schooled. Trevor wasn't losing his mind and Hattie didn't like to draw or think about swallowing a bottle of pills.

The Burton house – I was there for a week.

Oh, and I hate cartoons.

Those old bastards were tougher than they looked. I'll give them that. The Burtons were older and slower than I remembered from their stalking kids' playgrounds days. Now they were all grey hair and cardigans and fluffy slippers. Two monsters withering away.

I knocked on their door. She opened and I forced my way into the house. It was easy. I tied them up with their own rope. Tied them tight. Gagged them. You should've seen the look on their faces when I told them who I was. Now, I don't know if they remembered me specifically, but they knew I was one of their grabs come back to haunt them.

They both screamed behind their gags when they saw the knife.

I didn't hold back but at the same time, I had to be strategic about the wounds. They had to fit the story of the last supper. But the reality of what happened in that house was far more straightforward than the Darcy lie I fed the police. The Burtons paid the price for what they did to me. For what they did to all the children.

You see now, Mike?

This was personal but it was also laying the groundwork for the next stage. That is, for Darcy's revenge. And Darcy's revenge was all about finding the man in her drawings. The man with the gold watch. The man she couldn't forget.

I showered for a long time when it was over. Stood under a torrent of hot water, letting it rake down my back while I listened to their gagged screams still ringing in my head. Four people dead because of me. And still I felt numb. Neither good nor bad. Just nothing.

I washed most of the blood off but it was stubborn around my nails. No matter how hard I scrubbed with their shower brush, I couldn't get it all out.

I stepped out of the shower, my skin red and glowing from the heat. Dried off with a fresh towel. Wiped the mirror clear and then opened a window. I stood in front of the mirror, staring at my reflection.

Something had to change.

I found a pair of scissors in the Burtons' bathroom cabinet amongst all the medication. There were a *lot* of pill bottles in that house, and a pill crusher too. Without thinking about it too long, I began to cut my hair. I practiced my faces, remembering Darcy's smile. Recalling her voice, her shyness, her eyes and mannerisms. Even when I'd cut my hair down to the right length, I stood there for hours, trying to recreate the puzzle of Darcy. Letting go of myself. Slipping into her skin, which was so much easier than I'd expected.

It felt good to disappear into someone else.

The Burtons had a computer and monitor set up in their bedroom. I couldn't get in because there was a password blocking access. I'd used the internet a little at some of the parties I'd attended, always supervised, of course. But I did know that phones could be unlocked with facial recognition technology or even a fingerprint.

There was a phone on the bedside table. Sure enough, it asked for a fingerprint.

I walked downstairs into the kitchen where I'd left the bodies. Tried his finger, then hers. It was her phone.

I sat at the kitchen table and looked up my own disappearance. There wasn't much and it felt like the world had moved on perfectly well without me. I was tempted to type Mum's name into the box. See if there was a picture of her. But I couldn't do it. I didn't even know if she was alive or not. If she'd moved to another country.

Did she have other children now?

I read up on Darcy's story. Caught up with the latest news reports, and there were plenty of those kicking around because of the anniversary. I read and read. Took it all in. Reading about Darcy was hard but looking at happy childhood photos of her was even worse. I couldn't forget the sight of her withering away on that bed.

I took a lot of showers in that house but never felt clean. Some dirt you can't wash off.

And the blood was stuck in my nails.

I'd already moved the Burtons' bodies into position for the last supper story. Laid them out in the kitchen, trying to make it look like they'd just fallen that way. I had to cook. Thank God for the internet and YouTube – that's all I can say. My cooking skills were non-existent. I raided the pantry, the fridge and whatever. On top of everything else, I had to make a pot of soup, for God's sake, and although it tasted horrible, it looked the part. I tipped it over the bodies. Mostly on Hattie, because Trevor was supposed to push her backwards so she knocked the pot over.

I made the kitchen table look really nice. Presented everything perfectly, just like it was really happening. Trevor and Hattie's dead eyes watched me all the way. Then, I swept the plates, glasses and cutlery onto the floor. The candles too.

That bit was fun.

The scene was starting to take shape. Didn't matter that my fingerprints were everywhere. There was nothing in the story that prevented 'Poppy' from touching the bodies at any point.

All I had to do was wait a week. Poppy wasn't supposed to go to the police until one week after their deaths.

I lived off sandwiches and tea. Making food was pretty uncomfortable with the way the bodies were starting to stink up the place. Flies all over the house too. But I had to eat and I had to stay there for a week after the last supper. And that week allowed me the time to do the things I had to do.

For starters, I had to create Hattie's picture book. There was a drawer in the living room with several diaries, mostly outdated and unused. Some plain notepads and lined journals too. I picked one. Grabbed some colouring pens and crayons from another drawer and scribbled all sorts of crap in there, creating a backstory for the Burtons. Dating, falling in love, a wedding with no guests – all of it fictional. There was only one page that mattered. That was the bait for when I made it to the Drummond house.

The handover on the beach. The man in the gold watch.

As long as I could get 'Hattie's journal' into the Drummond house, someone in the immediate and extended family would eventually see the book. See *that* page. I wanted to provoke a reaction and I'd be looking out for it whilst playing the role of a kid who wasn't doing very much. A long shot maybe but if the person I was looking for did reveal themselves, I'd know where to strike.

And of course, there were others who had a price to pay. I hadn't forgotten about the men who ran the parties.

I logged on to the sisters' forums. One of the websites was gone but the second was still online and active. I opened a fresh account and made contact. There was a security check and I filled the box up with things that had happened – things only the sisters and I would know. Took a while to get a response and, at first, no one believed it was me. They thought it was the rich men trying to catch them out. Eventually, phone calls were made. They realised it was me and that I was trying to activate the plan.

Stacey. Jess. Katy. They all began to show up, and others too. They were nervous about taking this out of the realm of revenge fantasy, not surprising when you consider who we were going up against. Still, I reminded them of what I'd already done and what these powerful people had done to us at the parties. I realised I was the leader. I'd killed. There was so much more to come and I needed them with me. I needed that guarantee of sisterhood until the end.

They said yes. I wasn't convinced but what choice did I have but to believe them?

We all got ready.

One week passed. It was time to leave the Burtons' house.

I planted Darcy's teddy bear, hat and t-shirt in the Burtons' attic. That was a huge win for me when it came to getting into the Drummond house. No one would doubt me, and if they did, there was always the DNA test. I knew that was coming sooner or later, and if I played my cards right, it would be later. Once they'd taken me home. I could only hope that Darcy's belongings in the Burton house was enough to convince everyone until the test confirmed it one hundred percent. And it was.

So, how did I pass the DNA test?

Luck, mostly. But I didn't pass anything. It just looked that way.

Lola's a sweet girl. I'm glad I made friends with her but she *was* the obvious candidate when I researched your children. I had to make friends with one of them.

The mouth swab didn't touch me, Mike. Remember the fuss I kicked up in the days leading up to the test? Made quite the scene, didn't I? The neurotic child act. Exhausting but necessary. And who'd question it after what 'Darcy' had been through?

I think the guy from the accredited laboratory was a little starstruck.

You remember how it went, don't you? I pretended Lola was my comfort blanket. We went upstairs with DNA Guy to get away from everyone. I didn't want you or Sophie there. I insisted on that. And I didn't want DNA Guy putting a swab in my mouth, so I acted like I was scared. I

put my arm around Lola and she did the same. Such a
sweet girl – I wish she really was my sister. We sat side by
side on the bed. DNA Guy hesitated when I asked him to
look away. I cried when he said he couldn't. So I said I
couldn't do it with him watching because Trevor Burton
used to watch me like a hawk, jumping on every little
mistake I made. He was just a young guy. I could see he
was flustered and so I kept stalling. Finally, he turned his
head over his shoulder. Asked me if that was okay. Perfect, I
said. I nudged Lola, then pressed a finger to my lips.
Quickly, I ran the swab around the inside of her mouth. It
was funny. Kind of exciting. She almost gave it away by
laughing but I shook my head. Gave her a look that said it
was our secret.

Then, I told the man he could turn around. And just as
he did, I pulled the swab out of my mouth. But it never
touched me. It was Lola's DNA that went inside the
envelope.

I was lucky. It only worked because Darcy Drummond
was famous and her ordeal made everyone walk on
eggshells around her. Even DNA Guy. And I had Darcy's
things – the teddy bear, t-shirt and hat. I *was* Darcy. The
world wanted Darcy back. They *needed* her back. And so,
they got her.

Everything was ready to go. The house was ready, my
story was ready, the Burtons were ready on the kitchen floor,
and the sisters who'd escaped were waiting for me to signal
them on the forum. That's when they'd know it was time.
That's when they'd come to the designated location. Somewhere quiet. Somewhere close to the Drummond house in
Morningside, Edinburgh.

You should have seen the look I got from the woman

behind the front desk in Cathcart Police Station. Like I was crap on her shoes.

"I think you're looking for me," I said.

She arched her eyebrows. "Oh? And who might you be?"

I didn't hesitate.

"My name is Darcy Drummond."

47

I look at Mike slumped in the chair. He's bloody and exhausted, even more so after my story. But his eyes are wide open.

"So," I say, taking a step back. "Now you know what happened to Darcy after you handed her over. The newspapers said you were a big gambler. But still – you must have owed someone a *lot* of money."

He keeps shaking his head.

"I didn't–"

"I think she still loved you, Mike. After all, she never said your name in the hostel. Not once, even to her closest sisters. You were always 'the man with the gold watch' in her drawings. Weird that she'd try to protect you, especially after what you did to her."

He coughs and narrowly misses spraying blood on me.

"I didn't do it."

Fragments of sunlight find their way through cracks in the boarded-up windows. These cylindrical shapes are a hundred tiny spotlights on Mike's gruesome face, which looks like something out a horror movie.

"Liar."

His head wobbles from side to side. Eyes blinking furiously.

"I loved her."

"You killed her."

Mike is an explosion of movement. It's like his clothes have caught fire. He jerks back and forth, battling the rope that's tied around his chest and wrists. The knots hold and he tips the chair over.

"I LOVED HER."

I look down at him on the floor.

"Is that why you drink so much?" I ask. "Because of what you did?"

Mike sounds like a dying animal on the floor.

"They were...going to kill...Sophie and the boys."

He bawls like a child, his face buried in the floor.

I walk around the fallen chair. Lean over, grab the back and pull Mike back into an upright position. He makes a gagging noise on the way up and I'm sure he's about to puke all over me. He doesn't.

I glance at the graffiti on the wall. Colourful squiggles of spray paint, words and images combined, a gift from the teenagers who break in here after dark, looking for somewhere to drink cheap cider and beer. Remnants of their parties litter the far corner of the room. Broken glass. Plastic bags. Even a few needles.

"So," I say to Mike. "You confess?"

48

M y fingers on the knife handle are slippery with sweat. The grip uncertain as I press the blade against Mike's exposed jugular.

"You confess then?"

"It wasn't me," Mike says. "I loved her."

"You just said they were going to kill Sophie and the boys."

Mike's dazzling blue eyes narrow in confusion. "What?"

"You're a pathetic drunk," I tell him, leaning in closer. "Aren't you? You flew too close to the sun and burned your wings. Except, they weren't your wings. And yet you had to pay for them somehow."

We're eye to eye. Mike's chest heaves up and down and I can smell the whisky on his breath but despite that, I stay there until he finds the words.

"I've been in Hell all these years," he croaks.

"You don't know what Hell is."

He looks away.

"You confess then?" I ask.

It's a long time coming. A simple nod of the head.

"Don't tell Sophie. It'll kill her."

"What about the rest of it?"

That gets his attention. "What?"

"You've got more than one confession to make, haven't you?"

His face distorts with horror. "I don't...what are you talking about?"

"You remember the parties, Mike? Don't you? Back in the day, the parties with all the girls on the boats. In the big houses. The parties, Mike. Think."

"Parties?"

I slap his face. Hard.

"Don't play the fool. You and Edward Wallace might hate each other's guts but that doesn't mean you won't come together for special occasions. You getting me yet, Mike?"

His eyes flicker with confusion.

"I'll get revenge for Darcy," I whisper in his ear. "But I want it for so many others too."

I turn my back on him. Then I walk over to the windows and find a loose board. I pry it backwards as far as it'll go, just enough to see on to the driveway. I see Mike's Audi parked where I left it.

I look outside, not daring to blink.

Listening. Waiting.

"Let's wait until the others get here, shall we?"

49

It doesn't take long before I hear a car pull up outside Redhall House. There's a flicker of excitement and the whoosh of blood pulsing in my ear.

"HERE WE GO," I say, turning back to Mike. "They found us."

PART IV

Revenge

50

MARGO

The search for Mike and Darcy is still on. But we've had to come back to Sophie's house because she left in such a panic earlier that she forgot to take her phone with her.

She hurries into the kitchen ahead of Edward and me. The phone is charging on the kitchen counter.

I'm standing at the door. Edward and Sophie are side by side while Sophie scrolls through her phone checking for messages. Her thumbs are a blur as they tap the screen. The main reason for getting the phone, however, is to use the family tracking app that's been installed on all the Drummond phones. Mike, Sophie and the children all have it. It seems like the best chance of finding them. So far, we've driven around the outskirts of Edinburgh in search of Mike's car. Needle in a haystack feels like an understatement. We've called Mike on Edward's phone and it keeps going straight to voicemail.

Sophie's hands shake to the point of distraction. Edward

tries to take the phone off her but she snaps and refuses to hand it over.

"Give me some space, Dad."

I feel like doing something useful so I pour three glasses of water at the sink. No one touches them once I've lined them up on the counter. Not even me. I stand beside Sophie, and a map of the local area pops up on her screen. Different-coloured pins for each family member, most of the pins landing here on the house.

She pinches the screen and the names expand: Mike, Sophie, Maria, Tom and Nick. I guess Darcy doesn't have a phone yet.

Sophie zooms in on 'Mike'. Her chest is heaving.

"Where are you?" she mutters.

"I always knew he was scum," Edward says, his disdainful expression landing on me. "I didn't want to believe he was involved but there were so many signs."

"Shut up, Dad," Sophie says, not looking up from the screen. "I'm trying to track Mike's phone, for God's sake."

Edward rolls his eyes. "Look at the way he behaved after Darcy's disappearance. The grief was always too theatrical for my liking. Too rehearsed."

Sophie looks up this time. "SHUT UP!"

Edward sighs, then walks to the door. "I'll go check on the kids."

"Fuck!" Sophie yells after her father goes upstairs. She holds the phone up, waving it right and left.

"What is it?" I ask.

"It's not giving me the location. It's stuck or something."

I lift a glass of water off the counter. Force it into Sophie's hand, and it takes a few seconds for her fingers to grip the cold surface. She sips at my insistence.

"C'mon," I say. "Your router's in the living room, isn't it? Maybe we'll get a better signal in there."

We relocate and Sophie flops into the armchair like a ragged doll. After a moment, she sits forward and places her phone on the coffee table. She stares at the map. Waiting for Mike's location to reveal itself.

"Stupid thing."

"It'll work," I say.

"Maybe I should close the app down," she says after ten seconds. "Try again from scratch."

"Can't hurt."

While we're waiting for the app to sort itself out, I pick up one of the family photo albums still lying open on the coffee table. Sophie must have left them there for Darcy's benefit. *Look, this was you. This can be you again!* I get up with a book, walk around the living room and browse the images.

"C'mon," Sophie says through gritted teeth. She's holding the phone like she's about to smash it on the table. "Fucking work!"

I hear the toilet flush upstairs. Listen to Edward's footsteps on the landing. He's got heavy feet and the house sounds like it's under attack.

"Anything yet?" I ask Sophie.

She shakes her head.

I leave her to it. Browse through the first, then second album. Darcy's baby photos dominate. Then it's all about young Darcy and the baby twins. Birthdays. Kindergarten. All of it leading to that horrific and life-changing day on Bournemouth Beach. I wonder why Sophie kept so many photos from the Bournemouth trip, let alone put them in an album. I'm not sure I'd want to look back.

I dive into the Bournemouth photos. It was, in fact, a

road trip down the east coast of England that wound its way round to Bournemouth on the south. I feel a surge of anxiety looking at these photos, as if all of this is happening in real time. Building up to the moment their holiday came to a crashing halt.

Mike, Sophie, Darcy and the twins splashing around in a water park. Eating candy floss at a funfair. Sitting with Edward and Liz in a restaurant. The Drummonds visiting an animal sanctuary. Smiles for the camera. Visiting some kind of Lego-World playpark. And of course, photos on the beach. From that day.

I look through several beach shots. Stop. Go back.

My muscles are tensing up.

There it is. The gold watch on Mike's tanned wrist and all the confirmation I need that he was involved in Darcy's disappearance. The fucker gave his daughter away to clear his debts. He must have been planning it for a while. Someone (or several people) from the organisation he owed money to must have been there on the beach for the actual handover itself. The Burtons weren't up to the handover but that doesn't mean they weren't there. Watching from the sidelines, somehow. Hattie saw the gold watch and drew it in her journal. They must have known for a while they were getting a blonde child.

Fuck. It's horrible. That poor girl.

And now Mike's cracked. He's grabbed her and we've no idea what he's planning to do next. Am I next? Is he going after anyone who suspects his involvement in Darcy's kidnapping?

The hairs stand up on the back of my neck. Upstairs, I hear the creak of Edward's feet on the floor. He's up there walking from room to room, checking on the Drummond children.

I stare at the ceiling. Then, I look at Sophie, who's absorbed in the task of getting the app to work.

This is my chance. She needs to see Hattie's drawing.

Now.

51

MARGO

"We need to talk, Sophie," I say, putting the photo album down on the table. I sit down on the armchair and as the nerves engulf me, my right leg starts to shake.

She doesn't look up from the phone. "I'm kind of busy right now."

"Sophie–"

There's no warning. She snaps at me like I'm a five-year-old child pestering Mummy for attention. "Margo, will you *please* be quiet? I'm trying to get this fucking app to work so I can find my husband and daughter."

I want to yell and scream but someone in this room, in this entire fucked-up scenario, has to keep their shit together. I take a deep breath. Then, I pull the folded piece of paper out of my pocket. Unfold it. Quietly.

"You *have* to look at this."

"Margo–"

"Now."

Something about the way I say it makes Sophie look up

from the phone. She narrows her eyes at the piece of paper in my hand. I offer it to her.

"What's that?" she asks.

"It's the missing page from Hattie's journal."

Her face hardens and for the first time since we came back to the house, Sophie's really listening to me.

"Where did you get that?"

"Mike's coat pocket. He left it in the casino last night and the slimeball who runs the place gave it to me."

"You went to the casino?"

"Yes."

"Why?"

I shrug. "To talk to the slimeball."

Sophie shakes her head. "I don't understand. Why did you want to talk to him?"

"That's not important right now," I say, thrusting the slip of paper towards her. "Look at the picture, will you? Look what Hattie drew in her journal."

She takes it but doesn't look right away. The poor woman knows something terrible is waiting for her on that page.

"It's Bournemouth Beach," I say. "It's the handover, Sophie. Look at it. Look at *him*. Look what's he wearing on his wrist."

Sophie's lips move but nothing comes out. It's like her internal wiring has short-circuited.

"Sophie–"

"It's only a drawing, for God's sake."

"I know you and the kids were threatened. And they weren't idle threats either. Didn't you ever wonder why it just stopped?"

She doesn't answer and I snatch the paper out of her hand.

"Three child-sized coffins on your doorstep? Holy shit. These weren't back-alley loan sharks chasing a couple of grand. Mike borrowed too much money from the wrong people."

Sophie pushes herself slowly off the chair. Her eyes simmer with rage. "Margo, you should leave."

She's still my friend. I want to help her. I want to go over and put my arm around her but right now that'd be like trying to stroke an angry lioness.

"I'm not going anywhere," I say.

"Why would Mike take Darcy?" she says in a whisper. "If he *was* involved, why would he take her now?"

I shake my head. "Mike's not thinking very clearly right now. This latest fuck-up at the casino might have tipped him over the edge. We have to find them. And when we do–"

Sophie's phone chirps. We both stare at it before Sophie grabs it off the table. She studies the map and her eyes light up.

"I know where they are."

I nod.

"Shall we call your dad?"

Sophie glances at the ceiling.

"No. Dad's the last person in the world Mike needs to see right now."

52

SOPHIE

I'm at the end of my rope.

First, my long-lost daughter comes home and it still feels like everything's falling apart. Mike's drinking and gambling is worse than ever. My self-medicating isn't much better. The kids, apart from Lola, are wary of Darcy. So am I.

Nothing has been right for thirteen years.

Nothing.

And now this? The dawning realisation of what my parents and Margo have been trying to tell me and all those nasty online whispers that just might be true.

Did he do it?

Did Mike know someone was going to snatch her away from us?

I don't know how much more I can take. But something keeps me going – the truth. I want the truth. In fact, I *demand* the truth. As long as anger holds back my exhaustion, I'll keep hunting for answers.

Fuck this. Fuck being helpless all the time.

We're in my car. Margo's driving like a maniac, travelling west along Glenlockhart Road, following Mike's signal. A massive golf course whizzes past on the right. A wall of stooped, shedding trees leans over the road. Most of the scenery is a blur.

"We don't want to get pulled over," I say. "Margo?"

"I'll drive," she says, flooring the accelerator. "You just make sure I'm going in the right direction."

"What are we going to find when we get there?"

"They'll be alright."

"If...if Mike is involved, I don't care if he's alright."

"Let's just get there."

"And what if they aren't there? What if the phone was dumped and we're chasing an empty signal?"

"What if the sky falls on top of our heads?"

"What?"

"One thing at a time, Sophie."

I stare at the road ahead. Margo's got me thinking all kinds of crazy things. I know my family is a mess, and on top of all Mike's shit, my father is a serial cheater who likes fooling around with younger women. God help us. We're the epitome of rich and fucked up but we don't have to be *this* fucked up. I've got children who need some stability in their life. They're my priority now, no matter what I find out today. I haven't always been a good mother but if one positive thing comes out of this mess, it'll be my kids getting a mother who's got her shit together. And that starts with being present.

"Did you text your mum?" Margo asks.

I nod. "She's on her way to the house."

"Your dad will be wondering why we ran out on him."

"I don't care. Mum will calm him down. Anyway, he's

going to be ecstatic if his suspicions about Mike turn out to be true."

"Ecstatic?"

"Ecstatic. That's how much he loathes Mike. He'd do anything to get rid of him."

"Jesus."

"I know. We're messed up."

Margo's face is a picture of concentration as she grips the wheel. She doesn't drive much, to my knowledge, and yet she's tearing through the streets in my car like a Formula One driver fleeing a bank robbery. We're still going too fast.

"Tell me where I'm going, Sophie."

"Straight ahead," I say, following the map. "Nearly there. There's a left turn coming up in five hundred metres. Four hundred. Margo, time to slow down."

"We'll be fine."

Mercifully, she slows down. Then, out of nowhere, she hits the steering wheel.

"You know something?" she says. "This gets crazier the more I think about it."

"That's comforting."

"Your parents hate Mike's guts, right?"

"Yes."

"And your dad especially would love to prove that he was involved in Darcy's disappearance?"

I shake my head. "What are you going on about, Margo?"

Her foot touches the brake pedal, slowing the car to a crawl. Fortunately there's no traffic behind us.

Margo talks without pausing for breath. "An ex-boyfriend called me out of the blue recently. Bit of a conspiracy nut. Not one of my finest moments but never mind that now. Anyway, he's banging on about Mike all the time, about proving how he had something to do with Darcy's disappearance. He's fucking obsessed. Now, on the same night he makes contact, I get a weird voice-disguised phone call telling me I need to look at Hattie's picture book. Someone really wanted me to notice that missing page, Sophie. Well, I noticed it and then voilà! It shows up in Mike's pocket."

"What are you saying?"

Margo nods while looking at the road. "Steve was at the casino last night. And he knows I was there too."

"You were there last night too?"

"Long story. Anyway, what if, somehow, Steve got close and slipped the missing page in Mike's pocket?"

I feel sick. "What the fuck, Margo?"

"It's possible. It *is* possible."

"How?"

"The pocket was shallow. No one would put it in there for safekeeping. It could easily have slipped out in front of anyone, and in fact, that's what happened. Right? That's how I found it. I'll bet you a million pounds that Hattie's drawing was planted in Mike's pocket."

My head is throbbing. "And how would this Steve guy get his hands on a page from Hattie's journal in the first place?"

Margo stops the car in the middle of the road.

"Edward gave it to him. They're working together."

"*What?*"

"My mystery caller – I think it was your dad."

"Dad?"

Margo laughs and it's so inappropriate that I'm stunned into silence. "You fucking rich people," she says. "You're so weird."

She looks at me. Her expression has changed to all business.

"I think Edward wanted me to start digging around. I'm a journalist. Not a very good one, I'll admit, but I got a lot of publicity out of that Darcy article. If I was somehow to come to the conclusion that Mike was involved in Darcy's kidnapping, well, I could gather a lot of media attention, and fast. Edward would've loved that."

I think I'm going to pass out.

"Edward and Steve," Margo says, shaking her head. "My God, what a combo. I'll bet Edward gave Steve his cuts and bruises today too. Anything to make Mike look unstable."

"Margo," I say. "We better keep going."

The satnav talks to me, distracting me from the churning sensation in the pit of my stomach. I direct Margo straight ahead and we roll down a wide but quiet street with long rows of modern houses on either side. Nice-looking neighbourhood. Everything clean. Lawns neat, hedges trimmed.

"Redhall House. Take this right turn up here."

"What right turn?" Margo asks.

"That one. Turn right now!"

Margo spots the turn late but catches it. An ever-narrowing lane steers us away from civilisation. Crooked trees lean over us like curious strangers, blotting out the sun. It's like we've ventured into another world.

"Redhall House," I say. "It's down there."

"Creepy."

"Should we park here on the road and walk–"

But Margo's already accelerating and, before I know it, she's pulled up in front of the building. The car skids to a stop on the gravel.

"Nothing like a quiet entrance, is there?"

"That's the least of your worries right now," Margo says, unlocking her seatbelt.

We sit in silence, looking at Redhall House. It's boarded up at the front, cold and uninviting. Once, it had been beautiful. Now it's a piece of fading history, neglected year after year. There's a heavy air of sadness hanging over this place. I can feel it.

Margo kills the engine.

I unbuckle my seatbelt and reach for the door handle. Before stepping outside, I turn to Margo and feel my body shiver. "I'm scared."

"I know," she says, staring at the chilling exterior of Redhall House. "Me too."

53

MARGO

"How do we get in?" I ask Sophie as we approach the building.

Our feet crunch over the gravel.

Fuck this place. I mean, seriously. Talk about uninviting. It's all boarded up at the front and, I imagine, at the back too. It's one giant no-entry sign in the shape of a house, perfectly isolated from the surrounding neighbourhood. We're hidden by trees. There's no sun here. God knows what sort of lowlifes creep around after dark.

"Let's try the back," Sophie says.

There's something different about Sophie. Back at the house, telling her about Mike's involvement in Darcy's kidnapping, I thought she'd reached her limit – and who can blame her? A breakdown seemed imminent. But now, it's like she's got her second wind. Her eyes are clear. Focused. For the first time in a while, Sophie doesn't seem like a piece of glass that's about to break.

We hurry around the back of Redhall House. The windows here are boarded up too, with one exception. A downstairs window where the board's been wrenched off and dumped on the long grass like rubbish. Maybe the crackheads did it. This is probably their doorway.

"I'll go first," I say.

I use the torch on my phone to light the way. The ledge is rough and jagged. Something rakes against my knee as I try to balance my foot on the ledge. My jeans make a ripping noise.

"Shite."

I push upwards, clear the window and drop into the dark interior of Redhall House. My landing sounds like a plane crash as far as I'm concerned. I take a couple of steps forward. Sophie's a beat behind me. I feel her breath on the back of my neck after she lands.

"Are you okay?" I whisper.

She whispers back. "Yes. You?"

"I'm cold."

The smell of cat piss is unmistakable. Quite the treat for sensitive noses. I wince but start walking forward. Sophie's beside me as I shine the light onto the floor, illuminating fragments of debris at our feet. Anything goes in here. I see rocks, shards of glass, cardboard, bricks, a mangled-looking children's doll and plastic bottles. There's spray-paint on the wall. It's hardly the work of Banksy.

It's so quiet in here, except for the sound of our feet brushing the floor. Man, this place is creepy. We exit the back room, cover the hallway and notice a staircase up ahead. There's a door for the 'Ladies and Disabled Toilets' at the end of the hallway. A big room next to it, overlooking the front where we parked. We walk in, and along with pinpricks of daylight spilling through the boarded-up windows there's a hint of torch or lamplight. Sophie and I are not alone.

She greets us before we've fully turned the corner.

"Hello."

At last. We've found Mike and Darcy.

Sophie screams and I don't even think about it – I just grab hold of her because if I don't, she might collapse to the floor. It's like she's having a fit, her limbs jerking in a series of uncontrollable muscle movements. It lasts about five seconds. Then it's over and she's as still as a mannequin in my arms.

"Easy," I tell her. "I've got you."

Mike didn't take Darcy. *She* took him. And it's immediately after that first horrific glimpse inside Redhall House that I remember back to the beginning of all this. Back to the way I felt when I first heard that Darcy, aka Poppy, had stayed in the Burtons' house after overhearing their plan to kill her and discovering who she really was. And the way it made me feel.

That it was bullshit.

But I pushed my doubt away when she passed the DNA test.

Now, I know.

This isn't Darcy.

The girl stands in the centre of the room with a knife in hand. Blood drips from the blade. Mike's tied to a wooden chair beside her, barely conscious. His head flops around in a sluggish rhythm while he emits a low, continuous wheeze that makes it sound like he's deflating. His face looks like a sick art project.

"Mike," Sophie whispers.

I hold her back again and it's like fighting off a bear.

Mike groans. His handsome face is ruined forever. "S... S...Sophie."

The girl is eerily calm. It's obvious she's been waiting for us and that she must have known about the tracking app on Mike's phone. Still, the look on her face. I swear it's disapproval. Her voice cuts like a razor blade.

"Where's Edward?"

I let go of Sophie and she doesn't fall or try to make a run for it. She's holding strong, for now at least. And that's without the pills.

"We need to get Mike to a hospital," I say. "He's lost a lot of blood."

The girl doesn't seem to register my words. "Where's the old man? I thought he'd come with you."

"You thought Edward would be here with us?"

"Hoped."

It's not easy but I hold her gaze. In the dim light, she looks otherworldly.

"Darcy," Sophie says, stepping forward. She reaches a hand across the room, shivering like we're standing in a giant freezer. "Why–?"

The girl shakes her head. "Not Darcy."

Sophie lets out a low, miserable wail as the wall of grief crashes back down on top of her. There's a flicker of emotion in the girl's eyes. It might be regret.

"Who are you?" I ask.

The girl looks at me and nods. "Get Edward Drummond here if you want to know the answer. Get him here fast."

54

SOPHIE

Dad's tinny voice grates in my ear.

"Redhall House?"

"Yes," I say. "Can you please come over here?"

"Now?"

"NOW."

The phone is on loudspeaker and everyone in the room can hear our conversation. At this point, I'm numb. Automatic pilot is running the show. That's how I can function, that's how I can make a phone call. My husband is tied to a chair and slowly bleeding to death before my eyes. The girl who fooled me into thinking my daughter had come home is the one killing him. And although I don't understand anything anymore, I have to convince my dad to walk into the lion's den.

"Redhall House?" he repeats. "The children's home?"

"Please, Dad."

"What the hell is going on, Sophie? Why did you and Margo just run off without saying anything to me?"

"Dad," I say, staring at the girl. *Why won't she look at me?*

"I'm sorry we ran out but something's happened and I need you here. Just you. Leave the kids with Mum and come to Redhall House right away."

"Sophie–"

"When you get here, go around to the back of the house and climb in through the downstairs window. We're in the big room at the front."

"*We?*"

"You have to hurry, okay?"

I expect more protests, but there's a long silence instead.

"Dad?"

I can hear his raspy breathing down the line. At that moment, I have the overwhelming feeling that I'm talking to a stranger. After all, I don't know my husband. My eldest daughter is still gone. Family has never felt so fragile.

Finally, he speaks.

"Stay there, Sophie. I'm on my way."

55

THE GIRL

The others will be here soon.

None of us thought this would ever happen. We *wanted* it to but that's different than believing it ever would. We were just tired girls, fantasising about revenge during those horrific, demeaning parties and whenever we had a moment to ourselves at the hostel. I fantasised in my drawings. The dream was always there. It was far away but we kept it in sight. The girls who got out of the hostel set up the forums but still, nothing happened. It took Darcy and Emily being taken away from me to push me over the edge. That was the last straw.

But we still had such a mountain to climb. How could nobodies like us get back at such powerful men?

From the inside.

Those two stories would come together – the kidnapping of Darcy Drummond and the hostel. I never told Darcy who organised those depraved parties. If she hadn't been so famous, she would've found out for herself, and that's too horrible a thing to think about. Whenever I came back, tired and sore, she didn't ask and I didn't volunteer the information. It was no surprise, then, to discover that the man in the gold watch, the man who gave her away, was one of those same men who attended the parties.

I've used Mike's phone to go online and signal the forum. They already know where to come because a couple of the girls have been here before, dropping off the chairs, rope and other bits and pieces. But this is the main event. The scary bit.

Will anyone show?

Margo and Sophie ask me questions while we wait for Edward. I ignore them. They beg me to call an ambulance for Mike. I don't. In the end, we wait in silence. Silence, that is, apart from the sound of Mike's laboured breathing as he drifts in and out of consciousness. He's lost a lot of blood.

Finally, we hear a car pull up outside Redhall House. The engine cuts out and Margo goes to the window and pulls back a loose board.

"Is it him?" I ask.

She nods.

"And?"

"He's alone," Margo says.

"Good."

My legs are shaking. What if the others don't come?

"What are you going to do to him?" Sophie asks. "What are you going to do to my dad?"

I don't answer. Instead, I walk over to the corner of the room, push back an assortment of debris and pick up the second coil of rope. It's been here for weeks, hidden under a crumpled sheet of tarpaulin. The junkies have taken the other chairs though. God knows what they did that for. They're not upstairs. I'll just have to make do.

We hear footsteps on the gravel.

"Sophie?"

I press a finger to my lips. No one speaks.

We listen as the old man walks around for a bit. Then, as instructed by Sophie, he goes to the back of Redhall House and labours through the window that isn't boarded up. There's a sharp cry of pain at his landing. A scratching noise on the floor as he claws his way back to his feet. A final groan. Then, the assured footsteps of Edward Drummond return.

"Sophie?"

I look at Sophie. Shake my head.

Edward's footsteps come closer. I wipe the river of sweat off my brow. Squeeze down on the knife handle until it feels like my knuckles might pop.

He walks down the hallway for what feels like forever, then appears in the doorway. It's a casual dress day for Edward; he's wearing double denim and still holding the car key in his hand. His enormous gut strains against the light blue shirt. He's a statue. Motionless. Then, he sees Mike and the horror widens his eyes.

"What the hell is this?"

He looks at Sophie, then at me. His face is a picture of confusion and that's when I walk towards him, just to let him know who's in charge of all this. I make sure he sees the bloody knife.

"About time," I say.

"Darcy?"

I shake my head.

"Not Darcy."

His eyes hop back and forth between Sophie, Margo and the slumped figure of Mike in the chair. His ancient mind works overtime, scrambling for an explanation. But that's like trying to grab smoke. Here is a man who likes to be in control of everything, and today, he's an animal caught in a trap.

I know he doesn't recognise me. There were so many girls at the parties.

"Margo," I say. "Are you good with knots?"

She hesitates.

"Use the rope," I say, "and tie Edward's legs to the chair. Doesn't have to be fancy – just hook him up to Mike's chair."

"Have you gone mad?" Edward says, turning to me. The monster grows tall in my mind and widens, as if unfurling a set of hidden wings. I'm small and I'm scared but I won't let him see. He's seen enough fear in the eyes of young women.

"Darcy," he says.

"She's not Darcy," Sophie says in a grim voice.

I bring the bloody knife closer to him.

"Margo," I say.

Margo leads a bewildered-looking Edward over to Mike's chair. She sits him down, trying to avoid the blood puddles, and takes a deep breath. Then she loops one end of the rope around his ankles and the other around the chair. It'll do for now. She doesn't apologise to the old man as she secures the knots. Doesn't even look at him.

"There's a set of handcuffs over there," I say, pointing to the sheet of blue tarpaulin. "Look underneath it."

Margo straightens up. "What am I supposed to do with them?"

"Put them on the old man."

"This is outrageous!" Edward yells. He glances around the room. "Sophie, what's going on?"

Margo gets the cuffs and fastens them around Edward's

wrists. He doesn't notice that he's sitting on Mike's blood now.

"Did you ask Steve to follow me around?" Margo asks Edward.

He barks. "I don't know anyone called Steve."

Margo takes a step back. "Bullshit. You found out he was my ex and you told him to persuade me of Mike's guilt. Didn't you? I hope you gave him a good tip for the cuts and bruises on his face today. Mike didn't do that. You did, and he let you."

Edward glares at her. "I don't know what you're talking about."

"Mike *was* involved Darcy's kidnapping," Margo says. "But you didn't know that for sure. You've never known for sure. You just hate his guts because he's not good enough, as in rich enough, for your little girl."

"Nonsense."

"Nonsense? You saw that picture in Hattie's diary, the one with the gold watch, and you must have been as giddy as a schoolboy. *You* tore it out. *You* planted it in Mike's coat pocket where it was bound to fall out and be discovered. *You* called me and disguised your voice. Hoping to lead me to that book."

Edward looks up at Margo. "You just said so yourself. He *was* involved."

"Yes, he was involved. But you didn't know. And if he was innocent, you'd still happily see him go down for it. Fucking rich people. You're mad."

I'm impressed by the way Margo goes after the old man. As for Mike, I don't know if he can hear much of anything anymore. Maybe I cut him too much. I want him to look at me. He doesn't remember me either. That much was clear from when we first met at the police station several weeks ago. I was just another pretty face at a party. Another body. Another thing to be used.

I look at Sophie. "Darcy's dead. I'm sorry."

I don't tell her that it happened recently. Somehow, I think that would make it worse. If she wants the details, well, that's for another time. But she deserves that much.

Sophie's eyes are *clawing* at me. It's uncomfortable to look at. "You knew her? You know what happened?"

I nod.

"What about the DNA test?" Margo asks. "You passed."

"I cheated."

Sophie's leaning on Margo's shoulder for support. She's chalk-white on the face and neck and it looks like she's about to puke or pass out. She's lost Darcy twice and I wonder if she's strong enough to bear the load.

"Who are you?" Margo asks.

"A girl. Just one of many."

"One of many?"

"At Edward's parties."

Edward makes a loud scoffing noise before anyone can get a word in. He rattles his handcuffs in protest like a cartoon villain. "What do you want? Money?"

I don't answer. Instead, I turn my attention to Margo and a shellshocked-looking Sophie. "I know it's a lot to take in. You know about Mike's debts so you know why he gave up Darcy. But you don't know about the parties."

"What parties?" Margo asks.

"Edward and Mike *do* hate each other's guts," I say. "But they've both got the same weakness for young women. For *girls*. And when these stronger urges call, they're willing to put their mutual dislike aside."

Margo steps forward, bringing Sophie with her. It's like she's afraid to let go of her friend. "Mike?"

I nod.

Sophie stares at her bleeding husband.

"Mike showed me screenshots from a forum," Margo says. "There were these women or girls talking about Edward Drummond. About what he did to them."

"Taken from the first forum, I'll bet."

"I suppose. I don't know."

"That one was taken down but we've got others with less obvious URLs. And there were plenty of posts on that original forum that also mentioned Mike by name. He didn't show you those, no?"

Margo shakes her head. "No."

"There were lots of men named. Some of them are pretty famous by all accounts."

"What about Trevor and Hattie?" Margo says. "Where do they fit in?"

"Kidnappers. Not Darcy's. Mine."

"Right."

"You'd have to ask Mike who actually lifted Darcy off the beach that day. Someone hired by his creditors, I suppose. All Darcy remembered, or wanted to remember, was that her father was involved in the handover. She drew pictures of the scene, of that day, and it haunted her. It was always Daddy she saw in the betrayal."

Sophie runs to the corner, doubles over and throws up. There's a wet splattering noise. Sounds like she's just relinquished half her body weight.

"Shit," Margo whispers.

"Some of the girls were resourceful," I say, keeping an eye on the doubled-over Sophie. "Intelligent. Angry. We were young but we knew it was wrong. I told the others about Darcy and how they gave her another name in the hostel. As if we didn't have reason enough to hate Mike Drummond. He gave her away and exploited girls just like her."

Sophie straightens up, her eyes cloudy and distant. She wipes a hand over her mouth and walks over to me. "Where's Darcy? Where is she now?"

"I don't know."

"Is she buried? Did they...cremate her? Where can I find her?"

"I don't know. Really, I don't. I didn't even get to say goodbye."

"Me neither," Sophie says.

"I'm sorry we did this to you, Sophie. We had Darcy's belongings and that was a good start. It's not easy to get close to men like Mike and Edward. We had to come at them from the inside. We had to come up with this plan and hope for luck."

Margo nods. She closes her eyes like she's memorising a wall of text. "So, you escaped somehow. You got out. Then, you turned your kidnappers, Trevor and Hattie, into Darcy's kidnappers?"

"And I became Darcy."

"You killed them both," Margo says. "Didn't you?"

"Yes."

Sophie's hand is pressed over her stomach. Her chest rises and falls as she looks at her father and husband.

"Combine resourcefulness, determination and imagination," I say. "And you've got a shot at revenge. I resemble Darcy, so I volunteered. When I lost my roommates, I snapped. I went for it. I drew the picture book with the intent of drawing out the man in the gold watch. It was pretty obvious from the moment I saw Mike that he was the one. Still, I had to be sure. And–"

I look around the room.

"And what?" Margo asks.

"There's still one missing."

"One what?"

"The manager," I say. "The one who organised the parties. The one who dealt with the girls before they were thrown to the men. He's the devil. Maybe even the worst of them all."

"Who?" Margo asks. "Who is he?"

"Funny thing is," I say, "he's another 'gold watch man'. And we can't start the fun and games, not until he's here with his friends."

56

SOPHIE

I stand outside the door, ready to knock.

The girl and Margo are waiting in the car. It's parked on the street, tucked out of sight behind a tall, well-pruned hedge. I can hear the engine running.

She *must* be crazy to send me here. If she's crazy, I don't have to believe any of it. I don't have to believe that my husband gave our daughter away and that he and Dad have been organising depraved parties with young women, with *girls*, for years.

Mike *and* Dad?

I do believe her.

And I believe that she was Darcy's friend.

I should've cracked by now. The load is too heavy but I have a responsibility to my surviving children. They need me. My husband and father are sick and I don't want either one of them anywhere near my children ever again. I'm strong for my kids, but not just them – I'm strong for *myself*. I'm here. I'm still standing.

Redhall House. We have to go back there once I've led

the third man to the car. Whatever happens next, I'm not going to stop it.

My closed fist hovers in front of the door. Trembling.

My days of self-prescription are over, I swear to God. Clarity will be my best friend going forward.

At last, I knock. Take a couple of steps backwards and wait. A bird squawks on the roof and shatters the intense silence. I hear wings flapping. If only I could get away so easily.

Slow, plodding footsteps approach the door. The rattle of a key turning in the lock, which goes on for an eternity. Finally, the door opens and there he is, Jimmy Gold, my old nightwatchman. He's smiling at me. His eyes light up as he steps through the doorway.

"Sophie! Well, this is a pleasant surprise."

57

MARGO

W e're parked in a quiet, leafy suburb about five miles south of Edinburgh. Feels like we've been waiting for days for Sophie to come back with Jimmy Gold, the former nightwatchman.

Gold. Watch. Man.

The girl was right. There were two of them. Mike and Jimmy. What a fucked-up coincidence in a mightily fucked-up situation. Thanks a lot, universe.

I don't know what I'm supposed to do here. Am I supposed to stop all this? Or am I supposed to cheer it on because these twisted fuckers have caused so much suffering to Darcy, this girl, whatever her name is, and all the others?

What do I do?

Holy shit. What a tragedy.

I'm sitting behind the wheel and the engine is still running. The girl sits in the back, wearing Maria's Adidas hoodie (which was in the boot) to cover her blood-stained shirt.

I look through the windscreen. Such a nice day in

contrast to the unfolding horror. Birds chirp. There's only a scattering of clouds, none of which threaten rain. A teenage girl in a school uniform walks her Yorkshire terrier past the car. The dog stops at the back wheel. He lifts his head, nose twitching at the air. I wonder if he smells the blood.

I glance at my watch. Sophie's been gone less than three minutes but it feels like half an hour at least.

"What's your name?" I ask the girl.

"Doesn't matter."

"Fair enough. Can I ask you another question?"

"You can ask."

"How many girls were involved in this elaborate scheme?"

"Just the ones that got out."

"How did they get out?"

"Some managed to escape. Some got old. They don't want you if you're not attractive."

"And they just let them go?" I ask.

"In exchange for silence. Which means they'll kill you if you talk."

"Doesn't that scare you?"

"I don't feel much anymore."

I nod even though I know she's lying. "But you got the all-important job, eh? You went into the Burton house and you had to come back out, telling the world you were Darcy. That took serious guts."

"We had to get inside," she says. "How else would someone like me ever get close to the likes of Mike or Edward Drummond?"

"But you had to kill people."

"The legal system would never give us justice."

"How do you know for sure?"

"Can you imagine us versus the Drummond/Wallace empire in court?"

I don't answer because it's a rhetorical question. Instead, I glance at the top of the Gold house over the hedge. Still nothing. Maybe the sound of voices under the birdsong.

"Did you think you'd make it this far?" I ask. "When you walked into the police station and told them you were Darcy."

She laughs and it's a pleasant change. It's the first time she's sounded almost happy. Whatever else this is, it's an achievement, and I think she's proud of how far she's come. But she doesn't answer the question and when I look over my shoulder, the girl's eyes are closed. Her head leans back. Face screwed up in a tight grimace, like she's having a bad dream.

Where did you go, I wonder.

58

The 'superyacht' party was already in full swing when the girl arrived. The lights were down and the tables full of people, their faces cloaked in the deliberate gloom. On a tiny stage in the corner of the 'Function Room', a live band fed the audience a steady diet of fifties rock and roll classics. Edward Drummond, the man behind the party, had loved fifties music since he was a small boy – Buddy Holly, Jerry Lee Lewis, Elvis Presley, Fats Domino. There was always fifties rock and roll playing all night at Edward's parties. That was a sure thing, along with the girls.

The girl heard raucous laughter even though the boat hadn't begun its voyage onto the loch. But walking up the ramp, then into the Function Room, it seemed like the party had been going on for days.

She'd arrived with three other girls from the hostel. All first-timers, just like her. Mid-to-late teens. They all stood around in the doorway as instructed, awkward and frightened, waiting for someone to come along and tell them what to do. They'd barely spoken to one another in the van that brought them to the marina.

Sure, they'd exchanged a nervous smile here and there. Spoken a few words to ease the tension.

It was just a job. That's what Shug told her back at the hostel and that's what she told herself now. Just a job. Serving drinks. Laughing at their jokes and looking pretty. They'd dolled her up nice and there was always the reward of a nice boat trip on the loch. Forget the creeps. Same as it was in the hostel when she got the call to go upstairs. She was an attractive young girl who looked older than her years, especially with makeup on.

But she wasn't stupid. She wasn't fooled by the surface glamour.

The girls were standing there for about five minutes before someone came to see them. An old guy who called himself Jimmy. He seemed nice.

Jimmy led them to the staff area. Once there, he stood them in line and checked the girls over. Looked them up and down. Ran his hands up and down their bodies without a flicker of emotion. No one protested. A woman came into the room a few minutes later. She was about fifty, blonde-haired and dressed in a stunning red gown that showed off her voluptuous figure. She did the same checking thing that Jimmy did.

The woman explained what the girls had to do. Be good waitresses, she said. Hostesses. It was nothing they hadn't already heard: serve drinks, talk to the men, laugh at their jokes, etc. She opened the door and led them back towards the Function Room.

I Fought the Law was going down a storm with the partygoers. The bass shook the floor and throttled her insides.

The girl felt a tight knotting sensation in her stomach. There were so many 'waitresses' working on the yacht. How many of them were new arrivals? How many had been to other parties? She looked at the others who'd come with her. All in their tight dresses, as requested by the party organiser. The makeup didn't hide how young some of them were.

She glanced through the window. The boat was moving. Taking them to the centre of the loch.

Her companions set off, walking deeper into the Function Room. They were approached in seconds.

The girl stayed put. She'd heard a noise that didn't fit with everything else. It was lost in the music but she thought it was a scream.

She walked into the dark room. Things became clearer.

Girls sitting with older men. Drinking or being forced to drink. Girls who were clearly out of their heads, being dragged to their feet and led away. Some of the men looked familiar but she didn't know their names. She was pretty sure she'd seen some of them on TV.

It happened out of nowhere. Rough hands clamped on her shoulders.

"How's it going?"

He spun her around like she was a rotating rack in a shop. It was Jimmy Gold, with his salt and pepper hair. His thin and wiry frame squeezed into a dark suit. He was smiling again.

"My friends would like to meet you."

She didn't know what she was supposed to say. "Do your friends want a drink?"

He laughed and she saw the crooked shape of his teeth. Everything was so much clearer up close. "Oh aye, they're thirsty. But listen, darling, these are very special friends. Edward – he's the guy who puts these special events together. You play nice with him. Mike, his son-in-law, you'll like him. Some others, and me, of course. We've got a booth in the corner over there. Away from the music."

"I'm working," she said.

He didn't seem to like that.

"I know. That's why I'm asking you over."

Of course, she thought, this was her job. She had no right to say no.

He held his hand out. When she didn't take it right away, he grabbed her by the arm and started leading her to the booth in the corner. She could hear them laughing over there. It was too loud and she was scared.

"Remember my name," he said. "It's Jimmy."

He wasn't smiling anymore.

59

MARGO

I watch as Sophie leads Jimmy Gold out of the driveway and across the nature strip. They walk side by side towards the car with the engine idling. For anyone looking in from the outside, it's a harmless scene. Could be a loving daughter taking her elderly father out for lunch.

Judging by the smile on Gold's withered face and the relaxed manner of his walk, he has no idea what's coming.

The air is charged with tension. The girl breathes heavily behind me. She's whispering something to herself but I can't make out the words. Sounds like she's trying to motivate herself to carry on.

I glance over my shoulder to offer a reassuring smile. To my surprise, she's checking her phone. Or *a* phone. I've no idea if it's hers or not.

"Are you okay?" I ask.

What else can I say?

The poor girl looks exhausted. She manages a weak nod of the head, then turns back to the window, her eyes filling with tears. She wipes them dry. Her face hardens again.

"Almost there," she whispers.

Sophie and Jimmy Gold are still walking towards the car. Sophie clings to a ghoulish smile and I note the look of determination on her face as she tries to hang on to it. Back at Redhall House, I thought she was about to lose it. Since then, something else has taken over. She's fighting back.

"Why do I get the feeling he's the one you really want?" I ask.

"I want all of them."

"Okay."

And then it happens. Jimmy Gold sees us and he freezes on the edge of the kerb. His body is rigid and tall. *He knows something is wrong.* Sophie steps away, like there's a bad smell coming off the old man. For a second, I'm convinced that Gold's about to run but, after a slight wobble, his shoulders droop.

He looks at Sophie. She says something to him and he nods. After that, a sad glance back towards the house. Wondering if he'll ever see his wife again.

60

THE GIRL

Mike Drummond is half-dead. A pitiful sight, still tied to the chair in Redhall House. He's a sickly pale-blue colour that's hard to look at. But he's still there. Still floating in and out of consciousness, still begging for help when he can summon the strength to form words. That's good. I need him alive because Mike, the eternal gambler, has got more debts to pay off. This time, however, he won't clear his tab by handing over a child.

A second coil of rope binds Edward Drummond to the legs of the chair. He's cuffed and going nowhere. Head bowed, looking frail. Jimmy Gold is tied to the opposite legs. Also cuffed. Margo did a good job with the knots.

Their phones have been removed. Destroyed to avoid any potential tracking issues.

This thing is moving fast now.

I pull the phone out my pocket, log in to the forum and show Sophie and Margo a recently uploaded video. I requested this to be uploaded to the forum and the sisters delivered. It's the small sample of video evidence we have stitched together. It's not much but I want the two women, especially Sophie, to see it with their own eyes. Mike and Edward are both in there, both clearly visible at one of the many superyacht parties that took place in various locations over the years. The thumping music. Buddy fucking Holly. The raucous laughter. It still gives me nightmares.

Sophie watches with dead eyes. She sees both her husband and father sitting at a massive table covered in champagne bottles, tall glasses and empty food plates. Mike and Edward are surrounded by underage girls – sometimes sitting on their laps, sometimes pouring them drinks. The fake laughter of those girls – I'll never forget it. Jimmy Gold makes a brief appearance, leaning over the table and whispering something in Edward's ear. The clip is looped. Thirty-two seconds in total, repeated over and over. I wish we had more but it's enough for Sophie and Margo to see with their own eyes that Mike and Edward, sworn enemies, attended these parties together.

I stop the video. Check the forum for any updates.

"Are we expecting someone else?" Margo asks.

I don't answer.

Sophie's head is bowed. She stays like that for a long time, as if in prayer, and then finally looks up. She stares at the three men tied to the chair. "Why do I feel like I'm cursed?"

She walks into the centre of the room, her heels scraping on the floor. Her eyes shimmer with cold hatred. Finally, she comes to a stop in front of the chair.

"We played the part of victims for years," she says to Mike. "Our daughter, gone. Our *baby*. Darcy was kidnapped and it was *you*. You were responsible."

Mike's awake. His eyes wide with horror. He tries to

speak but Sophie presses a finger to her lips, shutting him down. Her voice is calm. Eerily quiet.

"All the nights we cried together."

"S-S-Sophie..."

"And all the while, you were going to these sick parties and abusing other children. Who the fuck are you, Mike? Girls just like Darcy. Girls who–"

Edward cuts her off. He raises his arms, showing her the cuffs. "Sophie! Get me out of this, for God's sake. I'm your father. Get me out–"

Sophie leans over Edward. She throws a fast, whip-like left hook that snaps the old man's head back. Years of resentment in a single strike. Edward cries out, more in shock than pain. Sophie straightens up and winces. Shakes out her hand, then leans over her father for a second time. His cheek is on fire where she hit him.

Edward looks at his daughter and it's the first time I've seen real fear in his eyes. He didn't look like that when Margot tied him up.

"All my life I've worshipped you," she hisses. "We pushed the bad things away but you're even worse than I thought. You're a monster. You're dead to me. And to Mum – I won't let you humiliate her anymore."

"Sophie–"

"Shut the fuck up."

She steps back from the chair. Eyes bright and clear. "Mum inherits the money when you're gone. Right? And as the only child, I'm next in line."

I smile and Edward sees me smiling. He's old and shrinking before my eyes. Jimmy Gold, the one who loved to hurt us the most, is crying like a child.

Sophie looks at me. "What will you do with them?"

"Everything."

She walks over to me. Stands at her full height, which is impressive. A giant of a woman, even without heels.

"I don't want them back," she says. "I don't want these men anywhere near my children. Do you understand?"

Mike makes a gargled protest.

Edward barks across the room but there's no bite in his voice anymore. He sounds scared and the fact that no one's listening drives him crazy. "Sophie! Sophie! Sophie! Have you lost your mind?"

Jimmy Gold just cries.

"Just make sure it doesn't come back to me," Sophie says to me. "My children need me. I've failed one already, but never again."

"Sophie," Margo says, her eyes darting back and forth across the room. "Are we really going to let this–?"

"Yes."

Margo stares down at the floor. "Okay."

The room goes quiet for a while, with the exception of Jimmy Gold's relentless sobbing. But even he shuts up when we hear a vehicle pulling up on the Redhall House driveway. Another vehicle follows seconds later. The engines purr in unison before they're switched off. Doors open and slam shut. There are no voices out front, only the sharp crunch of feet stepping on gravel. The footsteps get louder. They slip around the back where the window with the missing board is waiting.

To my surprise, Edward's laughing.

"You can smash our phones to pieces all you like," he says to me, his eyes cold and loathing. "But you can't control everything. I've got a wife. I'm an important man. Do you finally understand who you're meddling with, you stupid little girl?"

"What?" I ask.

"Did you really think no one would notice I was gone?"

Margo shakes her head. "I don't think it's the police out there, Edward."

The colour leaves his face.

There's a scratching noise from down the hall. They're at the window. They're climbing through the gap, avoiding the broken glass on the ledge. I listen to the soft thump of their landing. It's music to my ears because I'm not alone anymore.

Jimmy Gold is bawling again. He jerks at the rope around his ankles and the chair shudders. "What's happening?"

Margo looks at me. She whispers. "What *is* happening?"

I look towards the doorway.

The first girl appears and it's Stacey. She worked at my very first superyacht party. An old hand by that point. I'll always remember the way she held me at the end of the night. How she comforted me. Today, she looks good. She's about a year older than me. Ivory-white skin, red hair tied back in a ponytail. One of the first to get out, she was crucial in developing the forums.

She looks nervous. But she walks in. Looking at the men.

The others follow – Katy, then Jess, then Anna. I don't know all their names but fourteen young women in total, not including myself, fill the room. They look well. Healthy and strong. It's more than I'd hoped for. Still, this is only a tiny sample of the girls who were abused at Edward Drummond's parties. These are the girls who got out.

They spread out across the room, keeping their eyes on the three men. There's a look in their eyes. A *hungry* look.

Sophie and Margo exchange nervous glances. But no one talks. Not at first. After a moment, however, a few of the girls approach Sophie and I overhear hushed apologies for making her think that Darcy had come home. *It was our way in*, they say.

"Let's begin," I say.

Margo takes a dazed-looking Sophie by the arm. "I think that's our cue to leave."

Margo looks at me and I nod.

"SOPHIE! GET BACK HERE!"

Edward yells as his daughter walks away for the last time. His face contorts with terror, disgust and helplessness. It's the recognition that his bank account won't save him. Sophie is his last link to the world he knows, a world where he's treated like a king because of the wealth he was born into. That sun is setting and Edward knows it.

"SOPHIE!"

Mike and Jimmy Gold wrestle with their bonds, their limbs jerking back and forth. They're animals fuelled by panic. Tugging at the rope. Fighting the cuffs. The chair topples over, landing on Jimmy's right side. He howls in pain. Edward is yanked to the left, his ankles leading the way. He winces as his body is pulled into an impossible shape, but keeps screaming his daughter's name. His voice shoots up an octave until his vocal cords collapse. In the end, he can only manage a croak.

"Sophie."

But she's gone.

61

I don't know this particular girl's name. Online, she identifies as the username 'Panda'. That's about all I know for sure. That, and she's got scars.

Most notably, there's a long spine-shaped scar that runs down the back of her neck. It's hypopigmented and stands out in stark contrast to the rest of her pinkish-red skin. Panda has other scars that she keeps hidden. She's listed them in detail on the forum. Souvenirs from her years at the parties. She walks with a slight limp but she never spoke about that. Apparently, she sustains bruises easily even though she's only in her twenties.

What I do know for sure is that Panda has been waiting a long time for this. Even if none of the other girls showed up today, Panda would have. That much I'm certain of. I don't think she can get past the nightmares until we get this over with.

Candles have been lit. The men are gagged but still trying to scream.

Panda looks nervous as she walks into the centre of the

room. She's carrying a large duffel bag which she places on the floor with such care it could be a sacred relic. She squats down and winces at some sudden, shooting pain. The moment passes. Slowly, she unzips the bag and starts to pull out the items: the pliers, ice picks and sledgehammers.

The men scream. I barely hear it anymore – it's like a faint electrical hum in the background.

We cover the floor with plastic sheets. As I work, I think about Darcy and what she'd make of all this. She was such a good person. A sweet and gentle soul. She was better than all of us, so I hope she can forgive me.

One of the girls places a portable Panasonic stereo on the window ledge. She pops a CD inside and the electric motor rotates the disc at high speed. The men stop protesting when a surge of fifties-era rock and roll fills the front room of Redhall House. *Whole Lotta Shakin' Going On* by Jerry Lee Lewis.

We put our gloves on.

It's going to be a long night.

THANK YOU FOR READING

Did you enjoy reading *The Lost Girl*? Please consider leaving a review on Amazon. Your review will help other readers to discover the novel.

ABOUT THE AUTHOR

Mark Gillespie writes psychological thriller and suspense novels. He's a former professional musician (bass player) from Glasgow, Scotland who spent ten years touring the UK and Ireland, playing sessions and having the time of his life. Don't ask though. What happened on the road stays on the road.

He now lives in Auckland, New Zealand with his wife and a small menagerie of rescue creatures. If he's not writing, he's jamming with other musicians, running on the beach, watching mixed martial arts and boxing. Or devouring horror and thriller movies.

www.markgillespieauthor.com

ALSO BY MARK GILLESPIE

I Know Who You Are

The Lost Girl

Printed in Great Britain
by Amazon